SPOOKY STORIES TO TELL IN THE DARK

GHOSTS, GHOULS, AND OTHER HORRORS

Curated by Chris Ball

Chanthology

All rights reserved
Published by: Chanthology Limited
Communication House, Victoria Avenue, Camberley, Surrey. GU15 3HX.
United Kingdom

www.chanthology.com

Paperback Edition: ISBN 978-1-915449-65-8

Hardcover Edition: ISBN 978-1-915449-67-2

Kindle Edition: ISBN 978-1-915449-66-5

CONTENTS

INTRODUCTION

From the earliest moments I can recall, there was something inexplicably alluring about the dark and the mysteries it concealed. As a child, I would retreat beneath my bed covers, armed only with a dim light, to explore realms of fear and fascination through stories of the supernatural. This nightly ritual, though it often concluded with me in the grips of terror, unable to sleep and drenched in sweat, was a testament to the magnetic pull of the macabre. The stories that danced along the blurred line between reality and nightmare had a profound impact on me, shaping my early encounters with literature. It was this fascination that inspired the creation of "Spooky Stories to Tell in the Dark," a homage to the timeless appeal of being deliciously scared.

The essence of fear is a fundamental, primal emotion, hardwired into our very survival instincts.

Yet, paradoxically, within the security of our own homes, we seek it out through tales that set our hearts racing and palms sweating. There is something uniquely human about this controlled dance with fear. It sharpens our senses, heightens our awareness, and, in a profound way, makes us feel intensely alive. In the solitude of a dark room, with only the faint glow of a reading light to pierce the gloom, every shadow quivers with potential menace, and every sound could be the whisper of something otherworldly. This collection of stories draws from an era when such feelings were not just the stuff of fiction but woven into the fabric of daily life, when the supernatural was an accepted, even expected part of existence.

The tales within these pages are more than mere entertainment. They are a reflection of the darkness that resides within the human soul, of our deepest fears, and of desires so potent and taboo that we dare not voice them. They remind us of a time when the world brimmed with mysteries and the night itself was a realm of endless possibility and peril.

As you embark on this journey through "Spooky Stories to Tell in the Dark," you will encounter narratives that span the spectrum of horror and the supernatural. From the mournful spectre in "The Spectre Bride" by William Harrison Ainsworth to the eerie beauty of "The Red-Haired Girl" by Sabine Baring-Gould, and the unsettling "The Damned Thing" by Ambrose Bierce, each story has been carefully selected for its ability to unsettle and enchant. You will find tales of justice beyond the grave in "The Trial for Murder" by Charles Dickens, and feel the icy touch of the supernatural in "The Cold Embrace" by Mary Elizabeth Braddon.

This anthology is not merely a collection of horror stories; it is an odyssey into the shadows that lie just beyond the reach of the light. It is an invitation to explore the eerie calm of "Between the Lights" by E.F. Benson, and the other meticulously chosen gems that make up this collection. Each tale promises not just to frighten but to provoke thought and perhaps even introspection, challenging you to confront the unknown and to ponder the mysteries that have captivated humanity since time immemorial.

The older stories in this collection offer a unique window into the past, revealing a world steeped in the supernatural and the unexplained. They allow us to traverse time, experiencing the fears, beliefs, and dilemmas of bygone eras. Through these narratives, we are reminded of the universality of horror and its enduring appeal across cultures and centuries.

The true power of these stories, however, lies not just in their capacity to scare but in the skill with which they are told. The masters of horror understand the art of language, atmosphere, and suspense, weaving these elements together to create stories that linger in the imagination long after the last page has been turned. They reveal to us that the deepest horrors are those that reside in the shadows of our minds, suggested but never fully disclosed, leaving us to fill in the blanks with our own fears and anxieties.

Engaging with these stories offers a form of catharsis, providing a safe space to confront our darkest fears. They allow us to grapple with the unknown, to face the darkness within and without, and to find a peculiar sort of comfort in acknowledging our deepest anxieties. This collection is thus more than just an anthology of ghost stories; it is an invitation to step out of the light and into the darkness, to rediscover the thrill of the ghost story, the allure of the supernatural, and the seductive power of fear.

For those of us who, like me, found our first love in the chilling pages of a horror story, to those who know the exquisite terror of reading under the covers long after the world has gone to sleep, "Spooky Stories to Tell in the Dark" is a call to return to that world. It is a reminder of the joy and exhilaration that comes from allowing ourselves to be scared, from surrendering to the stories that make us check over our shoulders and question what might lurk in the shadows.

In these tales, you will find more than just ghosts and ghouls; you will find reflections of your own fears and curiosities, echoes of the age-old human quest to understand the unknown. You will be reminded that horror, at its core, is a deeply human genre, one that speaks to our most fundamental emotions and experiences. As you turn these pages and embark on this journey, remember that you are not just reading stories; you are participating in a tradition as old as humanity itself, the tradition of storytelling that seeks to explore the very limits of our understanding and to confront the darkness that lies at the heart of the human experience.

Welcome to "Spooky Stories to Tell in the Dark," where the shadows come alive and the familiar becomes eerily alien. Here, fear is not just an emotion to be avoided but a gateway to a deeper understanding of ourselves and the world around us. These stories invite you to join in the dance of light and darkness that has captivated the human imagination for centuries. So, I invite you to settle in, turn down the lights, and prepare to be transported to a world where the only limit is your own willingness to explore the depths of fear and fascination. Welcome, dear reader, to a journey through the night, to a celebration of the macabre, and to a rediscovery of the timeless appeal of being deliciously scared.

THE SPECTRE BRIDE

by William Harrison Ainsworth

The castle of Hernswolf, at the close of the year 1655, was the resort of fashion and gaiety. The baron of that name was the most powerful nobleman in Germany and was equally celebrated for the patriotic achievements of his sons and the beauty of his only daughter. The estate of Hernswolf, which was situated in the centre of the Black Forest, had been given to one of his ancestors by the gratitude of the nation and descended with other hereditary possessions to the family of the present owner. It was a castellated, gothic mansion built according to the fashion of the times in the grandest style of architecture. It consisted principally of dark winding corridors and vaulted tapestry rooms, magnificent indeed in their size but ill-suited to private comfort from the very circumstance of their dreary magnitude. A dark grove of pine and mountain ash encompassed the castle on every side and threw an aspect of gloom around the scene, which was seldom enlivened by the cheering sunshine of heaven.

* * * * *

The castle bells rang out a merry peal at the approach of a winter twilight, and the warder was stationed with his retinue on the battlements to announce the arrival of the company who were invited to share the amusements that reigned within the walls. Lady Clotilda, the baron's only daughter, had but just attained her seventeenth year, and a brilliant assembly was invited to celebrate the birthday. The large vaulted apartments were thrown open for the reception of the numerous guests, and the gaieties of the evening had scarcely commenced when the clock from the dungeon tower was heard to strike with unusual solemnity, and on the instant, a tall stranger, arrayed in a deep suit of black, made his appearance in the ballroom. He bowed courteously on every side but was received by all with the strictest reserve. No one knew who he was or whence he came, but it was evident from his appearance that he was a nobleman of the first rank, and though his introduction was accepted with distrust, he was treated by all with respect. He addressed himself, particularly to the daughter of the baron, and was so intelligent in his remarks, so lively in his sallies, and so fascinating in his address, that he quickly interested the feelings of his young and sensitive auditor. In fine, after some hesitation on the part of the host, who, with the rest of the company, was unable to approach the stranger with indifference, he was requested to remain a few days at the castle, an invitation which was cheerfully accepted.

The dead of the night drew on, and when all had retired to rest, the dull, heavy bell was heard swinging to and fro in the grey tower, though there was scarcely a breath to move the forest trees. Many of the guests, when they met the next morning at the breakfast table, averred that there had been sounds as of the most heavenly music, while all persisted in affirming that they had heard awful noises, proceeding, as it seemed, from the apartment which the stranger at that time occupied. He soon, however, made his appearance at the breakfast circle, and when the circumstances of the preceding night were alluded to, a dark smile of unutterable meaning played around his saturnine features and then relapsed into an expression of the deepest melancholy. He addressed his conversation principally to Clotilda, and when he talked of the different climes he had visited, of the sunny regions of Italy, where the very air breathes the fragrance of flowers, and the summer breeze sighed over a land of sweets when he spoke to her of those delicious countries, where the smile of the day sinks into the softer beauty of the night, and the loveliness of heaven is never for an instant obscured, he drew tears of regret from the bosom of his fair auditor, and for the first time, she regretted that she was yet at home

Days rolled on, and every moment increased the fervour of the inexpressible sentiments with which the stranger had inspired her. He never discoursed of love, but he looked it in his language, in his manner, in the insinuating tones of his voice, and in the slumbering softness of his smile, and when he found that he had succeeded in inspiring her with favourable sentiments, a sneer of the most diabolical meaning spoke for an instant and died again on his dark featured countenance. When he met her in the company of her parents, he was at once respectful and submissive, and it was only when alone with her, in her ramble through the dark recesses of the forest, that he assumed the guise of the more impassioned admirer.

As he was sitting one evening with the baron in the wainscotted apartment of the library, the conversation happened to turn upon the supernatural agency. The stranger remained reserved and mysterious during the discussion, but when the baron, in a jocular manner, denied the existence of spirits and satirically mocked their appearance, his eyes glowed with unearthly lustre, and his form seemed to dilate to more than its natural dimensions. When the conversation had ceased, a fearful pause of a few seconds and a chorus of celestial harmony was heard pealing through the dark forest glade. All were entranced with delight, but the stranger was disturbed and gloomy; he looked at his noble host with compassion, and something like a tear swam in his dark eye. After the lapse of a few seconds, the music died gently in the distance, and all was hushed as before. The baron soon after quit the apartment and was followed almost immediately by the stranger. He had not long been absent when an awful noise, as of a person in the agonies of death, was heard, and the Baron was discovered stretched dead along the corridors. His countenance was convulsed with pain, and the grip of a human hand was visible on his blackened throat. The alarm was instantly given, and the castle searched in every direction, but the stranger was seen no more. The body of the baron, in the meantime, was quietly committed to the earth, and the remembrance of the dreadful transaction was recalled but as a thing that once was.

* * * * *

After the departure of the stranger, who had indeed fascinated her very senses, the spirits of the gentle Clotilda evidently declined. She loved to walk early and late in the walks that he had once frequented, to recall his last words, to dwell on his sweet smile, and wander to the spot where she had once discoursed with him of love. She avoided all society and never seemed to be happy when left alone in the solitude of her chamber. It was then that she gave vent to her affliction in tears, and the love that the pride of maiden modesty concealed in public burst forth in the hours of privacy. So beauteous, yet so resigned was the fair mourner that she seemed already an angel freed from the trammels of the world and prepared to take her flight to heaven.

As she was one summer evening rambling to the sequestered spot that had been selected as her favourite residence, a slow step advanced towards her. She turned around and, to her infinite surprise, discovered the stranger. He stepped gaily to her side and commenced an animated conversation. 'You left me,' exclaimed the delighted girl; 'and I thought all happiness was fled from me forever; but you return, and shall we not again be happy?'—'Happy,' replied the stranger, with a scornful burst of derision, 'Can I ever be happy again—can there;—but excuse the agitation, my love, and impute it to the pleasure I experience at our meeting. Oh! I have many things to tell you aye! and many kind words to receive; is it not so, sweet one? Come, tell me truly, have you been happy in my absence? No! I see in that sunken eye, in that pallid cheek, that the poor wanderer has at least gained some slight interest in the heart of his beloved. I have roamed to other climes, I have seen other nations; I have met with other females, beautiful and accomplished, but I have met with but one angel, and she is here before me. Accept this simple offering of my affection, dearest,' continued the stranger, plucking a heath-rose from its stem; 'it is beautiful as the wild flowers that deck thy hair, and sweet as is the love I bear thee.'—'It is sweet, indeed,' replied Clotilda, 'but its sweetness must wither ere night closes around. It is beautiful, but its beauty is short-lived, as the love evinced by man. Let not this, then, be the type of thy attachment; bring me the delicate evergreen, the sweet flower that blossoms throughout the year, and I will say, as

I wreathe it in my hair, "The violets have bloomed and died—the roses have flourished and decayed; but the evergreen is still young, and so is the love of heart!"—you will not—cannot desert me. I live but in you; you are my hopes, my thoughts, my existence itself: and if I lose you, I lose my all—I was but a solitary wild flower in the wilderness of nature until you transplanted me to a more genial soil; and can you now break the fond heart you first taught to glow with passion?'—'Speak not thus,' returned the stranger, 'it rends my very soul to hear you; leave me—forget me—avoid me for ever—or your eternal ruin must ensue. I am a thing abandoned of God and man—and did you but see the scared heart that scarcely beats within this moving mass of deformity, you would flee me, as you would an adder in your path. Here is my heart, love, feel how cold it is; there is no pulse that betrays its emotion; for all is chilled and dead as the friends I once knew.'—'You are unhappy, love, and your poor Clotilda shall stay to succour you. Think not I can abandon you in your misfortunes. No! I will wander with thee through the wide world, and be thy servant, thy slave, if thou wilt have it so. I will shield thee from the night winds, that they blow not too roughly on thy unprotected head. I will defend thee from the tempest that howls around; and though the cold world may devote thy name to scorn—though friends may fall off, and associates wither in the grave, there shall be one fond heart who shall love thee better in thy misfortune, and cherish thee, bless thee still.' She ceased, and her blue eyes swam in tears as she turned it, glistening with affection towards the stranger. He averted his head from her gaze, and a scornful sneer of the darkest, the deadliest malice passed over his fine countenance. In an instant, the expression subsided; his fixed, glassy eye resumed its unearthly chillness, and he turned once again to his companion. 'It is the hour of sunset,' he exclaimed; 'the soft, the beauteous hour, when the hearts of lovers are happy, and nature smiles in unison with their feelings; but to me, it will smile no longer—ere the morrow dawns I shall very far, from the house of my beloved; from the scenes where my heart is enshrined, as in a sepulchre. But must I leave thee, the dearest flower of the wilderness, to be the sport of a whirlwind, the prey of the mountain blast?'—'No, we will not part,' replied the impassioned girl; 'where thou goest, will I go; thy home shall be my home, and thy God shall be my God.'—'Swear it, swear it,' resumed the stranger, wildly grasping her by the hand; 'swear to the fearful oath I shall dictate.' He then desired her to kneel, and holding his right hand in a menacing attitude towards heaven, and throwing back his dark raven locks, exclaimed in a strain of bitter imprecation with the ghastly smile of an incarnate fiend, 'May the curses of an offended God,' he cried, 'haunt thee, cling to thee for ever in the tempest and in the calm, in the day and in the night, in sickness and in sorrow, in life and in death, shouldst thou swerve from the promise thou hast here made to be mine. May the dark spirits of the damned howl in thine ears the accursed chorus of fiends—may the air rack thy bosom with the quenchless flames of hell!

May thy soul be as the lazar-house of corruption, where the ghost of departed pleasure sits enshrined, as in a grave: where the hundred-headed worm never dies and where the fire is never extinguished. May a spirit of evil lord it over thy brow, and proclaim, as thou passest by,

"THIS IS THE ABANDONED OF GOD AND MAN;"

may fearful spectres haunt thee in the night season; may thy dearest friends drop day by day into the grave, and curse thee with their dying breath: may all that is most horrible in human nature, more solemn than language can frame, or lips can utter, may this, and more than this, be thy eternal portion, shouldst thou violate the oath that thou has taken.' He ceased—hardly knowing what she did, the terrified girl acceded to the awful adjuration and promised eternal fidelity to him, who was henceforth to be her lord. 'Spirits of the damned, I thank thee for thine assistance,' shouted the stranger; 'I have wooed my fair bride bravely. She is mine—mine forever.—Aye, body and soul both mine; mine in life, and mine in death. What in tears, my sweet one, ere yet the honeymoon is passed? Why! indeed thou hast cause for weeping: but when next we meet, we shall meet to sign the nuptial bond.' He then imprinted a cold salute on the cheek of his young bride and, softening down the unutterable horrors of his countenance, requested her to meet him at eight o'clock on the ensuing evening in the chapel adjoining to the castle of Hernswolf. She turned round to him with a burning sigh as if to implore protection from himself, but the stranger was gone.

On entering the castle, she was observed to be impressed with deepest melancholy. Her relations vainly endeavoured to ascertain the cause of her uneasiness, but the tremendous oath she had sworn completely paralysed her faculties, and she was fearful of betraying herself by even the slightest intonation of her voice, or the least variable expression of her countenance. When the evening was concluded, the family retired to rest; but Clotilda, who was unable to take repose, from the restlessness of her disposition, requested to remain alone in the library that adjoined her apartment.

All was now deep midnight; every domestic had long since retired to rest, and the only sound that could be distinguished was the sullen howl of the ban-dog as he bayed, the waning moon Clotilda remained in the library in an attitude of deep meditation. The lamp that burnt on the table where she sat was dying away, and the lower end of the apartment was already more than half obscured. The clock from the northern angle of the castle tolled out the hour of twelve, and the sound echoed dismally in the solemn stillness of the night. Sudden the oaken door at the farther end of the room was gently lifted on its latch, and a bloodless figure, apparelled in the habiliments of the grave, advanced slowly up the apartment. No sound heralded its approach as it moved with noiseless steps to the table where the lady was stationed. She did not at first perceive it till she felt a death-cold hand fast grasped in her own and heard a solemn voice whisper in her ear, 'Clotilda.' She looked up a dark figure was standing beside her; she endeavoured to scream, but her voice was unequal to the exertion; her eye was fixed, as if by magic, on the form which slowly removed the garb that concealed its countenance and disclosed the livid eyes and skeleton shape of her father. It seemed to gaze on her with pity, regret and mournfully exclaimed—'Clotilda the dresses and the servants are ready, the church bell has tolled, and the priest is at the altar, but where is the affianced bride? There is room for her in the grave, and tomorrow shall she be with me.'—'Tomorrow?' faltered out the distracted girl; 'the spirits of hell shall have registered it, and tomorrow must the bond be cancelled.' The figure ceased—slowly retired and was soon lost in the obscurity of distance.

The morning—evening—arrived, and already as the hall clock struck eight, Clotilda was on her road to the chapel. It was a dark, gloomy night, thick masses of dun clouds sailed across the firmament, and the roar of the winter wind echoed awfully through the forest trees. She reached the appointed place; a figure was in waiting for her—it advanced—and discovered the features of the stranger. 'Why! this is well, my bride,' he exclaimed, with a sneer, 'and well will I repay thy fondness. Follow me.' They proceeded together in silence through the winding avenues of the chapel until they reached the adjoining cemetery. Here they paused for an instant, and the stranger, in a softened tone, said, 'But one hour more, and the struggle will be over. And yet this heart of incarnate malice can feel when it devotes so young, so pure a spirit to the grave. But it must—it must be,' he proceeded, as the memory of her past love rushed into her mind, 'for the fiend whom I obey has so willed it. Poor girl, I am leading thee indeed to our nuptials; but the priest will be death, thy parents the mouldering skeletons that rot in heaps around; and the witnesses to our union, the lazy worms that revel on the carious bones of the dead. Come, my young bride, the priest is impatient for his victim.' As they proceeded, a dim blue light moved swiftly before them and displayed at the extremity of the churchyard the portals of a vault. It was open, and they entered it in silence. The hollow wind came rushing through the gloomy abode of the dead, and on every side were piled the mouldering remnants of coffins, which dropped piece by piece upon the damp mud. Every step they took was on a dead body, and the bleached bones rattled horribly beneath their feet. In the centre of the vault rose a heap of unburied skeletons, whereon was seated, a figure too awful even for the darkest imagination to conceive. As they approached it, the hollow vault rung with a hellish peal of laughter; and every mouldering corpse seemed endued with unholy life. The stranger paused, and as he grasped his victim in his hand, one sigh burst from his heart—one tear glistened in his eye. It was but for an instant; the figure frowned awfully at his vacillation and waved his gaunt hand.

The stranger advanced; he made certain mystic circles in the air, uttered unearthly words, and paused in excess of terror. Of a sudden, he raised his voice and wildly exclaimed—'Spouse of the spirit of darkness, a few moments are yet thine; that thou may'st know to whom thou hast consigned thyself. I am the undying spirit of the wretch who curst his Saviour on the cross. He looked at me in the closing hour of his existence, and that look hath not yet passed away, for I am curst above all on earth. I am eternally condemned to hell and I must cater for my master's taste till the world is parched as is a scroll, and the heavens and the earth have passed away. I am he of whom thou may'st have read and of whose feats thou may'st have heard. A million souls has my master condemned me to ensnare, and then my penance is accomplished, and I may know the repose of the grave. Thou art the thousandth soul that I have damned. I saw thee in thine hour of purity, and I marked thee at once for my home. Thy father did I murder for his temerity, and permitted to warn thee of thy fate; and myself have I beguiled for thy simplicity. Ha! the spell works bravely, and thou shall soon see, my sweet one, to whom thou hast linked thine undying fortunes, for as long as the seasons shall move on their course of nature—as long as the lightning shall flash and the thunders roll, thy penance shall be eternal. Look below! and see to what thou art destined.' She looked. The vault split in a thousand different directions; the earth yawned asunder, and the roar of mighty waters was heard. A living ocean of molten fire glowed in the abyss beneath her and blended with the shrieks of the damned, and the triumphant shouts of the fiends rendered horror more horrible than imagination. Ten million souls were writhing in the fiery flames, and as the boiling billows dashed them against the blackened rocks of adamant, they cursed with the blasphemies of despair; and each curse echoed in thunder across the wave. The stranger rushed towards his victim. For an instant, he held her over the burning vista, looked fondly in her face and wept as if he were a child. This was but the impulse of a moment; again he grasped her in his arms, dashed her from him with fury; and as her last parting glance was cast in kindness on his face, shouted aloud, 'not mine is the crime, but the religion that thou professest; for is it not said that there is a fire of eternity prepared for the souls of the wicked; and hast not thou incurred its torments?' She, poor girl, heard not, heeded not the shouts of the blasphemer. Her delicate form bounded from rock to rock, over billow, and over foam; as she fell, the ocean lashed itself as it were in triumph to receive her soul, and as she sunk deep in the burning pit, ten thousand voices reverberated from the bottomless abyss, 'Spirit of evil! here indeed is an eternity of torments prepared for thee; for here the worm never dies, and the fire is never quenched.'

A MIDNIGHT VISITOR

by John Kendrick Bangs

I do not assert that what I am about to relate is, in all its particulars, absolutely true. Not understand me that it is not true, but I do not feel that I care to make an assertion that is more than likely to be received by a sceptical age with sneers of incredulity. I will content myself with a simple narration of the events of that evening, the memory of which is so indelibly impressed upon my mind and which, were I able to do so, I should forget without any sentiments of regret whatsoever.

The affair happened on the night before I fell ill with typhoid fever and is about the sole remaining remembrance of that immediate period left to me. Briefly, the story is as follows:

Notwithstanding the fact that I was overworked in the practice of my profession—it was early in March, and I was preparing my contributions for the coming Christmas issues of the periodicals for which I write—I had accepted the highly honourable position of Entertainment Committeeman at one of the small clubs to which I belonged. I accepted the office, supposing that the duties connected with it were easy to perform and with absolutely no notion that the faith of my fellow committeemen in my judgment was so strong that they would ultimately manifest a desire to leave the whole programme for the club's diversion in my hands. This, however, they did; and when the month of March assumed command of the calendar I found myself utterly fagged out and at my wits' end to know what style of entertainment to provide for the club meeting to be held on the evening of the 15th of that month. I had provided already an unusually taking variety of evenings, of which one, in particular, called the "Martyrs' Night," in which living authors writhed through selections from their own works while an inhuman audience, every man of whom had suffered even as the victims then suffered, sat on tenscore of camp-stools puffing the smoke of twenty-five score of free cigars into their faces, and gloating over their misery, was extremely successful, and had gained for me among my professional brethren the enviable title of "Machiavelli Junior." This performance, in fact, was the one now uppermost in the minds of the club members, has been the most recent of the series; and it had been prophesied by many men whose judgment was unassailable that no man, not even I, could ever conceive of anything that could surpass it. Disposed at first to question the accuracy of a prophecy to the effect that I was, like most others of my kind, possessed of limitations, I came finally to believe that perhaps, after all, these male Cassandras with whom I was thrown were right. Indeed, the more I racked my brains to think of something better than the "Martyrs' Night," the more I became convinced that in that achievement I had reached the zenith of my powers. The thing for me to do now was to hook myself securely onto the zenith and stay there. But how to do it? That was the question which drove sleep from my eyes and deprived me for a period of six weeks of my reason, my hair departing immediately upon the restoration thereof—a not uncommon after-symptom of typhoid.

It was a typical March night, this one upon which the extraordinary incident about to be related took place. It was the kind of night that novelists use when they are handling a mystery that, in the abstract, would amount to nothing but which, in the concrete of a bit of wild, weird, and windy nocturnalism sends the reader into hysterics. It may be—I shall not attempt to deny it—that had it happened upon another kind of an evening—a soft, mild, balmy June evening, for instance—my own experience would have seemed less worthy of preservation in the amber of publicity, but of that, the reader must judge for himself. The fact alone remains that upon the night when my uncanny visitor appeared, the weather department was apparently engaged in getting rid of its remnants. There was a large percentage of withering blast in the general make-up of the evening; there were rain and snow, which alternated in pattering upon my window pane and whitening the apology for a world that stands three blocks from my flat on Madison Square; the wind whistled as it always does upon occasions of this sort, and from all corners of my apartment, after the usual fashion, there seemed to come sounds of a supernatural order, the effect of which was to send cold chills off on their regular trips up and down the spine of their victim—in this instance myself. I wish that at the time, the hackneyed quality of these sensations had appealed to me. That it did not do so was shown by the highly nervous state in which I found myself as my clock struck eleven. If I could only have realized at that hour that these symptoms were the same old threadbare premonitions of the appearance of a supernatural being, I should have left the house and gone to the club, and so have avoided the visitation then imminent. Had I done this, I should doubtless also have escaped typhoid since the doctors attributed that misfortune to the shock of my experience, which, in my then-wearied state, I was unable to sustain—and what the escape of typhoid would have meant to me only those who have seen the bills of my physician and druggist for services rendered and prescriptions compounded are aware. That my mind unconsciously took thought of spirits was shown by the fact that when the first chill came upon me, I arose and poured out for myself a stiff bumper of old Reserve Rye, which I immediately swallowed, but beyond this, I did not go. I simply sat there before my fire and cudgelled my brains for an idea whereby my fellow members at the Gutenberg Club might be amused. How long I sat there, I do not know. It may have been ten minutes; it may have been an hour—I was barely conscious of the passing of time—but I do know that the clock in the Dutch Reformed Church steeple at Twenty-ninth Street and Fifth Avenue was clanging out the first stroke of the hour of midnight when my door-bell rang.

Theretofore—if I may be allowed the word—the tintinnabulation of my doorbell had been invariably pleasing unto me. I am fond of company, and company alone was betokened by its ringing since my creditors gratify their passion for interviews at my office if perchance, they happen to find me there. But on this occasion—I could not at the moment tell why—its clanging seemed the very essence of discord. It jangled with my nervous system, and as it ceased, I was conscious of a feeling of irritability which is utterly at variance with my nature outside of business hours. In the office, for the sake of discipline, I frequently adopt a querulous manner, finding it necessary in dealing with office boys, but the moment I leave shop behind me, I become a different individual entirely and have been called a moteless sunbeam by those who have seen only that side of my character. This, by the way, must be regarded as a confidential communication since I am at present engaged in preparing a vest-pocket edition of the philosophical works of Schopenhauer in words of one syllable and were it known that the publisher had intrusted the magnificent pessimism of that illustrious juggler of words and theories to a "moteless sunbeam" it might seriously interfere with the sale of the work; and I may say, too, that this request that my confidence be respected is entirely disinterested, inasmuch as I declined to do the work on the royalty plan, insisting upon the payment of a lump sum, considerably in advance.

But to return. I heard the bell ring with a sense of profound disgust. I did not wish to see anybody. My whiskey was low, my quinine pills few in number; my chills alone were present in a profusion bordering upon ostentation.

"I'll pretend not to hear it," I said to myself, resuming my work of gazing at the flickering light of my fire—which, by the way, was the only light in the room.

"Ting-a-ling-a-ling", went the bell, as if in answer to my resolve.

"Confound the luck!" I cried, jumping from my chair and going to the door with the intention of opening it, an intention, however, which was speedily abandoned, for as I approached it a sickly fear came over me—a sensation I never had before known seemed to take hold of my being, and instead of opening the door, I pushed the bolt to make it the more secure.

"There's a hint for you, whoever you are!" I cried. "Do you hear that bolt slide, you?" I added tremulously, for, from the other side, there came no reply—only a more violent ringing of the bell.

"See here!" I called out, as loudly as I could, "Who are you, anyhow? What do you want?"

There was no answer except the bell, which began again.

"Bell-wire's too cheap to steal!" I called again. "If you want wire, go buy it; don't try to pull mine out. It isn't mine, anyhow. It belongs to the house."

Still, there was no reply, only the clanging of the bell; and then my curiosity overcame my fear, and with a quick movement, I threw open the door.

"Are you satisfied now?" I said angrily. But I addressed an empty vestibule. There was absolutely no one there, and then I sat down on the mat and laughed. I never was so glad to see no one in my life. But my laugh was short-lived.

"What made that bell ring?" I suddenly asked myself, and then the feeling of fear came upon me again. I gathered my somewhat shattered self together, sprang to my feet, slammed the door with such force that the corridors echoed to the sound, slid the bolt once more, turned the key, moved a heavy chair in front of it, and then fled like a frightened hare to the sideboard in my dining room. There I grasped the decanter holding my whiskey, seized a glass from the shelf, and started to pour out the usual dram, when the glass fell from my hand, and was shivered into a thousand pieces on the hardwood floor; for, as I poured, I glanced through the open door, and there in my sanctum the flicker of a random flame divulged the form of a being, the eyes of whom seemed fixed on mine, piercing me through and through. To say that I was petrified dimly expresses the situation. I was granitized, and so I remained until, by a more luminous flicker from the burning wood, I perceived that the being wore a flaring red necktie.

"He is human," I thought; and with the thought, the tension in my nervous system relaxed, and I was able to feel a sufficiently well-developed sense of indignation to demand an explanation. "This is a mighty cool proceeding on your part," I said, leaving the sideboard and walking into the sanctum.

"Yes," he replied in a tone that made me jump. It was so extremely sepulchral—a tone that seemed as if it might have been acquired in a damp corner of some cave off the earth. "But it's a cool evening."

"I wonder that a man of your coolness doesn't hire himself out to some refrigerating company," I remarked with a sneer which would have delighted the soul of Cassius himself.

"I have thought of it," returned the being calmly. "But never went any further. Summer-hotel proprietors have always outbid the refrigerating people, and they in turn have been laid low by millionaires, who have hired me on occasion to freeze out people they didn't like, but who have persisted in calling. I must confess, though, my dear Hiram, that you are not much warmer yourself— this greeting is hardly what I expected."

"Well, if you want to make me warmer," I retorted hotly, "just keep on calling me Hiram. How the deuce did you know of that blot on my escutcheon, anyhow?" I added, for Hiram was one of the crimes of my family that I had tried to conceal, my parents, having fastened the name of Hiram Spencer Carrington upon me at baptism for no reason other than that my rich bachelor uncle, who subsequently failed and became a charge upon me, was so named.

"I was standing at the door of the church when you were baptized," returned the visitor, "and as you were an interesting baby, I have kept an eye on you ever since. Of course I knew that you discarded Hiram as soon as you got old enough to put away childish things, and since the failure of your uncle I have been aware that you desired to be known as Spencer Carrington, but to me you are, always have been, and always will be, Hiram."

"Well, don't give it away," I pleaded. "I hope to be famous some day, and if the American newspaper paragrapher ever got hold of the fact that once in my life I was Hiram, I'd have to Hiram to let me alone."

"That's a bad joke, Hiram," said the visitor, "and for that reason I like it, though I don't laugh. There is no danger of your becoming famous if you stick to humor of that sort."

"Well, I'd like to know," I put in, my anger returning—"I'd like to know who in Brindisi you are, what in Cairo you want, and what in the name of the seventeen hinges of the gates of Singapore you are doing here at this time of night?"

"When you were a baby, Hiram, you had blue eyes," said my visitor. "Bonny blue eyes, as the poet says."

"What of it?" I asked.

"This," replied my visitor. "If you have them now, you can very easily see what I am doing here. I am sitting down and talking to you."

"Oh, are you?" I said with fine scorn. "I had not observed that. The fact is, my eyes were so weakened by the brilliance of that necktie of yours that I doubt I could see anything—not even one of my own jokes. It's a scorcher, that tie of yours. In fact, I never saw anything so red in my life."

"I do not see why you complain of my tie," said the visitor. "Your own is just as bad."

"Blue is never so withering as red," I retorted, at the same time caressing the scarf I wore.

"Perhaps not—but—ah—if you will look in the glass, Hiram, you will observe that your point is not well taken," said my vis-a-vis calmly.

I acted upon the suggestion and looked upon my reflection in the glass, lighting a match to facilitate the operation. I was horrified to observe that my beautiful blue tie, of which I was so proud, had in some manner changed and was now of the same aggressive hue as was that of my visitor, red even as a brick is red. To grasp it firmly in my hands and tear it from my neck was the work of a moment, and then in a spirit of rage, I turned upon my companion.

"See here," I cried, "I've had quite enough of you. I can't make you out, and I can't say that I want to. You know where the door is—you will oblige me by putting it to its proper use."

"Sit down, Hiram," said he, "and don't be foolish and ungrateful. You are behaving in a most extraordinary fashion, destroying your clothing and acting like a madman generally. What was the use of ripping up a handsome tie like that?"

"I despise loud hues. Red is a jockey's color," I answered.

"But you did not destroy the red tie," said he with a smile. "You tore up your blue one—look. There it is on the floor. The red one you still have on."

Investigation showed the truth of my visitor's assertion. That flaunting streamer of anarchy still made my neck infamous, and before me on the floor, an almost unrecognizable mass of shreds lay my cherished cerulean tie. The revelation stunned me; tears came into my eyes and trickled down my cheeks, fairly hissed with the feverish heat of my flesh. My muscles relaxed, and I fell limp into my chair.

"You need stimulant," said my visitor kindly. "Go take a drop of your Old

Reserve, and then come back here to me. I've something to say to you."

"Will you join me?" I asked faintly.

"No," returned the visitor. "I am so fond of whiskey that I never molest it. That act which is your stimulant is death to the rye. Never realized that, did you?"

"No, I never did," I said meekly.

"And yet you claim to love it. Bah!" he said.

And then I obeyed his command, drained my glass to the dregs, and returned. "What is your mission?" I asked when I had made myself as comfortable as possible under the circumstances.

"To relieve you of your woes," he said.

"You are a homoeopath, I observe," said I, with a sneer. "You are a homoeopath in theory and an allopath in practice."

"I am not usually unintelligent," said he. "I fail to comprehend your meaning. Perhaps you express yourself badly."

"I wish you'd express yourself for Zulu-land," I retorted hotly. "What I mean is, you believe in the similia similibus business, but you prescribe large doses. I don't believe troubles like mine can be cured on your plan. A man can't get rid of his stock by adding to it."

"Ah, I see. You think I have added to your troubles?"

"I don't think so," I answered, with a fond glance at my ruined tie. "I know so."

"Well, wait until I have laid my plan before you, and see if you won't change your mind," said my visitor, significantly.

"All right," I said. "Proceed. Only hurry. I go to bed early, as a rule, and it's getting quite early now."

"It's only one o'clock," said the visitor, ignoring the sarcasm. "But I will hasten, as I've several other calls to make before breakfast."

"Are you a milkman?" I asked.

"You are flippant," he replied. "But, Hiram," he added, "I have come here to aid you in spite of your unworthiness. You want to know what to provide for your club night on the 15th. You want something that will knock the 'Martyr's Night' silly."

"Not exactly that," I replied, "I don't want anything so abominably good as to make all the other things I have done seem failures. That is not good business."

"Would you like to be hailed as the discoverer of genius? Would you like to be the responsible agent for the greatest exhibition of skill in a certain direction ever seen? Would you like to become the most famous impresario the world has ever known?"

"Now," I said, forgetting my dignity under the enthusiasm with which I was inspired by my visitor's words, and infected more or less with his undoubtedly magnetite spirit—"now you're shouting."

"I thought so, Hiram. I thought so, and that's why I am here. I saw you on Wall Street to-day, and read your difficulty at once in your eyes, and I resolved to help you. I am a magician, and one or two little things have happened of late to make me wish to prestidigitate in public. I knew you were after a show of some kind, and I've come to offer you my services."

"Oh, pshaw!" I said. "The members of the Gutenberg Club are men of brains—not children. Card tricks are hackneyed, and sleight-of-hand shows pall."

"Do they, indeed?" said the visitor. "Well, mine won't. If you don't believe it, I'll prove to you what I can do."

"I have no paraphernalia," I said.

"Well, I have," said he, and as he spoke, a pack of cards seemed to grow out of my hands. I must have turned pale at this unexpected happening, for my visitor smiled and said:

"Don't be frightened. That's only one of my tricks. Now choose a card," he added, "and when you have done so, toss the pack in the air. Don't tell me what the card is; it alone will fall to the floor."

"Nonsense!" said I. "It's impossible."

"Do as I tell you."

I did as he told me, to a degree only. I tossed the cards in the air without choosing one, although I made a feint of doing so.

Not a card fell back to the floor. They every one disappeared from view in the ceiling. If it had not been for the heavy chair, I would have rolled in front of the door. I think I should have fled.

"How's that for a trick?" asked my visitor.

I said nothing, for the very good reason that my words stuck in my throat.

"Give me a little creme de menthe, will you, please?" said he after a moment's pause.

"I haven't a drop in the house," I said, relieved to think that this wonderful being could come down to anything so earthly.

"Pshaw, Hiram!" he ejaculated, apparently in disgust. "Don't be mean, and, above all, don't lie. Why, man, you've got a bottle full of it in your hand! Do you want it all?"

He was right. Where it came from, I do not know, but beyond question, the graceful, slim-necked bottle was in my right hand, and my left held a liqueur glass of exquisite form.

"Say," I gasped as soon as I was able to collect my thoughts, "what are your terms?"

"Wait a moment," he answered. "Let me do a little mind-reading before we arrange preliminaries."

"I haven't much of a mind to read tonight," I answered wildly.

"You're right there," said he. "It's like a dime novel, that mind of yours tonight. But I'll do the best I can with it. Suppose you think of your favourite poem, and after turning it over in your mind carefully for a few minutes, select two lines from it, concealing them, of course, from me, and I will tell you what they are."

Now my favourite poem, I regret to say, is Lewis Carroll's "Jabberwock," a fact I was ashamed to confess to an utter stranger, so I tried to deceive him by thinking of some other lines. The effort was hardly successful, for the only other lines I could call to mind at the moment were from Rudyard Kipling's rhyme, "The Post that Fitted," and which ran,

"Year by year, in pious patience, vengeful Mrs Boffin sits

Waiting for the Sleary babies to develop Sleary's fits."

"Humph!" ejaculated my visitor. "You're a great Hiram, you are."

And then, rising from his chair and walking to my "poet's corner," the magician selected two volumes.

"There," said he, handing me the Departmental Ditties. "You'll find the lines you tried to fool me with at the foot of page thirteen. Look."

I looked, and there lay that vile Sleary sentiment, in all the majesty of type, staring me in the eyes.

"And here," added my visitor, opening Alice in the Looking-Glass—"here is the poem that to your mind holds all the philosophy of life:

"'Come to my arms, my beamish boy,

He chortled in his joy.'"

I blushed and trembled. Blushed that he should discover the weakness of my taste, I trembled at his power.

"I don't blame you for coloring," said the magician. "But I thought you said Gutenberg was made up of men of brains? Do you think you could stay on the rolls a month if they were aware that your poetic ideals are summed up in the 'Jabberwock' and 'Sleary's Fits'?"

"My taste might be far worse," I answered.

"Yes, it might. You might have stooped to liking some of your own verses. I ought really to congratulate you, I suppose," retorted the visitor with a sneering laugh.

This roused my ire again.

"Who are you, anyhow, that you come here and take me to the task?" I demanded angrily. "I'll like anything I please, and without asking your permission. If I cared more for the Peterkin Papers than I do for Shakespeare, I wouldn't be accountable to you, and that's all there is about it."

"Never mind who I am," said the visitor. "Suffice to say that I am myself. You'll know my name soon enough. In fact, you will pronounce it involuntarily the first thing when you wake in the morning, and then—" Here, he shook his head ominously, and I felt myself grow rigid with fright in my chair. "Now for the final trick," he said after a moment's pause. "Think of where you would most like to be at this moment, and I'll exert my power to put you there. Only close your eyes first."

I closed my eyes and wished. When I opened them, I was in the billiard room of the Gutenberg Club with Perkins and Tompson.

"For Heaven's sake, Spencer," they said, in surprise, "where did you drop in from? Why, man, you are as white as a sheet. And what a necktie! Take it off!"

"Grab hold of me, boys, and hold me fast," I pleaded, falling to my knees in terror. "If you don't, I believe I'll die."

The idea of returning to my sanctum was intolerably dreadful to me.

"Ha! ha!" laughed the magician, for even as I spoke to Perkins and Tompson,

I found myself seated opposite my infernal visitor in my room once more.

"They couldn't keep you an instant with me summoning you back."

His laughter was terrible; his frown was pleasanter, and I felt myself gradually losing control of my senses.

"Go," I cried. "Leave me, or you will have the crime of murder on your conscience."

"I have no con—" he began, but I heard no more.

That is the last I remember of that fearful night. I must have fainted and then fallen into a deep slumber.

When I woke, it was morning, and I was alone but undressed and in bed, unconscionably weak and surrounded by medicine bottles of many kinds. The clock on the mantle on the other side of the room indicated that it was after ten o'clock.

"Great Beelzebub!" I cried, taking note of the hour. "I have an engagement with Barlow at nine."

And then a sweet-faced woman, who, I afterwards learned, was a professional nurse, entered the room, and within an hour, I realized two facts. One was that I had lain ill for many days and that my engagement with Barlow was now for six weeks unfulfilled; the other, that my midnight visitor was none other than—

And yet I don't know. His tricks certainly were worthy of that individual, but Perkins and Tompson assert that I never entered the club that night, and surely if my visitor was Beelzebub himself, he would not have omitted so importantly, a factor of success as my actual presence in the billiard room on that occasion would have been; and, besides, he was altogether too cool to have come from his reputed residence.

Altogether I think the episode most unaccountable, particularly when I reflect that while no trace of my visitor was discoverable in my room the next morning, as my nurse tells me, my blue necktie was, in reality, found upon the floor, crushed and torn into a shapeless bundle of frayed rags.

As for the club entertainment, I am told that, despite my absence, it was a wonderful success, redeemed from failure, the treasurer of the club said, by the voluntary services of a guest, who secured admittance on one of my cards, and who executed some sleight-of-hand tricks that made the members tremble, and whose mind-reading feats performed on the club's butler not only made it necessary for him to resign his office but disclosed to the House Committee the whereabouts of several cases of rare wines that had mysteriously disappeared.

THE RED-HAIRED GIRL

by Sabine Baring-Gould

In 1876, we took a house in one of the best streets and parts of B——. I do not give the name of the street or the number of the house because the circumstances that occurred in that place were such as to make people nervous and shy—unreasonably so—of taking those lodgings after reading our experiences therein.

We were a small family—my husband, a grown-up daughter, and myself; and we had two maids—a cook and the other house- and a parlourmaid in one. We had not been a fortnight in the house before my daughter said to me one morning:

"Mamma, I do not like Jane"—that was our house parlourmaid.

"Why so?" I asked. "She seems respectable, and she does her work systematically. I have no fault to find with her, none whatever."

"She may do her work," said Bessie, my daughter, "but I dislike inquisitiveness."

"Inquisitiveness!" I exclaimed. "What do you mean? Has she been looking into your drawers?"

"No, mamma, but she watches me. It is hot weather now, and when I am in my room, occasionally, I leave my door open whilst writing a letter or doing any little bit of needlework, and then I am almost certain to hear her outside. If I turn sharply round, I see her slipping out of sight. It is most annoying. I really was unaware that I was such an interesting personage as to make it worth anyone's while to spy out my proceedings."

"Nonsense, my dear. You are sure it is Jane?"

"Well—I suppose so." There was a slight hesitation in her voice. "If not Jane, who can it be?"

"Are you sure it is not cook?"

"Oh, no, it is not cook; she is busy in the kitchen. I have heard her there, when I have gone outside my room upon the landing, after having caught that girl watching me."

"If you have caught her," said I, "I suppose you spoke to her about the impropriety of her conduct."

"Well, caught is the wrong word. I have not actually caught her at it. Only today I distinctly heard her at my door, and I saw her back as she turned to run away when I went towards her."

"But you followed her, of course?"

"Yes, but I did not find her on the landing when I got outside."

"Where was she, then?"

"I don't know."

"But did you not go and see?"

"She slipped away with astonishing celerity," said Bessie.

"I can take no steps in the matter. If she does it again, speak to her and remonstrate."

"But I never have a chance. She is gone in a moment."

"She cannot get away so quickly as all that."

"Somehow she does."

"And you are sure it is Jane?" again I asked, and again she replied: "If not Jane, who else can it be? There is no one else in the house."

So this unpleasant matter ended for the time being. The next intimation of something of the sort proceeded from another quarter—in fact, from Jane herself. She came to me some days later and said, with some embarrassment in her tone—

"If you please, ma'am, if I do not give satisfaction, I would rather leave the situation."

"Leave!" I exclaimed. "Why, I have not given you the slightest cause. I have not found fault with you for anything as yet, have I, Jane? On the contrary, I have been much pleased with the thoroughness of your work. And you are always tidy and obliging."

"It isn't that, ma'am; but I don't like being watched whatever I do."

"Watched!" I repeated. "What do you mean? You surely do not suppose that I am running after you when you are engaged on your occupations. I assure you I have other and more important things to do."

"No, ma'am, I don't suppose you do."

"Then who watches you?"

"I think it must be Miss Bessie."

"Miss Bessie!" I could say no more. I was so astounded.

"Yes, ma'am. When I am sweeping out a room, and my back is turned, I hear her at the door; and when I turn myself about, I just catch a glimpse of her running away. I see her skirts——"

"Miss Bessie is above doing anything of the sort."

"If it is not Miss Bessie, who is it, ma'am?"

There was a tone of indecision in her voice.

"My good Jane," said I, "set your mind at rest. Miss Bessie could not act as you suppose. Have you seen her on these occasions and assured yourself that it is she?"

"No, ma'am, I've not, so to speak, seen her face; but I know it ain't cook, and I'm sure it ain't you, ma'am; so who else can it be?"

I considered for some moments, and the maid stood before me in a dubious mood.

"You say you saw her skirts. Did you recognize the gown? What did she wear?"

"It was a light cotton print—more like a maid's morning dress."

"Well, set your mind at ease; Miss Bessie has not got such a frock as you describe."

"I don't think she has," said Jane, "but there was someone at the door, watching me, who ran away when I turned myself about."

"Did she run upstairs or down?"

"I don't know. I did go out on the landing, but there was no one there. I'm sure it wasn't cook, for I heard her clattering the dishes down in the kitchen at the time."

"Well, Jane, there is some mystery in this. I will not accept your notice; we will let matters stand over till we can look into this complaint of yours and discover the rights of it."

"Thank you, ma'am. I'm very comfortable here, but it is unpleasant to suppose that one is not trusted, and is spied on wherever one goes and whatever one is about."

A week later, after dinner one evening, when Bessie and I had quitted the table and left my husband to his smoke, Bessie said to me, when we were in the drawing room together: "Mamma, it is not Jane."

"What is not Jane?" I asked.

"It is not Jane who watches me."

"Who can it be, then?"

"I don't know."

"And how is it that you are confident that you are not being observed by Jane?"

"Because I have seen her—that is to say, her head."

"When? where?"

"Whilst dressing for dinner, I was before the glass doing my hair, when I saw in the mirror someone behind me. I had only the two candles lighted on the table, and the room was otherwise dark. I thought I heard someone stirring—just the sort of stealthy step I have come to recognize as having troubled me so often. I did not turn, but looked steadily before me into the glass, and I could see reflected therein someone—a woman with red hair. Then I moved from my place quickly. I heard steps of some person hurrying away, but I saw no one then."

"The door was open?"

"No, it was shut."

"But where did she go?"

"I do not know, mamma. I looked everywhere in the room and could find no one. I have been quite upset. I cannot tell what to think of this. I feel utterly unhinged."

"I noticed at table that you did not appear well, but I said nothing about it. Your father gets so alarmed, and fidgets and fusses, if he thinks that there is anything the matter with you. But this is a most extraordinary story."

"It is an extraordinary fact," said Bessie.

"You have searched your room thoroughly?"

"I have looked into every corner."

"And there is no one there?"

"No one. Would you mind, mamma, sleeping with me to-night? I am so frightened. Do you think it can be a ghost?"

"Ghost? Fiddlesticks!"

I made some excuses to my husband and spent the night in Bessie's room. There was no disturbance that night of any sort. Although my daughter was excited and unable to sleep till long after midnight, she did fall into refreshing slumber at last and, in the morning, said to me: "Mamma, I think I must have fancied that I saw something in the glass. I dare say my nerves were over-wrought."

I was greatly relieved to hear this, and I arrived at much the same conclusion as did Bessie but was again bewildered and my mind unsettled by Jane, who came to me just before lunch when I was alone and said—

"Please, ma'am, it's only fair to say, but it's not Miss Bessie."

"What is not Miss Bessie? I mean, who is not Miss Bessie?"

"Her as is spying on me."

"I told you it could not be she. Who is it?"

"Please, ma'am, I don't know. It's a red-haired girl."

"But, Jane, be serious. There is no red-haired girl in the house."

"I know there ain't, ma'am. But for all that, she spies on me."

"Be reasonable, Jane," I said, disguising the shock her words produced in me. "If there be no red-haired girl in the house, how can you have one watching you?"

"I don't know, but one does."

"How do you know that she is red-haired?"

"Because I have seen her."

"When?"

"This morning."

"Indeed?"

"Yes, ma'am. I was going upstairs, when I heard steps coming softly after me—the backstairs, ma'am; they're rather dark and steep, and there's no carpet on them, as on the front stairs, and I was sure I heard someone following me; so I twisted about, thinking it might be cook, but it wasn't. I saw a young woman in a print dress, and the light as came from the window at the side fell on her head, and it was carrots—reg'lar carrots."

"Did you see her face?"

"No, ma'am; she put her arm up and turned and ran downstairs, and I went after her, but I never found her."

"You followed her—how far?"

"To the kitchen. Cook was there. And I said to the cook, says I: 'Did you see a girl come this way?' And she said, short-like: 'No.'"

"And cook saw nothing at all?"

"Nothing. She didn't seem best pleased at my axing. I suppose I frightened her, as I'd been telling her about how I was followed and spied on."

I mused a moment only and then said solemnly—

"Jane, what you want is a pill. You are suffering from hallucinations. I know a case very much like yours and take my word for it that, in your condition of liver or digestion, a pill is a sovereign remedy. Set your mind at rest; this is a mere delusion caused by pressure on the optic nerve. I will give you a pill tonight when you go to bed, another tomorrow, a third on the day after, and that will settle the red-haired girl. You will see no more of her."

"You think so, ma'am?"

"I am sure of it."

On consideration, I thought it as well to mention the matter to the cook, a strange, reserved woman, not given to talking, who did her work admirably, but whom, for some inexplicable reason, I did not like. If I had considered a little further as to how to broach the subject, I should perhaps have proved more successful; but by not doing so, I rushed the question and obtained no satisfaction.

I had gone down to the kitchen to order dinner, and the difficult question had arisen about how to dispose of the scraps from yesterday's joint.

"Rissoles, ma'am?"

"No," said I, "not rissoles. Your master objects to them."

"Then perhaps croquettes?"

"They are only rissoles in disguise."

"Perhaps cottage pie?"

"No; that is inorganic rissole, a sort of protoplasm out of which rissoles are developed."

"Then, ma'am, I might make a hash."

"Not an ordinary, barefaced, rudimentary hash?"

"No, ma'am, with French mushrooms, or truffles, or tomatoes."

"Well—yes—perhaps. By the way, talking of tomatoes, which is that red-haired girl who has been about the house?"

"Can't say, ma'am."

I noticed at once that the eyes of the cook contracted, her lips tightened, and her face assumed a half-defiant, half-terrified look.

"You have not many friends in this place, have you, cook?"

"No, ma'am, none."

"Then who can she be?"

"Can't say, ma'am."

"You can throw no light on the matter? It is very unsatisfactory having a person about the house —and she has been seen upstairs—of whom one knows nothing."

"No doubt, ma'am."

"And you cannot enlighten me?"

"She is no friend of mine."

"Nor is she of Jane's. Jane spoke to me about her. Has she remarked concerning this girl to you?"

"Can't say, ma'am, as I notice all Jane says. She talks a good deal."

"You see, there must be someone who is a stranger and who has access to this house. It is most awkward."

"Very so, ma'am."

I could get nothing more from the cook. I might as well have talked to a log, and, indeed, her face assumed a wooden look as I continued to speak to her on the matter. So I sighed and said—

"Very well, hash with tomato," and went upstairs.

A few days later, the house parlourmaid said to me, "Please, ma'am, may I have another pill?"

"Pill!" I exclaimed. "Why?"

"Because I have seen her again. She was behind the curtains, and I caught her putting out her redhead to look at me."

"Did you see her face?"

"No; she up with her arm over it and scuttled away."

"This is strange. I do not think I have more than two podophyllin pills left in the box, but to those you are welcome. Only I should recommend a different treatment. Instead of taking them yourself, the moment you see, or fancy that you see, the red-haired girl, go at her with the box and threaten to administer the pills to her. That will rout her, if anything will."

"But she will not stop for the pills."

"The threat of having them forced on her every time she shows herself will disconcert her. Conceive, I am supposing that on each occasion Miss Bessie, or I, were to meet you on the stairs, in a room, on the landing, in the hall, we were to rush on you and force, let us say, castor-oil globules between your lips. You would give notice at once."

"Yes; so I should, ma'am."

"Well, try this upon the red-haired girl. It will prove infallible."

"Thank you, ma'am; what you say seems reasonable."

Whether Bessie saw more of the puzzling apparition, I cannot say. She spoke no further on the matter to me, but that may have been so as to cause me no further uneasiness. I was unable to resolve the question to my own satisfaction—whether what had been seen was a real person, who obtained access to the house in some unaccountable manner, or whether it was, what I have called it, an apparition.

As far as I could ascertain, nothing had been taken away. The movements of the red-haired girl were not those of one who sought to pilfer. They seemed to me rather those of one not in her right mind, and on this supposition, I made inquiries in the neighbourhood as to the existence in our street, in any of the adjoining houses, of a person wanting in her wits, who was suffered to run about at will. But I could obtain no information that at all threw light on a point to me so perplexing.

Hitherto I had not mentioned the topic to my husband. I knew so well that I should obtain no help from him that I made no effort to seek it. He would "Pish!" and "Pshaw!" and make some slighting reference to women's intellects and not further trouble himself about the matter.

But one day, to my great astonishment, he referred to it himself.

"Julia," said he, "do you observe how I have cut myself in shaving?"

"Yes, dear," I replied. "You have cotton-wool sticking to your jaw, as if you were growing a white whisker on one side."

"It bled a great deal," said he.

"I am sorry to hear it."

"And I mopped up the blood with the new toilet-cover."

"Never!" I exclaimed. "You haven't been so foolish as to do that?"

"Yes. And that is just like you. You are much more concerned about your toilet-cover being stained than about my poor cheek which is gashed."

"You were very clumsy to do it," was all I could say. Married people are not always careful to preserve the amenities in private life. It is a pity, but it is so.

"It was due to no clumsiness on my part," said he, "though I do allow my nerves have been so shaken, broken, by married life, that I cannot always command my hand, as was the case when I was a bachelor. But this time it was due to that new, stupid, red-haired servant you have introduced into the house without consulting me or my pocket."

"Red-haired servant!" I echoed.

"Yes, that red-haired girl I have seen about. She thrusts herself into my study in a most offensive and objectionable way. But the climax of all was this morning, when I was shaving. I stood in my shirt before the glass, and had lathered my face, and was engaged on my right jaw, when that red-haired girl rushed between me and the mirror with both her elbows up, screening her face with her arms, and her head bowed. I started back, and in so doing cut myself."

"Where did she come from?"

"How can I tell? I did not expect to see anyone."

"Then where did she go?"

"I do not know; I was too concerned about my bleeding jaw to look about me. That girl must be dismissed."

"I wish she could be dismissed," I said.

"What do you mean?"

I did not answer my husband, for I really did not know what answer to make.

I was now the only person in the house who had not seen the red-haired girl, except possibly the cook, from whom I could gather nothing but whom I suspected of knowing more concerning this mysterious apparition than she chose to admit. That what had been seen by Bessie and Jane was a supernatural visitant, I now felt convinced, seeing that it had appeared to that least imaginative and most commonplace of all individuals, my husband. By no mental process could he have been got to imagine anything. He certainly did see this red-haired girl and that no living, corporeal maid had been in his dressing room at the time, I was perfectly certain.

I was soon. However, I myself to be included in the number of those before whose eyes she appeared. It was in this wise.

Cook had gone out to do some marketing. I was in the breakfast room when, wanting a funnel to fill a little phial of brandy I always keep on the washstand in case of emergencies, I went to the head of the kitchen stairs to descend and fetch what I required. Then I was aware of a great clattering of the fire irons below and a banging about of the boiler and grate. I went down the steps very hastily and entered the kitchen.

There I saw a figure of a short, set girl in a shabby cotton gown, not over clean and slipshod, stooping before the stove and striking the fender with the iron poker. She had fiery red hair, very untidy.

I uttered an exclamation.

Instantly she dropped the poker, and, covering her face with her arms, uttering a strange, low cry, she dashed round the kitchen table, making nearly the complete circuit, and then swept past me, and I heard her clattering up the kitchen stairs.

I was too much taken aback to follow. I stood as one, petrified. I felt dazed and unable to trust either my eyes or my ears.

Something like a minute must have elapsed before I had sufficiently recovered to turn and leave the kitchen. Then I ascended slowly and, I confess, nervously. I was fearful lest I should find the red-haired girl cowering against the wall and that I should have to pass her.

But nothing was to be seen. I reached the hall and saw that no door was open from it except that of the breakfast room. I entered and thoroughly examined every recess, corner, and conceivable hiding place but could find no one there. Then I ascended the staircase, with my hand on the balustrade, and searched all the rooms on the first floor without the least success. Above were the servants' apartments, and I now resolved on mounting to them. Here the staircase was uncarpeted. As I was ascending, I heard Jane at work in her room. I then heard her come out hastily upon the landing. At the same moment, with a rush past me, uttering the same moan, went the red-haired girl. I am sure I felt her skirts sweep my dress. I did not notice her till she was close to me, but I did distinctly see her as she passed. I turned and saw no more.

I at once mounted to the landing where Jane was.

"What is it?" I asked.

"Please, ma'am, I've seen the red-haired girl again, and I did as you recommended. I went at her rattling the pill-box, and she turned and ran downstairs. Did you see her, ma'am, as you came up?"

"How inexplicable!" I said. I would not admit to Jane that I had seen the apparition.

The situation remained unaltered for a week. The mystery was unsolved. No fresh light had been thrown on it. I did not again see or hear anything out of the way, nor did my husband, I presume, for he made no further remarks relative to the extra servant who had caused him so much annoyance. I presume he supposed that I had summarily dismissed her. This I conjectured from a smugness assumed by his face, such as it always acquired when he had carried a point against me—which was not often.

However, one evening, abruptly, we had a new sensation. My husband, Bessie, and I were at dinner, and we were partaking of the soup, Jane standing by, waiting to change our plates and to remove the tureen, when we dropped our spoons, alarmed by fearful screams issuing from the kitchen. By the way, characteristically, my husband finished his soup before he laid down the spoon and said

—

"Good gracious! What is that?"

Bessie, Jane, and I were by this time at the door, and we rushed together to the kitchen stairs and, one after the other, ran down them. I was the first to enter, and I saw a cook wrapped in flames, a paraffin lamp on the floor broken, and the blazing oil flowing over it.

I had sufficient presence of mind to catch up the cocoanut matting, which was not impregnated with the oil and to throw it around cook, wrap her tightly in it, and force her down on the floor were not overflowed by the oil. I held her thus, and Bessie succoured me. Jane was too frightened to do other than scream. The cries of the burnt woman were terrible. Presently my husband appeared.

"Dear me! Bless me! Good gracious!" he said.

"You go away and fetch a doctor," I called to him; "you can be of no possible service here—you only get in our way."

"But the dinner?"

"Bother the dinner! Run for a surgeon."

In a little while, we had removed the poor woman to her room, she shrieking the whole way upstairs; and, when there, we laid her on the bed and kept her folded in the cocoanut matting till a medical man arrived, in spite of her struggles to be free. My husband, on this occasion, acted with commendable promptness; but whether because he was impatient for the completion of his meal or whether his sluggish nature was for once touched with human sympathy, it is not for me to say.

All I know is that, so soon as the surgeon was there, I dismissed Jane with, "There, go and get your master the rest of his dinner, and leave us with cook."

The poor creature was frightfully burnt. She was attended to devotedly by Bessie and myself till a nurse was obtained from the hospital. For hours she was as mad with terror as much as with pain.

The next day she was quieter and sent for me. I hastened to her, and she begged the nurse to leave the room. I took a chair and seated myself by her bedside, expressed my profound commiseration, and told her that I should like to know how the accident had taken place.

"Ma'am, it was the red-haired girl did it."

"The red-haired girl!"

"Yes, ma'am. I took a lamp to look how the fish was getting on, and all at once I saw her rush straight at me, and I—I backed, thinking she would knock me down, and the lamp fell over and smashed, and my clothes caught, and——"

"Oh, cook! you should not have taken the lamp."

"It's done. And she would never leave me alone till she had burnt or scalded me. You needn't be afraid—she don't haunt the house. It is me she has haunted, because of what I did to her."

"Then you know her?"

"She was in service with me, as kitchenmaid, at my last place, near Cambridge. I took a sort of hate against her, she was such a slattern and so inquisitive. She peeped into my letters, and turned out my box and drawers, she was ever prying; and when I spoke to her, she was that saucy! I reg'lar hated her. And one day she was kneeling by the stove, and I was there, too, and I suppose the devil possessed me, for I upset the boiler as was on the hot-plate right upon her, just as she looked up, and it poured over her face and bosom, and arms, and scalded her that dreadful, she died. And since then she has haunted me. But she'll do so no more. She won't trouble you further. She has done for me, as she has always minded to do, since I scalded her to death."

The unhappy woman did not recover.

"Dear me! no hope?" said my husband when informed that the surgeon despaired of her. "And good cooks are so scarce. By the way, that red-haired girl?"

"Gone—gone for ever," I said.

BETWEEN THE LIGHTS

by E.F. Benson

The day had been one unceasing fall of snow from sunrise until the gradual withdrawal of the vague white light outside indicated that the sun had set again. But as usual, at this hospitable and delightful house of Everard Chandler, where I often spent Christmas and was spending it now, there had been no lack of entertainment, and the hours had passed with a rapidity that had surprised us. A short billiard tournament had filled up the time between breakfast and lunch with Badminton and the morning papers for those who were temporarily not engaged, while afterwards, the interval till tea-time had been occupied by the majority of the party in a huge game of hide-and-seek all over the house, barring the billiard-room, which was a sanctuary for any who desired peace. But few had done that; the enchantment of Christmas, I must suppose, had, like some spell, made children of us again, and it was with palsied terror and trembling misgivings that we had tip-toed up and down the dim passages from any corner of which some wild screaming form might dart out on us. Then, wearied with exercise and emotion, we had assembled again for tea in the hall, a room of shadows and panels on which the light from the wide open fireplace, where there burned a divine mixture of peat and logs, flickered and grew bright again on the walls. Then, as was proper, ghost stories, for the narration of which the electric light was put out so that the listeners might conjecture anything they pleased to be lurking in the corners, succeeded, and we vied with each other in blood, bones, skeletons, armour and shrieks. I had just given my contribution and was reflecting with some complacency that probably the worst was now known when Everard, who had not yet administered to the horror of his guests, spoke. He was sitting opposite me in the full blaze of the fire, looking, after the illness he had gone through during the autumn, still rather pale and delicate. All the same, he had been among the boldest and best in the exploration of dark places that afternoon, and the look on his face now rather startled me.

"No, I don't mind that sort of thing," he said. "The paraphernalia of ghosts has become somehow rather hackneyed, and when I hear of screams and skeletons I feel I am on familiar ground, and can at least hide my head under the bed-clothes."

"Ah, but the bed-clothes were twitched away by my skeleton," said I, in self-defence.

"I know, but I don't even mind that. Why, there are seven, eight skeletons in this room now, covered with blood and skin and other horrors. No, the nightmares of one's childhood were the really frightening things, because they were vague. There was the true atmosphere of horror about them because one didn't know what one feared. Now if one could recapture that—"

Mrs Chandler got quickly out of her seat.

"Oh, Everard," she said, "surely you don't wish to recapture it again. I should have thought once was enough."

This was enchanting. A chorus of invitations asked him to proceed: the real true ghost-story first-hand, which was what seemed to be indicated, was too precious a thing to lose.

Everard laughed. "No, dear, I don't want to recapture it again at all," he said to his wife.

Then to us: "But really the—well, the nightmare perhaps, to which I was referring, is of the vaguest and most unsatisfactory kind. It has no apparatus about it at all. You will probably all say that it was nothing, and wonder why I was frightened. But I was; it frightened me out of my wits. And I only just saw something, without being able to swear what it was, and heard something which might have been a falling stone."

"Anyhow, tell us about the falling stone," said I.

There was a stir of movement about the circle around the fire, and the movement was not of purely physical order. It was as if—this is what I personally felt—it was as if the childish gaiety of the hours we had passed that day was suddenly withdrawn; we had jested on certain subjects, we had played hide-and-seek with all the power of earnestness that was in us. But now—so it seemed to me—there was going to be real hide-and-seek, real terrors were going to lurk in dark corners, or if not real terrors, terrors so convincing as to assume the garb of reality were going to pounce on us. And Mrs Chandler's exclamation as she sat down again, "Oh, Everard, won't it excite you?" tended in any case to excite us. The room still remained in dubious darkness except for the sudden lights disclosed on the walls by the leaping flames on the hearth, and there was the wide field for conjecture as to what might lurk in the dim corners. Everard, moreover, who had been sitting in bright light before, was banished by the extinction of some flaming log into the shadows. A voice alone spoke to us as he sat back in his low chair, a voice rather slow but very distinct.

"Last year," he said, "on the twenty-fourth of December, we were down here, as usual, Amy and I, for Christmas. Several of you who are here now were here then. Three or four of you at least."

I was one of these, but like the others kept silent for the identification, so it seemed to me was not asked for. And he went on again without a pause.

"Those of you who were here then," he said, "and are here now, will remember how very warm it was this day year. You will remember, too, that we played croquet that day on the lawn. It was perhaps a little cold for croquet, and we played it rather in order to be able to say—with sound evidence to back the statement—that we had done so."

Then he turned and addressed the whole little circle.

"We played ties of half-games," he said, "just as we have played billiards to-day, and it was certainly as warm on the lawn then as it was in the billiard-room this morning directly after breakfast, while to-day I should not wonder if there was three feet of snow outside. More, probably; listen."

A sudden draught fluted in the chimney, and the fire flared up as the current of air caught it.

The wind also drove the snow against the windows, and as he said, "Listen," we heard a soft scurry of the falling flakes against the panes, like the soft tread of many little people who stepped lightly but with the persistence of multitudes who were flocking to some rendezvous. Hundreds of little feet seemed to be gathering outside; only the glass kept them out. And of the eight skeletons present, four or five, anyhow, turned and looked at the windows. These were small-paned, with leaden bars. On the leaden bars, little heaps of snow had accumulated, but there was nothing else to be seen.

"Yes, last Christmas Eve was very warm and sunny," went on Everard. "We had had no frost that autumn, and a temerarious dahlia was still in flower. I have always thought that it must have been mad."

He paused a moment.

"And I wonder if I were not mad, too," he added.

No one interrupted him; there was something arresting, I must suppose, in what he was saying; it chimed in anyhow with the hide-and-seek, with the suggestions of the lonely snow.

Mrs Chandler had sat down again, but I heard her stir in her chair. But never was there a gay party so reduced as we had been in the last five minutes. Instead of laughing at ourselves for playing silly games, we were all taking a serious game seriously.

"Anyhow, I was sitting out," he said to me, "while you and my wife played your half-game of croquet. Then it struck me that it was not as warm as I had supposed because, quite suddenly, I shivered. And shivering, I looked up. But I did not see you and her playing croquet at all. I saw something which had no relation to you and her—at least, I hope not."

Now the angler lands his fish, the stalker kills his stag, and the speaker holds his audience.

And as the fish is gaffed, and as the stag is shot, so were we held. There was no getting away till he had finished with us.

"You all know the croquet lawn," he said, "and how it is bounded all round by a flower border with a brick wall behind it, through which, you will remember, there is only one gate.

"Well, I looked up and saw that the lawn—I could for one moment see it was still a lawn—was shrinking, and the walls were closing in upon it. As they closed in, too, they grew higher, and simultaneously the light began to fade and be sucked from the sky till it grew quite dark overhead and only a glimmer of light came in through the gate.

"There was, as I told you, a dahlia in flower that day, and as this dreadful darkness and bewilderment came over me, I remember that my eyes sought it in a kind of despair, holding on, as it were, to any familiar object. But it was no longer a dahlia, and for the red of its petals I saw only the red of some feeble firelight. And at that moment the hallucination was complete. I was no longer sitting on the lawn watching croquet, but I was in a low-roofed room, something like a cattle-shed, but round. Close above my head, though I was sitting down, ran rafters from wall to wall. It was nearly dark, but a little light came in from the door opposite to me, which seemed to lead into a passage that communicated with the exterior of the place.

Little, however, of the wholesome air came into this dreadful den; the atmosphere was oppressive and foul beyond all telling, it was as if for years it had been the place of some human menagerie, and for those years had been uncleaned and unsweetened by the winds of heaven. Yet that oppressiveness was nothing to the awful horror of the place from the view of the spirit. Some dreadful atmosphere of crime and abomination dwelt heavy in it, its denizens, whoever they were, were scarce human, so it seemed to me, and though men and women, were akin more to the beasts of the field. And in addition there was present to me some sense of the weight of years; I had been taken and thrust down into some epoch of dim antiquity."

He paused a moment, and the fire on the hearth leapt up for a second and then died down again. But in that gleam, I saw that all faces were turned to Everard and that all wore some look of dreadful expectancy. Certainly, I felt it myself and waited in a sort of shrinking horror for what was coming.

"As I told you," he continued, "where there had been that unseasonable dahlia, there now burned a dim firelight, and my eyes were drawn there. Shapes were gathered round it; what they were I could not at first see. Then perhaps my eyes got more accustomed to the dusk, or the fire burned better, for I perceived that they were of the human form, but very small, for when one rose with a horrible chattering, to his feet, his head was still some inches off the low roof. He was dressed in a sort of shirt that came to his knees, but his arms were bare and covered with hair.

"Then the gesticulation and chattering increased, and I knew that they were talking about me, for they kept pointing in my direction. At that, my horror suddenly deepened, for I became aware that I was powerless and could not move hand or foot; a helpless, nightmare impotence had possession of me. I could not lift a finger or turn my head. And in the paralysis of that fear, I tried to scream, but not a sound could I utter.

"All this I suppose took place with the instantaneousness of a dream, for at once, and without transition, the whole thing had vanished, and I was back on the lawn again, while the stroke for which my wife was aiming was still unplayed. But my face was dripping with perspiration, and I was trembling all over.

"Now, you may all say that I had fallen asleep and had a sudden nightmare. That may be so, but I was conscious of no sense of sleepiness before, and I was conscious of none afterwards. It was as if someone had held a book before me, whisked the pages open for a second and closed them again."

Somebody, I don't know, who got up from his chair with a sudden movement that made me start and turn on the electric light. I do not mind confessing that I was rather glad of this.

Everard laughed.

"Really, I feel like Hamlet in the play scene," he said, "and as if there was a guilty uncle present. Shall I go on?"

I don't think anyone replied, and he went on.

"Well, let us say for the moment that it was not a dream exactly but a hallucination.

"Whichever it was, in any case, it haunted me; for months, I think, it was never quite out of my mind but lingered somewhere in the dusk of consciousness, sometimes sleeping quietly, so to speak, but sometimes stirring in its sleep. It was no good my telling myself that I was disquieting myself in vain, for it was as if something had actually entered into my very soul as if some seed of horror had been planted there. And as the weeks went on, the seed began to sprout so that I could no longer even tell myself that that vision had been a moment's disorderment only. I can't say that it actually affected my health. I did not, as far as I know, sleep or eat insufficiently, but the morning after morning, I used to wake, not gradually and through pleasant dozings into full consciousness, but with absolute suddenness, and find myself plunged in an abyss of despair.

"Often, too, eating or drinking, I used to pause and wonder if it was worthwhile.

"Eventually, I told two people about my trouble, hoping that perhaps the mere communication would help matters, hoping also, but very distantly, that though I could not believe at present that digestion or the obscurities of the nervous system were at fault, a doctor by some simple dose might convince me of it. In other words, I told my wife, who laughed at me, and my doctor, who laughed also and assured me that my health was quite unnecessarily robust.

"At the same time, he suggested that the change of air and scene does wonder for the delusions that exist merely in the imagination. He also told me, in answer to a direct question, that he would stake his reputation on the certainty that I was not going mad.

"Well, we went up to London as usual for the season, and though nothing whatever occurred to remind me in any way of that single moment on Christmas Eve, the reminding was seen to all right, the moment itself took care of that, for instead of fading as is the way of sleeping or waking dreams, it grew every day more vivid, and ate, so to speak, like some corrosive acid into my mind, etching itself there. And to London succeeded Scotland.

"I took last year for the first time a small forest up in Sutherland called Glen Callan, very remote and wild but affording excellent stalking. It was not far from the sea, and the gillies always used to warn me to carry a compass on the hill because sea mists were liable to come up with frightful rapidity, and there was always a danger of being caught by one and of having perhaps to wait hours till it cleared again. This, at first, I always used to do, but, as everyone knows, any precaution that one takes which continues to be unjustified gets gradually relaxed. At the end of a few weeks, since the weather had been uniformly clear, it was natural that, as often as not, my compass remained at home.

"One day the stalk took me on to a part of my ground that I had seldom been on before, a very high table-land on the limit of my forest, which went down very steeply on one side to a loch that lay below it, and on the other, by gentler gradations, to the river that came from the loch, six miles below which stood the lodge. The wind had necessitated our climbing up—or so my stalker had insisted—not by the easier way, but up the crags from the loch. I had argued the point with him for it seemed to me that it was impossible that the deer could get our scent if we went by the more natural path, but he still held to his opinion; and therefore, since after all this was his part of the job, I yielded. A dreadful climb we had of it, over big boulders with deep holes in between, masked by clumps of heather, so that a wary eye and a prodding stick were necessary for each step if one wished to avoid broken bones. Adders also literally swarmed in the heather; we must have seen a dozen at least on our way up, and adders are a beast for which I have no manner of use. But a couple of hours saw us to the top, only to find that the stalker had been utterly at fault, and that the deer must quite infallibly have got wind of us, if they had remained in the place where we last saw them. That, when we could spy the ground again, we saw had happened; in any case they had gone. The man insisted the wind had changed, a palpably stupid excuse, and I wondered at that moment what other reason he had—for reason I felt sure there must be—for not wishing to take what would clearly now have been a better route. But this piece of bad management did not spoil our luck, for within an hour we had spied more deer, and about two o'clock I got a shot, killing a heavy stag. Then sitting on the heather I ate lunch, and enjoyed a well-earned bask and smoke in the sun. The pony meantime had been saddled with the stag, and was plodding homewards.

"The morning had been extraordinarily warm, with a little wind blowing off the sea, which lay a few miles off sparkling beneath a blue haze, and all morning in spite of our abominable climb, I had had an extreme sense of peace, so much so that several times I had probed my mind, so to speak, to find if the horror still lingered there. But I could scarcely get any response from it.

"Never since Christmas had I been so free of fear, and it was with a great sense of repose, both physical and spiritual, that I lay looking up into the blue sky, watching my smoke-whorls curl slowly away into nothingness. But I was not allowed to take my ease long, for Sandy came and begged that I would move. The weather had changed, he said, the wind had shifted again, and he wanted me to be off this high ground and on the path again as soon as possible, because it looked to him as if a sea-mist would presently come up."

"'And yon's a bad place to get down in the mist,' he added, nodding towards the crags we had come up.

"I looked at the man in amazement, for to our right lay a gentle slope down onto the river, and there was now no possible reason for again tackling those hideous rocks up which we had climbed this morning. More than ever, I was sure he had some secret reason for not wishing to go the obvious way. But about one thing, he was certainly right, the mist was coming up from the sea, and I felt in my pocket for the compass and found I had forgotten to bring it.

"Then there followed a curious scene which lost us time that we could really ill afford to waste, I insisting on going down by the way that common sense directed, he imploring me to take his word for it that the crags were the better way. Eventually, I marched off to the easier descent, and told him not to argue any more but follow. What annoyed me about him was that he would only give the most senseless reasons for preferring the crags. There were mossy places, he said, on the way I wished to go, a thing patently false, since the summer had been one spell of unbroken weather; or it was longer, also obviously untrue; or there were so many vipers about.

"But seeing that none of these arguments produced any effect, at last, he desisted and came after me in silence.

"We were not yet half down when the mist was upon us, shooting up from the valley like the broken water of a wave, and in three minutes we were enveloped in a cloud of fog so thick that we could barely see a dozen yards in front of us. It was therefore another cause for self-congratulation that we were not now, as we should otherwise have been, precariously clambering on the face of those crags up which we had come with such difficulty in the morning, and as I rather prided myself on my powers of generalship in the matter of direction, I continued leading, feeling sure that before long we should strike the track by the river. More than all, the absolute freedom from fear elated me; since Christmas I had not known the instinctive joy of that; I felt like a schoolboy home for the holidays. But the mist grew thicker and thicker, and whether it was that real rain-clouds had formed above it, or that it was of an extraordinary density itself, I got wetter in the next hour than I have ever been before or since. The wet seemed to penetrate the skin, and chill the very bones. And still there was no sign of the track for which I was making.

"Behind me, muttering to himself, followed the stalker, but his arguments and protestations were dumb, and it seemed as if he kept close to me, as if afraid.

"Now, there are many unpleasant companions in this world; I would not, for instance, care to be on the hill with a drunkard or a maniac, but worse than either, I think, is a frightened man because his trouble is infectious, and, insensibly. I began to be afraid of being frightened too.

"From that, it is but a short step to fear. Other perplexities, too, beset us. At one time, we seemed to be walking on flat ground. At another, I felt sure we were climbing again, whereas all the time, we ought to have been descending unless we had missed the way very badly indeed. Also, for the month was October, it was beginning to get dark, and it was with a sense of relief that I remembered that the full moon would rise soon after sunset. But it had grown very much colder, and soon, instead of rain, we found we were walking through a steady fall of snow.

"Things were pretty bad, but then for the moment, they seemed to mend. Far, far away to the left, I suddenly heard the brawling of the river. It should, it is true, have been straight in front of me, and we were perhaps a mile out of our way, but this was better than the blind wandering of the last hour, and turning to the left, I walked towards it. But before I had gone a hundred yards, I heard a sudden choked cry behind me and just saw Sandy's form flying as if in terror of pursuit, into the mists. I called him but got no reply and heard only the spurned stones of his running.

"What had frightened him, I had no idea, but certainly with his disappearance, the infection of his fear disappeared also, and I went on, I may almost say, with gaiety. At the moment, however, I saw a sudden well-defined blackness in front of me, and before I knew what I was doing, I was half stumbling, half walking up a very steep grass slope.

"During the last few minutes, the wind had got up, and the driving snow was peculiarly uncomfortable, but there had been a certain consolation in thinking that the wind would soon disperse these mists, and I had nothing more than a moonlight walk home. But as I paused on this slope, I became aware of two things, one, that the blackness in front of me was very close, and the other that, whatever it was, it sheltered me from the snow. So I climbed on a dozen yards into its friendly shelter, for it seemed to me to be friendly.

"A wall some twelve feet high crowned the slope, and exactly where I struck it, there was a hole in it, or door rather, through which a little light appeared. Wondering at this, I pushed on, bending down, for the passage was very low, and in a dozen yards, came out on the other side.

"Just as I did this, the sky suddenly grew lighter, the wind, I suppose, having dispersed the mists, and the moon, though not yet visible through the flying skirts of cloud, made sufficient illumination.

"I was in a circular enclosure, and above me, there projected from the walls some four feet from the ground, broken stones which must have been intended to support a floor. Then simultaneously, two things occurred.

"The whole of my nine months' terror came back to me, for I saw that the vision in the garden was fulfilled, and at the same moment, I saw stealing towards me a little figure as of a man, but only about three foot six in height. That my eyes told me; my ears told me that he stumbled on a stone; my nostrils told me that the air I breathed was of an overpowering foulness, and my soul told me that it was sick unto death. I think I tried to scream but could not; I know I tried to move and could not. And it crept closer.

"Then I suppose the terror which held me spellbound so spurred me that I must move, for next moment I heard a cry break from my lips and was stumbling through the passage. I made one leap of it down the grass slope and ran as I hoped never to have to run again. What direction I took I did not pause to consider, so long as I put distance between me and that place. Luck, however, favoured me, and before long, I struck the track by the river and, an hour afterwards, reached the lodge.

"Next day, I developed a chill, and as you know, pneumonia laid me on my back for six weeks.

"Well, that is my story, and there are many explanations. You may say that I fell asleep on the lawn and was reminded of that by finding myself, under discouraging circumstances, in an old Picts' castle, where a sheep or a goat that, like myself, had taken shelter from the storm was moving about. Yes, there are hundreds of ways in which you may explain it. But the coincidence was an odd one, and those who believe in second sight might find an instance of their hobby in it."

"And that is all?" I asked.

"Yes, it was nearly too much for me. I think the dressing bell has sounded."

THE DAMNED THING

by Ambrose Bierce

By the light of a tallow candle, which had been placed on one end of a rough table, a man was reading something written in a book. It was an old account book, greatly worn, and the writing was not, apparently, very legible, for the man sometimes held the page close to the flame of the candle to get a stronger light upon it. The shadow of the book would then throw into obscurity half of the room, darkening a number of faces and figures; for besides the reader, eight other men were present. Seven of them sat against the rough log walls, silent and motionless, and the room was small, not very far from the table. By extending an arm, any one of them could have touched the eighth man, who lay on the table, face upward, partly covered by a sheet, his arms at his sides. He was dead.

The man with the book was not reading aloud, and no one spoke; all seemed to be waiting for something to occur; the dead man only was without expectation. From the blank darkness outside came in, through the aperture that served for a window, all the ever-unfamiliar noises of the night in the wilderness—the long, nameless note of a distant coyote; the stilly pulsing thrill of tireless insects in trees; strange cries of night birds, so different from those of the birds of the day; the drone of great blundering beetles, and all that mysterious chorus of small sounds that seem always to have been but half heard when they have suddenly ceased, as if conscious of an indiscretion. But nothing of all this was noted in that company; its members were not overmuch addicted to idle interest in matters of no practical importance; that was obvious in every line of their rugged faces—obvious even in the dim light of the single candle. They were evidently men of the vicinity—farmers and woodmen.

The person reading was a trifle different; one would have said of him that he was of the world, worldly, albeit there was that in his attire which attested a certain fellowship with the organisms of his environment. His coat would hardly have passed muster in San Francisco: his footgear was not of urban origin, and the hat that lay by him on the floor (he was the only one uncovered) was such that if one had considered it as an article of mere personal adornment, he would have missed its meaning. In countenance, the man was rather prepossessing, with just a hint of sternness, though that he may have assumed or cultivated as appropriate to one in authority. For he was a coroner. It was by virtue of his office that he had possession of the book in which he was reading; it had been found among the dead man's effects—in his cabin, where the inquest was now taking place.

When the coroner had finished reading, he put the book into his breast pocket. At that moment, the door was pushed open, and a young man entered. He, clearly, was not of mountain birth and breeding: he was clad as those who dwell in cities. His clothing was dusty, however, as from travel. He had, in fact, been riding hard to attend the inquest.

The coroner nodded; no one else greeted him.

"We have waited for you," said the coroner. "It is necessary to have done with this business to-night."

The young man smiled. "I am sorry to have kept you," he said. "I went away, not to evade your summons, but to post to my newspaper an account of what I suppose I am called back to relate."

The coroner smiled.

"The account that you posted to your newspaper," he said, "differs probably from that which you will give here under oath."

"That," replied the other, rather hotly and with a visible flush, "is as you choose. I used manifold paper and have a copy of what I sent. It was not written as news, for it is incredible, but as fiction. It may go as a part of my testimony under oath."

"But you say it is incredible."

"That is nothing to you, sir, if I also swear that it is true."

The coroner was apparently not greatly affected by the young man's manifest resentment. He was silent for some moments, his eyes upon the floor. The men about the sides of the cabin talked in whispers but seldom withdrew their gaze from the face of the corpse. Presently the coroner lifted his eyes and said: "We will resume the inquest."

The men removed their hats. The witness was sworn in.

"What is your name?" the coroner asked.

"William Harker."

"Age?"

"Twenty-seven."

"You knew the deceased, Hugh Morgan?"

"Yes."

"You were with him when he died?"

"Near him."

"How did that happen—your presence, I mean?"

"I was visiting him at this place to shoot and fish. A part of my purpose, however, was to study him, and his odd, solitary way of life. He seemed a good model for a character in fiction. I sometimes write stories."

"I sometimes read them."

"Thank you."

"Stories in general—not yours."

Some of the jurors laughed. Against a sombre background, humour shows highlights. Soldiers in the intervals of battle laugh easily, and a jest in the death chamber conquers by surprise.

"Relate the circumstances of this man's death," said the coroner. "You may use any notes or memoranda that you please."

The witness understood. Pulling a manuscript from his breast pocket, he held it near the candle and, turning the leaves until he found the passage that he wanted, began to read.

II

"...The sun had hardly risen when we left the house. We were looking for quail, each with a shotgun, but we had only one dog. Morgan said that our best ground was beyond a certain ridge that he pointed out, and we crossed it by a trail through the chaparral. On the other side was comparatively level ground, thickly covered with wild oats. As we emerged from the chaparral, Morgan was but a few yards in advance. Suddenly, we heard, at a little distance to our right, and partly in front, a noise as of some animal thrashing about in the bushes, which we could see were violently agitated.

"'We've started a deer,' said. 'I wish we had brought a rifle.'

"Morgan, who had stopped and was intently watching the agitated chaparral, said nothing, but had cocked both barrels of his gun, and was holding it in readiness to aim. I thought him a trifle excited, which surprised me, for he had a reputation for exceptional coolness, even in moments of sudden and imminent peril.

"'O, come!' I said. 'You are not going to fill up a deer with quail-shot, are you?'

"Still he did not reply; but, catching a sight of his face as he turned it slightly toward me, I was struck by the pallor of it. Then I understood that we had serious business on hand, and my first conjecture was that we had 'jumped' a grizzly. I advanced to Morgan's side, cocking my piece as I moved.

"The bushes were now quiet, and the sounds had ceased, but Morgan was as attentive to the place as before.

"'What is it? What the devil is it?' I asked.

"'That Damned Thing!' he replied, without turning his head. His voice was husky and unnatural. He trembled visibly.

"I was about to speak further, when I observed the wild oats near the place of the disturbance moving in the most inexplicable way. I can hardly describe it. It seemed as if stirred by a streak of wind, which not only bent it, but pressed it down—crushed it so that it did not rise, and this movement was slowly prolonging itself directly toward us.

"Nothing that I had ever seen had affected me so strangely as this unfamiliar and unaccountable phenomenon, yet I am unable to recall any sense of fear. I remember—and tell it here because, singularly enough, I recollected it then—that once, in looking carelessly out of an open window, I momentarily mistook a small tree close at hand for one of a group of larger trees at a little distance away. It looked the same size as the others but, being more distinctly and sharply defined in mass and detail, seemed out of harmony with them. It was a mere falsification of the law of aerial perspective, but it startled, almost terrified me. We so rely upon the orderly operation of familiar natural laws that any seeming suspension of them is noted as a menace to our safety, a warning of unthinkable calamity. So now, the apparently causeless movement of the herbage and the slow, undeviating approach of the line of disturbance were distinctly disquieting. My companion appeared actually frightened, and I could hardly credit my senses when I saw him suddenly throw his gun to his shoulders and fire both barrels at the agitated grass! Before the smoke of the discharge had cleared away, I heard a loud savage cry—a scream like that of a wild animal—and, flinging his gun upon the ground, Morgan sprang away and ran swiftly from the spot. At the same instant, I was thrown violently to the ground by the impact of something unseen in the smoke—some soft, heavy substance that seemed thrown against me with great force.

"Before I could get upon my feet and recover my gun, which seemed to have been struck from my hands, I heard Morgan crying out as if in mortal agony, and mingling with his cries were such hoarse savage sounds as one hears from fighting dogs. Inexpressibly terrified, I struggled to my feet and looked in the direction of Morgan's retreat; and may heaven in mercy spare me from another sight like that! At a distance of less than thirty yards was my friend, down upon one knee, his head thrown back at a frightful angle, hatless, his long hair in disorder and his whole body in violent movement from side to side, backward and forward. His right arm was lifted and seemed to lack the hand—at least, I could see none. The other arm was invisible. At times, as my memory now reports this extraordinary scene, I could discern but a part of his body; it was as if he had been partly blotted out—I can not otherwise express it—then a shifting of his position would bring it all into view again.

"All this must have occurred within a few seconds, yet in that time, Morgan assumed all the postures of a determined wrestler vanquished by superior weight and strength. I saw nothing but him, and him not always distinctly. During the entire incident, his shouts and curses were heard, as if through an enveloping uproar of such sounds of rage and fury as I had never heard from the throat of man or brute!

"For a moment only I stood irresolute, then, throwing down my gun, I ran forward to my friend's assistance. I had a vague belief that he was suffering from a fit or some form of convulsion. Before I could reach his side he was down and quiet. All sounds had ceased, but, with a feeling of such terror as even these awful events had not inspired, I now saw the same mysterious movement of the wild oats prolonging itself from the trampled area about the prostrate man toward the edge of a wood. It was only when it had reached the wood that I was able to withdraw my eyes and look at my companion. He was dead."

III

The coroner rose from his seat and stood beside the dead man. Lifting an edge of the sheet, he pulled it away, exposing the entire body, altogether naked and showing in the candlelight a clay-like yellow. It had, however, broad maculations of bluish-black, obviously caused by extravasated blood from contusions. The chest and sides looked as if they had been beaten with a bludgeon. There were dreadful lacerations; the skin was torn in strips and shreds.

The coroner moved round to the end of the table and undid a silk handkerchief, which had been passed under the chin and knotted on the top of the head. When the handkerchief was drawn away, it exposed what had been the throat. Some of the jurors who had risen to get a better view repented their curiosity and turned away their faces. Witness Harker went to the open window and leaned out across the sill, faint and sick. Dropping the handkerchief upon the dead man's neck, the coroner stepped to an angle of the room and, from a pile of clothing, produced one garment after another, each of which he held up a moment for inspection. All were torn and stiff with blood. The jurors did not make a closer inspection. They seemed rather uninterested. They had, in truth, seen all this before; the only thing that was new to them was Harker's testimony.

"Gentlemen," the coroner said, "we have no more evidence, I think. Your duty has been already explained to you; if there is nothing you wish to ask, you may go outside and consider your verdict."

The foreman rose—a tall, bearded man of sixty, coarsely clad.

"I should like to ask one question, Mr Coroner," he said. "What asylum did this yer last witness escape from?"

"Mr Harker," said the coroner, gravely and tranquilly, "from what asylum did you last escape?"

Harker flushed crimson again but said nothing, and the seven jurors rose and solemnly filed out of the cabin.

"If you have done insulting me, sir," said Harker, as soon as he and the officer were left alone with the dead man, "I suppose I am at liberty to go?"

"Yes."

Harker started to leave but paused, with his hand on the door latch. The habit of his profession was strong in him—stronger than his sense of personal dignity. He turned about and said:

"The book that you have there—I recognize it as Morgan's diary. You seemed greatly interested in it; you read it while I was testifying. May I see it? The public would like—"

"The book will cut no figure in this matter," replied the official, slipping it into his coat pocket; "all the entries in it were made before the writer's death."

As Harker passed out of the house, the jury reentered and stood about the table on which the now-covered corpse showed under the sheet with sharp definition. The foreman seated himself near the candle, produced from his breast pocket a pencil and scrap of paper, and wrote rather laboriously the following verdict, which with various degrees of effort, all signed:

"We, the jury, do find that the remains come to their death at the hands of a mountain lion, but some of us think, all the same, they had fits."

IV

In the diary of the late Hugh Morgan are certain interesting entries having, possibly, a scientific value as suggestions. At the inquest upon his body, the book was not put in evidence; possibly, the coroner thought it not worthwhile to confuse the jury. The date of the first of the entries mentioned can not be ascertained; the upper part of the leaf is torn away; the part of the entry remaining is as follows:

"... would run in a half circle, keeping his head always turned toward the centre, and again he would stand still, barking furiously. At last, he ran away into the brush as fast as he could go. I thought at first that he had gone mad but, on returning to the house, found no other alteration in his manner than what was obviously due to fear of punishment.

"Can a dog see with his nose? Do odours impress some olfactory centre with images of the thing emitting them?. .

"Sept 2.—Looking at the stars last night as they rose above the crest of the ridge east of the house, I observed them successively disappear—from left to right. Each was eclipsed but an instant, and only a few at the same time, but along the entire length of the ridge, all that were within a degree or two of the crest were blotted out. It was as if something had passed along between them and me, but I could not see it, and the stars were not thick enough to define its outline. Ugh! I don't like this...."

Several weeks' entries are missing, and three leaves are being torn from the book.

"Sept. 27.—It has been about here again—I find evidence of its presence every day. I watched again all of last night in the same cover, gun in hand, double-charged with buckshot. In the morning, the fresh footprints were there, as before. Yet I would have sworn that I did not sleep—indeed, I hardly sleep at all. It is terrible, insupportable! If these amazing experiences are real, I shall go mad; if they are fanciful, I am mad already.

"Oct. 3.—I shall not go—it shall not drive me away. No, this is my house, my land. God hates a coward...

"Oct. 5.—I can stand it no longer; I have invited Harker to pass a few weeks with me—he has a level head. I can judge from his manner if he thinks me mad.

"Oct. 7.—I have the solution of the problem; it came to me last night—suddenly, as by revelation. How simple—how terribly simple!

"There are sounds that we can not hear at either end of the scale note that stir no chord of that imperfect instrument, the human ear. They are too high or too grave. I have observed a flock of blackbirds occupying an entire treetop—the tops of several trees—and all in full song. Suddenly—in a moment—at absolutely the same instant—all spring into the air and fly away. How? They could not all see one another—whole treetops intervened. At no point could a leader have been visible to all. There must have been a signal of warning or command, high and shrill above the din, but by me unheard. I had observed, too, the same simultaneous flight when all were silent, among not only blackbirds but other birds—quail, for example, widely separated by bushes—even on opposite sides of a hill.

"It is known to seamen that a school of whales basking or sporting on the surface of the ocean, miles apart, with the convexity of the earth between them, will sometimes dive at the same instant—all gone out of sight in a moment. The signal has been sounded—too grave for the ear of the sailor at the masthead and his comrades on the deck—who nevertheless feel its vibrations in the ship as the stones of a cathedral are stirred by the bass of the organ.

"As with sounds, so with colors. At each end of the solar spectrum, the chemist can detect the presence of what are known as 'actinic' rays. They represent colors—integral colors in the composition of light—which we are unable to discern. The human eye is an imperfect instrument; its range is but a few octaves of the real 'chromatic scale' I am not mad; there are colors that we can not see.

"And, God help me! the Damned Thing is of such a color!"

THE COLD EMBRACE

by Mary Elizabeth Braddon

He was an artist—such things as happened to him sometimes happen to artists.

He was a German—such things as happened to him sometimes happen to Germans.

He was young, handsome, studious, enthusiastic, metaphysical, reckless, unbelieving, and heartless.

And being young, handsome and eloquent, he was beloved.

He was an orphan under the guardianship of his dead father's brother, his uncle Wilhelm, in whose house he had brought up from a little child, and she who loved him was his cousin—his cousin Gertrude, whom he swore he loved in return.

Did he love her? Yes, when he first swore it. It soon wore out, this passionate love; how threadbare and wretched a sentiment it became at last in the selfish heart of the student! But in its first golden dawn, when he was only nineteen and had just returned from his apprenticeship to a great painter at Antwerp, and they wandered together in the most romantic outskirts of the city at a rosy sunset, by holy moonlight, or bright and joyous morning, how beautiful a dream!

They keep it a secret from Wilhelm, as he has the father's ambition of a wealthy suitor for his only child—a cold and dreary vision beside the lover's dream.

So they are betrothed, and standing side by side when the dying sun and the pale rising moon divide the heavens, he puts the betrothal ring upon her finger, the white and taper finger whose slender shape he knows so well. This ring is a peculiar one, a massive golden serpent, its tail in its mouth, the symbol of eternity; it had been his mother's, and he would know it amongst a thousand. If he were to become blind tomorrow, he could select it from amongst a thousand by the touch alone.

He places it on her finger, and they swear to be true to each other forever and ever—through trouble and danger—sorrow and change—-in wealth or poverty. Her father must need to be won to consent to their union by and by, for they were now betrothed, and death alone could part them.

But the young student, the scoffer at the revelation, yet the enthusiastic adorer of the mystical, asks:

'Can death part us? I would return to you from the grave, Gertrude. My soul would come back to be near my love. And you—you, if you died before me —the cold earth would not hold you from me; if you loved me, you would return, and again these fair arms would be clasped round my neck as they are now.'

But she told him, with a holier light in her deep-blue eyes than had ever shone in his—she told him that the dead who die at peace with God is happy in heaven, and cannot return to the troubled earth; and that it is only the suicide—the lost wretch on whom sorrowful angels shut the door of Paradise—whose unholy spirit haunts the footsteps of the living.

The first year of their betrothal is passed, and she is alone, for he has gone to Italy, on a commission for some rich man, to copy Raphaels, Titians, and Guidos, in a gallery at Florence. He has gone to win fame, perhaps, but it is not the less bitter—he is gone!

Of course, her father misses his young nephew, who has been a son to him; and he thinks his daughter's sadness no more than a cousin should feel for a cousin's absence.

In the meantime, the weeks and months pass. The lover writes—often at first, then seldom—at last, not at all.

How many excuses she invents for him! How many times she goes to the distant little post office, to which he is to address his letters! How many times she hopes, only to be disappointed!

How many times she despairs, only to hope again!

But real despair comes at last and will not be put off anymore. The rich suitor appears on the scene, and her father is determined. She is to marry at once. The wedding day is fixed—the fifteenth of June.

The date seems burnt into her brain.

The date, written in fire, dances forever before her eyes.

The date, shrieked by the Furies, sounds continually in her ears.

But there is time yet—it is the middle of May—there is time for a letter to reach him at Florence; there is time for him to come to Brunswick, to take her away and marry her, in spite of her father—in spite of the whole world.

But the days and weeks fly by, and he does not write—he does not come. This is indeed despair which usurps her heart and will not be put away.

It is on the fourteenth of June. For the last time, she goes to the little post office; for the last time, she asks the old question, and they give her for the last time the dreary answer, 'No; no letter.'

For the last time—tomorrow is the day appointed for her bridal. Her father will hear no entreaties; her rich suitor will not listen to her prayers. They will not be put off a day—an hour; tonight alone is hers—this night, which she may employ as she will.

She takes another path than that which leads home; she hurries through some by-streets of the city, out onto a lonely bridge, where he and she had stood so often in the sunset, watching the rose-colored light glow fade and die upon the river.

He returns from Florence. He had received her letter. That letter, blotted with tears, entreating, despairing—he had received it, but he loved her no longer. A young Florentine, who has sat to him for a model, had bewitched his fancy—that fancy which with him stood in place of a heart—and Gertrude had been half-forgotten. If she had a rich suitor, good; let her marry him; better for her, better far for himself. He had no wish to fetter himself with a wife. Had he not his art always?—his eternal bride, his unchanging mistress.

Thus he thought it wiser to delay his journey to Brunswick so that he should arrive when the wedding was over—arrive in time to salute the bride.

And the vows—the mystical fancies—the belief in his return, even after death, to the embrace of his beloved? O, gone out of his life, melted away forever, those foolish dreams of his boyhood.

So on the fifteenth of June, he enters Brunswick, by that very bridge on which she stood, the stars looking down on her the night before. He strolls across the bridge and down by the water's edge, a great rough dog at his heels, and the smoke from his short meerschaum-pipe curling in blue wreaths fantastically in the pure morning air. He has his sketch-book under his arm, and, attracted now and then by some object that catches his artist's eye. He stops to draw: a few weeds and pebbles on the river's brink—a crag on the opposite shore—a group of pollard willows in the distance. When he has done this, he admires his drawing, shuts his sketchbook, empties the ashes from his pipe, refills from his tobacco pouch, sings the refrain of a gay drinking song, calls to his dog, smokes again, and walks on. Suddenly he opens his sketchbook again; this time, that which attracts him is a group of figures: but what is it? It is not a funeral, for there are no mourners.

It is not a funeral, but a corpse lying on a rough bier, covered with an old sail, carried between two bearers.

It is not a funeral, for the bearers are fishermen —fishermen in their everyday garb.

About a hundred yards from him, they rest their burden on a bank——one stands at the head of the bier, and the other throws himself down at the foot of it.

And thus, they form a perfect group; he walks back two or three paces, selects his point of sight, and begins to sketch a hurried outline. He has finished it before they move; he hears their voices, though he cannot hear their words, and wonders what they can be talking of. Presently he walks on and joins them.

'You have a corpse there, my friends?' he says.

'Yes; a corpse washed ashore an hour ago.'

'Drowned?'

'Yes, drowned. A young girl, very handsome.'

'Suicides are always handsome,' says the painter, and then he stands for a little while idly smoking and meditating, looking at the sharp outline of the corpse and the stiff folds of the rough canvas covering.

Life is such a golden holiday for him—young, ambitious, clever——that it seems as though sorrow and death could have no part in his destiny.

At last, he says that, as this poor suicide is so handsome, he should like to make a sketch of her.

He gives the fishermen some money, and they offer to remove the sailcloth that covers her features.

No, he will do it himself. He lifts the rough, coarse, wet canvas from her face. What face?

The face that shone on the dreams of his foolish boyhood; the face which once was the light of his uncle's home. His cousin Gertrude—his betrothed!

He sees, as in one glance, while he draws one breath, the rigid features—the marble arms—the hands crossed on the cold bosom; and, on the third finger of the left hand, the ring which had been his mother's—the golden serpent; the ring which, if he were to become blind, he could select from a thousand others by the touch alone.

But he is a genius and a metaphysician—grief, true grief, is not for such as he. His first thought is the flight—flight anywhere out of that accursed city —anywhere far from the brink of that hideous river —-anywhere away from remorse—anywhere to forget.

He is miles on the road that leads away from Brunswick before he knows that he has walked a step.

It is only when his dog lies down panting at his feet that he feels how exhausted he is himself and sits down upon a bank to rest, how the landscape spins round and round before his dazzled eyes while his morning's sketch of the two fishermen and the canvas-covered bier glares redly at him out of the twilight!

At last, after sitting a long time by the roadside, idly playing with his dog, idly smoking, idly lounging, looking as any idle, light-hearted travelling student might look, yet all the while acting over that morning's scene in his burning brain a hundred times a minute; at last, he grows a little more composed and tries presently to think of himself as he is, apart from his cousin's suicide.

Apart from that, he was no worse off than he was yesterday. His genius was not gone; the money he had earned at Florence still lined his pocketbook; he was his own master, free to go whither he would.

And while he sits on the roadside, trying to separate himself from the scene of that morning—trying to put away the image of the corpse covered with the damp canvas sail—trying to think of what he should do next, where he should go, to be farthest away from Brunswick and remorse, the old diligence comes rumbling and jingling along. He remembers it; it goes from Brunswick to Aix-la-Chapelle.

He whistles to his dog shouts to the postillion to stop, and springs into the coupé.

During the whole evening, through the long night, though he does not once close his eyes, he never speaks a word; but when morning dawns and the other passengers awake and begin to talk to each other, he joins in the conversation. He tells them that he is an artist, that he is going to Cologne and to Antwerp to copy Rubenses and the great picture by Quentin Matsys in the museum. He remembered afterwards that he talked and laughed boisterously and that when he was talking and laughing loudest, a passenger, older and graver than the rest, opened the window near him and told him to put his head out. He remembered the fresh air blowing in his face, the singing of the birds in his ears, and the flat fields and roadside reeling before his eyes. He remembered this and then fell in a lifeless heap on the floor of the diligence.

It is a fever that keeps him for six long weeks in a bed at a hotel in Aix-la-Chapelle.

He gets well and, accompanied by his dog, starts on foot for Cologne. By this time, he is his former self once more. Again the blue smoke from his short meerschaum curls upwards in the morning air—again, he sings some old university drinking song—again stops here and there, meditating and sketching.

He is happy and has forgotten his cousin—and so on to Cologne.

It is by the great cathedral he is standing, with his dog at his side. It is night, the bells have just chimed the hour, and the clocks are striking eleven; the moonlight shines full upon the magnificent pile, over which the artist's eye wanders, absorbed in the beauty of form.

He is not thinking of his drowned cousin, for he has forgotten her and is happy.

Suddenly someone, something from behind him, puts two cold arms around his neck and clasps its hands on his breast.

And yet there is no one behind him, for, on the flags bathed in the broad moonlight, there are only two shadows, his own and his dog's. He turns quickly round—there is no one—nothing to be seen in the broad square but himself and his dog, and though he feels, he cannot see the cold arms clasped round his neck.

It is not ghostly, this embrace, for it is palpable to the touch—it cannot be real, for it is invisible.

He tries to throw off the cold caress. He clasps the hands in his own to tear them asunder and to cast them off his neck. He can feel the long delicate fingers cold and wet beneath his touch, and on the third finger of his left hand, he can feel the ring which was his mother's—the golden serpent—the ring which he has always said he would know among a thousand by the touch alone. He knows it now!

His dead cousin's cold arms are round his neck—his dead cousin's wet hands are clasped upon his breast. He asks himself if he is mad. 'Up, Leo!' he shouts. 'Up, up, boy!' and the Newfoundland leaps to his shoulders—the dog's paws are on the dead hands, and the animal utters a terrific howl and springs away from his master.

The student stands in the moonlight, the dead arms around his neck, and the dog at a little distance moaning piteously.

Presently a watchman, alarmed by the howling of the dog, comes into the square to see what is wrong.

In a breath, the cold arms are gone.

He takes the watchman home to the hotel with him and gives him money; in his gratitude, he could have given that man half his little fortune.

Will it ever come to him again, this embrace of the dead?

He tries never to be alone; he makes a hundred acquaintances and shares the chamber with another student. He starts up if he is left by himself in the public room at the inn where he is staying and runs into the street. People notice his strange actions and begin to think that he is mad.

But, in spite of all, he is alone once more; for one night, the public room is empty for a moment when on some idle pretence, he strolls into the street, the street is empty too, and for the second time, he feels the cold arms round his neck, and for the second time, when he calls his dog, the animal slinks away from him with a piteous howl.

After this, he leaves Cologne, still travelling on foot—of necessity now, for his money is getting low. He joins travelling hawkers, walks side by side with labourers, talks to every foot passenger he falls in with, and tries from morning till night to get the company on the road.

At night he sleeps by the fire in the kitchen of the inn, at which he stops but does what he will, he is often alone, and it is now a common thing for him to feel the cold arms around his neck.

Many months have passed since his cousin's death—autumn, winter, and early spring. His money is nearly gone, his health is utterly broken, he is the shadow of his former self, and he is getting near to Paris. He will reach that city at the time of the Carnival. To this, he looks forward. In Paris, in Carnival time, he need never, surely, be alone, never feel that deadly caress; he may even recover his lost gaiety, and his lost health, once more resume his profession, once more earn fame and money by his art.

How hard he tries to get over the distance that divides him from Paris, while day by day, he grows weaker, and his step slower and heavier!

But there is an end at last; the long dreary roads are passed. This is Paris, which he enters for the first time—Paris, of which he has dreamed so much—Paris, whose million voices are to exorcise his phantom.

To him, tonight Paris seems one vast chaos of lights, music, and confusion—lights which dance before his eyes and will not be still—-music that rings in his ears and deafens him—-confusion which makes his head whirl round and round.

But, in spite of all this, he finds the opera house, where there is a masked ball. He has enough money left to buy a ticket for admission and to hire a domino to throw over his shabby dress. It seems only a moment after his entering the gates of Paris that he is in the very midst of all the wild gaiety of the opera-house ball.

No more darkness, no more loneliness, but a mad crowd, shouting and dancing, and a lovely Débardeuse hanging on his arm.

The boisterous gaiety he feels sure is his old light-heartedness come back. He hears the people around him talking of the outrageous conduct of some drunken student, and it is to him they point when they say this to him, who has not moistened his lips since yesterday at noon, for even now he will not drink; though his lips are parched, and his throat burning, he cannot drink.

His voice is thick and hoarse, and his utterance indistinct, but still, this must be his old light-heartedness come back that makes him so wildly gay.

The little Débardeuse is wearied out—her arm rests on his shoulder heavier than lead—the other dancers, one by one, drop off.

The lights in the chandeliers, one by one, die out.

The decorations look pale and shadowy in that dim light which is neither night nor day.

A faint glimmer from the dying lamps, a pale streak of cold grey light from the newborn day, creeping in through half-opened shutters.

And by this light, the bright-eyed Débardeuse fades sadly. He looks her in the face how the brightness of her eyes dies out! Again he looks her in the face. How white that face has grown!

Again—and now it is the shadow of a face alone that looks in his.

Again—and they are gone—the bright eyes, the face, the shadow of the face. He is alone, alone in that vast saloon.

Alone and, in the terrible silence, he hears the echoes of his own footsteps in that dismal dance which has no music.

No music but the beating of his breast. For the cold arms are round his neck—they whirl him round, they will not be flung off or cast away; he can no more escape from their icy grasp than he can escape from death. He looks behind him—there is nothing but himself in the great empty salle, but he can feel—cold, deathlike, but O, how palpable!—the long slender fingers and the ring which was his mother's.

He tries to shout, but he has no power in his burning throat. The silence of the place is only broken by the echoes of his own footsteps in the dance from which he cannot extricate himself.

Who says he has no partner? The cold hands are clasped on his breast, and now he does not shun their caress. No! One more polka if he drops down dead.

The lights are all out, and half an hour after, the gendarmes come in with a lantern to see that the house is empty; they are followed by a great dog that they have found seated howling on the steps of the theatre. Near the principal entrance, they stumble over——The body of a student, who has died from want of food, exhaustion, and the breaking of a blood vessel.

THE TRAVELLER'S STORY OF A TERRIBLY STRANGE BED

by Wilkie Collins

Shortly after my education at college was finished, I happened to be staying in Paris with an English friend. We were both young men then and lived, I am afraid, rather a wild life in the delightful city of our sojourn. One night we were idling about the neighbourhood of the Palais Royal, doubtful to what amusement we should next betake ourselves. My friend proposed a visit to Frascati's, but his suggestion was not to my taste. I knew Frascati's, as the French saying is, by heart;

had lost and won plenty of five-franc pieces there, merely for amusement's sake, until it was amusement no longer, and was thoroughly tired, in fact, of all the ghastly respectabilities of such a social anomaly as a respectable gambling-house. "For Heaven's sake," said I to my friend, "let us go somewhere where we can see a little genuine, blackguard, poverty-stricken gaming with no false gingerbread glitter thrown over it all. Let us get away from fashionable Frascati's, to a house where they don't mind letting in a man with a ragged coat, or a man with no coat, ragged or otherwise." "Very well," said my friend, "we needn't go out of the Palais Royal to find the sort of company you want. Here's the place just before us; as blackguard a place, by all report, as you could possibly wish to see." In another minute, we arrived at the door and entered the house, the back of which you have drawn in your sketch.

When we got upstairs and left our hats and sticks with the doorkeeper, we were admitted into the chief gambling room. We did not find many people assembled there. But, few as the men were who looked up at us on our entrance, they were all types—lamentably true types—of their respective classes.

We had come to see blackguards, but these men were something worse. There is a comic side, more or less appreciable, in all blackguardism— here, there was nothing but tragedy—mute, weird tragedy. The quiet in the room was horrible. The thin, haggard, long-haired young man, whose sunken eyes fiercely watched the turning up of the cards, never spoke; the flabby, fat-faced, pimply player, who pricked his piece of pasteboard perseveringly, to register how often black won and how often red—never spoke; the dirty, wrinkled old man, with the vulture eyes and the darned great-coat, who had lost his last sou, and still looked on desperately, after he could play no longer—never spoke. Even the voice of the croupier sounded as if it were strangely dulled and thickened in the atmosphere of the room. I had entered the place to laugh, but the spectacle before me was something to weep over. I soon found it necessary to take refuge in excitement from the depression of spirits which was fast stealing on me. Unfortunately, I sought the nearest excitement by going to the table and beginning to play. Still more, unfortunately, as the event will show, I won—won prodigiously; won incredibly; won at such a rate that the regular players at the table crowded around me; and staring at my stakes with hungry, superstitious eyes, whispered to one another that the English stranger was going to break the bank.

The game was Rouge et Noir. I had played at it in every city in Europe without, however, the care or the wish to study the Theory of Chances—that philosopher's stone of all gamblers! And a gambler, in the strict sense of the word, I had never been. I was heart-whole from the corroding passion for play. My gaming was a mere idle amusement. I never resorted to it by necessity because I never knew what it was to want money. I never practised it so incessantly as to lose more than I could afford or to gain more than I could coolly pocket without being thrown off my balance by my good luck. In short, I had hitherto frequented gambling tables—just as I frequented ballrooms and opera houses—because they amused me and because I had nothing better to do with my leisure hours.

But on this occasion, it was very different—now, for the first time in my life, I felt what the passion for play really was. My success first bewildered and then, in the most literal meaning of the word, intoxicated me. Incredible as it may appear, it is nevertheless true that I only lost when I attempted to estimate chances and played according to the previous calculation. If I left everything to luck and staked without any care or consideration, I was sure to win—to win in the face of every recognized probability in favour of the bank. At first, some of the men present ventured their money safely enough on my color, but I speedily increased my stakes to sums they dared not risk. One after another, they left off playing and breathlessly looked on at my game.

Still, time after time, I staked higher and higher and still won. The excitement in the room rose to a fever pitch. The silence was interrupted by a deep-muttered chorus of oaths and exclamations in different languages every time the gold was shovelled across to my side of the table—even the imperturbable croupier dashed his rake on the floor in a (French) fury of astonishment at my success. But one man presents preserved his self-possession, and that man was my friend. He came to my side and, whispering in English, begged me to leave the place, satisfied with what I had already gained. I must do him the justice to say that he repeated his warnings and entreaties several times and only left me and went away after I had rejected his advice (I was, to all intents and purposes, gambling drunk) in terms which rendered it impossible for him to address me again that night.

Shortly after he had gone, a hoarse voice behind me cried: "Permit me, my dear sir—permit me to restore to their proper place two napoleons which you have dropped. Wonderful luck, sir! I pledge you my word of honour, as an old soldier, in the course of my long experience in this sort of thing, I never saw such luck as yours—never! Go on, sir—Sacre mille bombes! Go on boldly, and break the bank!"

I turned round and saw, nodding and smiling at me with inveterate civility, a tall man dressed in a frogged and braided surtout.

If I had been in my senses, I should have considered him, personally, as being rather a suspicious specimen of an old soldier. He had goggling, bloodshot eyes, mangy moustaches, and a broken nose. His voice betrayed a barrack-room intonation of the worst order, and he had the dirtiest pair of hands I ever saw—even in France. These little personal peculiarities exercised, however, no repelling influence on me. In the mad excitement, the reckless triumph of that moment, I was ready to "fraternise" with anybody who encouraged me in my game. I accepted the old soldier's offered pinch of snuff, clapped him on the back, and swore he was the most honest fellow in the world—the most glorious relic of the Grand Army that I had ever met with. "Go on!" cried my military friend, snapping his fingers in ecstasy—"Go on and win! Break the bank—Mille tonnerres! my gallant English comrade, break the bank!"

And I did go on—went on at such a rate that in another quarter of an hour, the croupier called out, "Gentlemen, the bank has discontinued for tonight." All the notes and all the gold in that "bank" now lay in a heap under my hands; the whole floating capital of the gambling house was waiting to pour into my pockets!

"Tie up the money in your pocket-handkerchief, my worthy sir," said the old soldier as I wildly plunged my hands into my heap of gold. "Tie it up, as we used to tie up a bit of dinner in the Grand Army; your winnings are too heavy for any breeches-pockets that ever were sewed. There! that's it—shovel them in, notes and all! Credie! what luck! Stop! another napoleon on the floor! Ah! sacre petit polisson de Napoleon! have I found thee at last? Now then, sir—two tight double knots each way with your honourable permission, and the money's safe. Feel it! feel it; fortunate sir! hard and round as a cannonball—Ah, bah! if they had only fired such cannonballs at us at Austerlitz—nom d'une pipe! if they only had! And now, as an ancient grenadier, as an ex-brave of the French army, what remains for me to do? I ask what? Simply this: to entreat my valued English friend to drink a bottle of Champagne with me and toast the goddess Fortune in foaming goblets before we part!"

Excellent ex-brave! Convivial ancient grenadier! Champagne, by all means! An English cheer for an old soldier! Hurrah! hurrah! Another English cheer for the goddess Fortune! Hurrah! hurrah! hurrah!

"Bravo! the Englishman; the amiable, gracious Englishman, in whose veins circulates the vivacious blood of France! Another glass? Ah, bah!—the bottle is empty! Never mind! Vive le vin! I, the old soldier, order another bottle and half a pound of bonbons with it!"

"No, no, ex-brave; never—ancient grenadier! Your bottle last time; my bottle this. Behold it! Toast away! The French Army! the great Napoleon! the present company! the croupier! the honest croupier's wife and daughters—if he has any! the Ladies generally! everybody in the world!"

By the time the second bottle of Champagne was emptied, I felt as if I had been drinking liquid fire—my brain seemed all aflame. No excess in wine had ever had this effect on me before in my life. Was it the result of a stimulant acting upon my system when I was in a highly excited state? Was my stomach in a particularly disordered condition? Or was the Champagne amazingly strong?

"Ex-brave of the French Army!" cried I, in a mad state of exhilaration, "I am on fire! how are you? You have set me on fire! Do you hear, my hero of Austerlitz? Let us have a third bottle of Champagne to put the flame out!"

The old soldier wagged his head, rolled his goggle-eyes, until I expected to see them slip out of their sockets; placed his dirty forefinger by the side of his broken nose; solemnly ejaculated "Coffee!" and immediately ran off into an inner room.

The word pronounced by the eccentric veteran seemed to have a magical effect on the rest of the company present. With one accord, they all rose to depart. Probably they had expected to profit by my intoxication, but finding that my new friend was benevolently bent on preventing me from getting dead drunk, had now abandoned all hope of thriving pleasantly on my winnings. Whatever their motive might be, at any rate, they went away in a body. When the old soldier returned and sat down again opposite me at the table, we had the room to ourselves. I could see the croupier, in a sort of vestibule which opened out of it, eating his supper in solitude. The silence was now deeper than ever.

A sudden change, too, had come over the "ex-brave." He assumed a portentously solemn look, and when he spoke to me again, his speech was ornamented by no oaths, enforced by no finger-snapping, enlivened by no apostrophes or exclamations.

"Listen, my dear sir," said he, in mysteriously confidential tones—"listen to an old soldier's advice. I have been to the mistress of the house (a very charming woman with a genius for cookery!) to impress on her the necessity of making us some particularly strong and good coffee. You must drink this coffee in order to get rid of your little amiable exaltation of spirits before you think of going home —you must, my good and gracious friend! With all that money to take home tonight, it is a sacred duty to yourself to have your wits about you. You are known to be a winner to an enormous extent by several gentlemen present tonight, who, in a certain point of view, are very worthy and excellent fellows; but they are mortal men, my dear sir, and they have their amiable weaknesses. Need I say more? Ah, no, no! you understand me! Now, this is what you must do—send for a cabriolet when you feel quite well again—draw up all the windows when you get into it—and tell the driver to take you home only through the large and well-lighted thoroughfares. Do this, and you and your money will be safe. Do this; and tomorrow you will thank an old soldier for giving you a word of honest advice."

Just as the ex-brave ended his oration in very lachrymose tones, the coffee came in; ready poured out in two cups. My attentive friend handed me one of the cups with a bow. I was parched with thirst and drank it off at a draught. Almost instantly afterwards, I was seized with a fit of giddiness and felt more completely intoxicated than ever. The room whirled round and round furiously; the old soldier seemed to be regularly bobbing up and down before me like the piston of a steam engine. I was half deafened by a violent singing in my ears; a feeling of utter bewilderment, helplessness, and idiocy overcame me. I rose from my chair, holding on by the table to keep my balance, and stammered out that I felt dreadfully unwell—so unwell that I did not know how I was to get home.

"My dear friend," answered the old soldier—and even his voice seemed to be bobbing up and down as he spoke—"my dear friend, it would be madness to go home in your state; you would be sure to lose your money; you might be robbed and murdered with the greatest ease. I am going to sleep here; do you sleep here, too—they make up capital beds in this house—take one; sleep off the effects of the wine, and go home safely with your winnings to-morrow—to-morrow, in broad daylight."

I had, but two ideas left: one, that I must never let go of hold of my handkerchief full of money; the other, that I must lie down somewhere immediately and fall off into a comfortable sleep. So I agreed to the proposal about the bed and took the offered arm of the old soldier, carrying my money with my disengaged hand. Preceded by the croupier, we passed along some passages and up a flight of stairs into the bedroom which I was to occupy. The ex-brave shook me warmly by the hand, proposed that we should breakfast together, and then, followed by the croupier, left me for the night.

I ran to the wash-hand stand; drank some of the water in my jug; poured the rest out, and plunged my face into it; then, I sat down in a chair and tried to compose myself. I soon felt better. The change for my lungs, from the fetid atmosphere of the gambling room to the cool air of the apartment I now occupied, the almost equally refreshing change for my eyes, from the glaring gaslights of the "salon" to the dim, quiet flicker of one bedroom-candle, aided wonderfully the restorative effects of cold water. The giddiness left me, and I began to feel a little like a reasonable being again. My first thought was of the risk of sleeping all night in a gambling house; my second of the still greater risk of trying to get out after the house was closed and of going home alone at night through the streets of Paris with a large sum of money about me. I had slept in worse places than this on my travels, so I determined to lock, bolt, and barricade my door and take my chance till the next morning.

Accordingly, I secured myself against all intrusion; looked under the bed and into the cupboard; tried the fastening of the window; and then, satisfied that I had taken every proper precaution, pulled off my upper clothing, put my light, which was a dim one, on the hearth among a feathery litter of wood-ashes, and got into bed, with the handkerchief full of money under my pillow.

I soon felt not only that I could not go to sleep but that I could not even close my eyes. I was wide awake and in a high fever. Every nerve in my body trembled—every one of my senses seemed to be preternaturally sharpened. I tossed and rolled, tried every kind of position, and perseveringly sought out the cold corners of the bed, and all to no purpose. Now I thrust my arms over the clothes; now I poked them under the clothes; now I violently shot my legs straight out down to the bottom of the bed; now I convulsively coiled them up as near my chin as they would go; now I shook out my crumpled pillow, changed it to the cool side, patted it flat, and lay down quietly on my back; now I fiercely doubled it in two, set it up on end, thrust it against the board of the bed, and tried a sitting posture. Every effort was in vain; I groaned with vexation as I felt that I was in for a sleepless night.

What could I do? I had no book to read. And yet, unless I found out some method of diverting my mind, I felt certain that I was in the condition to imagine all sorts of horrors; to rack my brain with forebodings of every possible and impossible danger; in short, to pass the night in suffering all conceivable varieties of nervous terror.

I raised myself on my elbow and looked about the room—which was brightened by a lovely moonlight pouring straight through the window— to see if it contained any pictures or ornaments that I could at all clearly distinguish. While my eyes wandered from wall to wall, a remembrance of Le Maistre's delightful little book, "Voyage autour de ma Chambre," occurred to me. I resolved to imitate the French author, and find occupation and amusement enough to relieve the tedium of my wakefulness, by making a mental inventory of every article of furniture I could see, and by following up to their sources the multitude of associations which even a chair, a table, or a wash-hand stand may be made to call forth.

In the nervous unsettled state of my mind at that moment, I found it much easier to make my inventory than to make my reflections, and thereupon soon gave up all hope of thinking in Le Maistre's fanciful track—or, indeed, of thinking at all. I looked about the room at the different articles of furniture and did nothing more.

There was, first, the bed I was lying in; a four-post bed, of all things in the world to meet with in Paris—yes, a thorough clumsy British four-poster, with the regular top lined with chintz—the regular fringed valance all round—the regular stifling, unwholesome curtains, which I remembered having mechanically drawn back against the posts without particularly noticing the bed when I first got into the room. Then there was the marble-topped wash-hand stand, from which the water I had spilt, in my hurry to pour it out, was still dripping, slowly and more slowly, onto the brick floor. Then two small chairs, with my coat, waistcoat, and trousers flung on them. Then a large elbow chair covered with dirty-white dimity, with my cravat and shirt collar thrown over the back. Then a chest of drawers with two of the brass handles off and a tawdry, broken china inkstand placed on it by way of ornament for the top. Then the dressing table, adorned by a very small looking glass and a very large pincushion. Then the window—an unusually large window. Then a dark old picture, which the feeble candle dimly showed me. It was a picture of a fellow in a high Spanish hat crowned with a plume of towering feathers. A swarthy, sinister ruffian, looking upward, shading his eyes with his hand, and looking intently upward—it might be at some tall gallows at which he was going to be hanged. At any rate, he had the appearance of thoroughly deserving it.

This picture put a kind of constraint upon me to look upward, too—at the top of the bed. It was a gloomy and not interesting object, and I looked back at the picture. I counted the feathers in the man's hat—they stood out in relief—three white, two green. I observed the crown of his hat, which was of conical shape, according to the fashion supposed to have been favoured by Guido Fawkes. I wondered what he was looking up at. It couldn't be at the stars; such a desperado was neither astrologer nor an astronomer. It must be at the high gallows, and he was going to be hanged presently. Would the executioner come into possession of his conical crowned hat and plume of feathers? I counted the feathers again—three white, two green.

While I still lingered over this very improving and intellectual employment, my thoughts insensibly began to wander. The moonlight shining into the room reminded me of a certain moonlight night in England—the night after a picnic party in a Welsh valley. Every incident of the drive homeward, through lovely scenery, which the moonlight made lovelier than ever, came back to my remembrance, though I had never given the picnic a thought for years; though, if I had tried to recollect it, I could certainly have recalled little or nothing of that scene long past. Of all the wonderful faculties that help to tell us we are immortal, which speaks the sublime truth more eloquently than memory? Here was I, in a strange house of the most suspicious character, in a situation of uncertainty, and even of peril, which might seem to make the cool exercise of my recollection almost out of the question; nevertheless, remembering, quite involuntarily, places, people, conversations, minute circumstances of every kind, which I had thought forgotten forever; which I could not possibly have recalled at will, even under the most favourable auspices. And what cause had produced in a moment the whole of this strange, complicated, mysterious effect? Nothing but some rays of moonlight shining in at my bedroom window.

I was still thinking of the picnic—of our merriment on the drive home—of the sentimental young lady who would quote "Childe Harold" because it was moonlight. I was absorbed by these past scenes and past amusements, when, in an instant, the thread on which my memories hung snapped asunder; my attention immediately came back to present things more vividly than ever, and I found myself, I neither knew why nor wherefore, looking hard at the picture again.

Looking for what?

Good God! the man had pulled his hat down on his brows! No! The hat itself was gone! Where was the conical crown? Where are the feathers— three white, two green? Not there! In place of the hat and feathers, what dusky object was it that now hid his forehead, his eyes, his shading hand?

Was the bed moving?

I turned on my back and looked up. Was I mad? or drunk? Dreaming? Giddy again? or was the top of the bed really moving down—sinking slowly, regularly, silently, horribly, right down throughout the whole of its length and breadth—right down upon me, as I lay underneath?

My blood seemed to stand still. A deadly paralysing coldness stole all over me as I turned my head round on the pillow and determined to test whether the bed-top was really moving or not by keeping my eye on the man in the picture.

The next look in that direction was enough. The dull, black, frowzy outline of the valance above me was within an inch of being parallel with his waist. I still looked breathlessly. And steadily and slowly—very slowly—I saw the figure, and the line of the frame below the figure, vanish as the valance moved down before it.

I am, constitutionally, anything but timid. I have been on more than one occasion in peril of my life and have not lost my self-possession for an instant, but when the conviction first settled on my mind that the bed-top was really moving, was steadily and continuously sinking down upon me, I looked up shuddering, helpless, panic-stricken, beneath the hideous machinery for murder, which was advancing closer and closer to suffocate me where I lay.

I looked up, motionless, speechless, breathless. The candle, fully spent, went out, but the moonlight still brightened the room. Down and down, without pausing and without sounding, came the bed-top, and still my panic-terror seemed to bind me faster and faster to the mattress on which I lay—down and down it sank, till the dusty odour from the lining of the canopy came stealing into my nostrils.

At that final moment, the instinct of self-preservation startled me out of my trance, and I moved at last. There was just room for me to roll myself sidewise off the bed. As I dropped noiselessly to the floor, the edge of the murderous canopy touched me on the shoulder.

Without stopping to draw my breath, without wiping the cold sweat from my face, I rose instantly on my knees to watch the bed-top. I was literally spellbound by it. If I had heard footsteps behind me, I could not have turned around; if a means of escape had been miraculously provided for me, I could not have moved to take advantage of it. The whole life in me was, at that moment, concentrated in my eyes.

It descended—the whole canopy, with the fringe around it, came down—down—close down; so close that there was not room now to squeeze my finger between the bed-top and the bed. I felt at the sides and discovered that what had appeared to me from beneath to be the ordinary light canopy of a four-post bed was, in reality, a thick, broad mattress, the substance of which was concealed by the valance and its fringe. I looked up and saw the four posts rising hideously bare. In the middle of the bed-top was a huge wooden screw that had evidently worked it down through a hole in the ceiling, just as ordinary presses are worked down on the substance selected for compression. The frightful apparatus moved without making the faintest noise. There had been no creaking as it came down; there was now not the faintest sound from the room above. Amid a dead and awful silence, I beheld before me—in the nineteenth century, and in the civilized capital of France—such a machine for secret murder by suffocation as might have existed in the worst days of the Inquisition, in the lonely inns among the Hartz Mountains, in the mysterious tribunals of Westphalia! Still, as I looked at it, I could not move. I could hardly breathe, but I began to recover the power of thinking, and in a moment, I discovered the murderous conspiracy framed against me in all its horror.

My cup of coffee had been drugged and drugged too strongly. I had been saved from being smothered by having taken an overdose of some narcotic. How I had chafed and fretted at the fever fit which had preserved my life by keeping me awake! How recklessly I had confided myself to the two wretches who had led me into this room, determined, for the sake of my winnings, to kill me in my sleep by the surest and most horrible contrivance for secretly accomplishing my destruction! How many men, winners like me, had slept, as I had proposed to sleep, in that bed, and had never been seen or heard of more! I shuddered at the bare idea of it.

But, ere long, all thought was again suspended by the sight of the murderous canopy moving once more. After it had remained on the bed—as nearly as I could guess—for about ten minutes, it began to move up again. The villains who worked it from above evidently believed that their purpose was now accomplished. Slowly and silently, as it had descended, that horrible bed-top rose towards its former place. When it reached the upper extremities of the four posts, it reached the ceiling, too. Neither hole nor screw could be seen; the bed became in appearance an ordinary bed again—the canopy an ordinary canopy—even to the most suspicious eyes.

Now, for the first time, I was able to move—to rise from my knees—to dress in my upper clothing —and to consider how I should escape. If I betrayed by the smallest noise that the attempt to suffocate me had failed, I was certain to be murdered. Had I made any noise already? I listened intently, looking towards the door.

No! no footsteps in the passage outside—no sound of a tread, light or heavy, in the room above —absolute silence everywhere. Besides locking and bolting my door, I had moved an old wooden chest against it, which I had found under the bed. To remove this chest (my blood ran cold as I thought of what its contents might be!) without making some disturbance was impossible, and, moreover, to think of escaping through the house, now barred up for the night, was sheer insanity. Only one chance was left for me—the window. I stole to it on tiptoe.

My bedroom was on the first floor, above an entresol, and looked into a back street, which you have sketched in your view. I raised my hand to open the window, knowing that on that action hung, by the merest hair-breadth, my chance of safety. They keep vigilant watch in a House of Murder. If any part of the frame cracked, if the hinge creaked, I was a lost man! It must have occupied me at least five minutes, reckoning by time —five hours, reckoning by suspense—to open that window. I succeeded in doing it silently—in doing it with all the dexterity of a house-breaker—and then looked down into the street. To leap the distance beneath me would be almost certain destruction! Next, I looked around at the sides of the house.

Down the left side ran a thick water pipe which you have drawn—it passed close by the outer edge of the window. The moment I saw the pipe, I knew I was saved. My breath came and went freely for the first time since I had seen the canopy of the bed moving down upon me!

To some men, the means of escape which I had discovered might have seemed difficult and dangerous enough—to me, the prospect of slipping down the pipe into the street did not suggest even a thought of peril. I had always been accustomed, by the practice of gymnastics, to keep up my school-boy powers as a daring and expert climber; and knew that my head, hands, and feet would serve me faithfully in any hazards of ascent or descent. I had already got one leg over the window sill when I remembered the handkerchief filled with money under my pillow. I could well have afforded to leave it behind me, but I was revengefully determined that the miscreants of the gambling house should miss their plunder as well as their victim. So I went back to the bed and tied the heavy handkerchief at my back by my cravat.

Just as I had made it tight and fixed it in a comfortable place, I thought I heard a sound of breathing outside the door. The chill feeling of horror ran through me again as I listened. No! dead silence still in the passage—I had only heard the night air blowing softly into the room. The next moment I was on the window sill—and the next, I had a firm grip on the water pipe with my hands and knees.

I slid down into the street easily and quietly, as I thought I should, and immediately set off at the top of my speed to a branch "Prefecture" of Police, which I knew was situated in the immediate neighbourhood. A "Sub-prefect," and several picked men among his subordinates happened to be up, maturing, I believe, some scheme for discovering the perpetrator of a mysterious murder which all Paris was talking of just then. When I began my story, in a breathless hurry and in very bad French, I could see that the Sub-prefect suspected me of being a drunken Englishman who had robbed somebody; but he soon altered his opinion as I went on, and before I had anything like concluded, he shoved all the papers before him into a drawer, put on his hat, supplied me with another (for I was bareheaded), ordered a file of soldiers, desired his expert followers to get ready all sorts of tools for breaking open doors and ripping up brick flooring, and took my arm, in the most friendly and familiar manner possible, to lead me with him out of the house. I will venture to say that when the Sub-prefect was a little boy and was taken for the first time to the play, he was not half as much pleased as he was now at the job in prospect for him at the gambling house!

Away we went through the streets, the Sub-prefect cross-examining and congratulating me in the same breath as we marched at the head of our formidable posse comitatus. Sentinels were placed at the back and front of the house the moment we got to it; a tremendous battery of knocks was directed against the door; a light appeared at a window; I was told to conceal myself behind the police—then came more knocks and a cry of "Open in the name of the law!" At that terrible summons, bolts and locks gave way before an invisible hand, and the moment after the Sub-prefect was in the passage, confronting a waiter half-dressed and ghastly pale. This was the short dialogue which immediately took place:

"We want to see the Englishman who is sleeping in this house?"

"He went away hours ago."

"He did no such thing. His friend went away; he remained. Show us to his bedroom!"

"I swear to you, Monsieur le Sous-prefect, he is not here! he—"

"I swear to you, Monsieur le Garcon, he is. He slept here—he didn't find your bed comfortable—he came to us to complain of it—here he is among my men—and here am I ready to look for a flea or two in his bedstead. Renaudin! (calling to one of the subordinates, and pointing to the waiter) collar that man and tie his hands behind him. Now, then, gentlemen, let us walk upstairs!"

Every man and woman in the house was secured—the "Old Soldier" the first. Then I identified the bed in which I had slept, and then we went into the room above.

No object that was at all extraordinary appeared in any part of it. The Sub-prefect looked around the place, commanded everybody to be silent, stamped twice on the floor, called for a candle, looked attentively at the spot he had stamped on, and ordered the flooring there to be carefully taken up. This was done in no time. Lights were produced, and we saw a deep raftered cavity between the floor of this room and the ceiling of the room beneath. Through this cavity, there ran a sort of case of iron perpendicularly thickly greased; and inside the case appeared the screw, which communicated with the bed-top below. Extra lengths of a screw, freshly oiled; levers covered with felt; all the complete upper works of a heavy press —constructed with infernal ingenuity so as to join the fixtures below, and, when taken to pieces again, to go into the smallest possible compass—were next discovered and pulled out on the floor. After some difficulty, the Sub-prefect succeeded in putting the machinery together and, leaving his men to work it, descended with me to the bedroom. The smothering canopy was lowered, but not so noiselessly as I had seen it lowered. When I mentioned this to the Sub-prefect, his answer, simple as it was, had a terrible significance. "My men," said he, "are working down the bed-top for the first time—the men whose money you won were in better practice."

We left the house in the sole possession of two police agents—every one of the inmates being removed to prison on the spot. The Sub-prefect, after taking down my "proces verbal" in his office, returned with me to my hotel to get my passport. "Do you think," I asked, as I gave it to him, "that any men have really been smothered in that bed, as they tried to smother me?"

"I have seen dozens of drowned men laid out at the Morgue," answered the Sub-prefect, "in whose pocket-books were found letters stating that they had committed suicide in the Seine, because they had lost everything at the gaming table. Do I know how many of those men entered the same gambling-house that you entered? won as you won? took that bed as you took it? slept in it? were smothered in it? and were privately thrown into the river, with a letter of explanation written by the murderers and placed in their pocket-books? No man can say how many or how few have suffered the fate from which you have escaped. The people of the gambling-house kept their bedstead machinery a secret from us—even from the police! The dead kept the rest of the secret for them. Good-night, or rather good-morning, Monsieur Faulkner! Be at my office again at nine o'clock—in the meantime, au revoir!"

The rest of my story is soon told. I was examined and re-examined; the gambling house was strictly searched all through from top to bottom; the prisoners were separately interrogated, and two of the less guilty among them made a confession. I discovered that the Old Soldier was the master of the gambling house—justice discovered that he had been drummed out of the army as a vagabond years ago; that he had been guilty of all sorts of villainies since; that he was in possession of the stolen property, which the owners identified; and that he, the croupier, another accomplice, and the woman who had made my cup of coffee, were all in the secret of the bedstead. There appeared some reason to doubt whether the inferior persons attached to the house knew anything of the suffocating machinery, and they received the benefit of that doubt by being treated simply as thieves and vagabonds. As for the Old Soldier and his two head myrmidons, they went to the galleys; the woman who had drugged my coffee was imprisoned for I forget how many years; the regular attendants at the gambling house were considered "suspicious" and placed under "surveillance"; and I became, for one whole week (which is a long time) the head "lion" in Parisian society. My adventure was dramatized by three illustrious play makers but never saw theatrical daylight; for the censorship forbade the introduction on the stage of a correct copy of the gambling-house bedstead.

One good result was produced by my adventure, which any censorship must have approved: it cured me of ever again trying "Rouge et Noir" as an amusement. The sight of green cloth, with packs of cards and heaps of money on it, will henceforth be forever associated in my mind with the sight of a bed canopy descending to suffocate me in the silence and darkness of the night.

Just as Mr Faulkner pronounced these words, he started in his chair and resumed his stiff, dignified position in a great hurry. "Bless my soul!" cried he, with a comic look of astonishment and vexation, "while I have been telling you what is the real secret of my interest in the sketch you have so kindly given to me, I have altogether forgotten that I came here to sit for my portrait. For the last hour or more I must have been the worst model you ever had to draw from!"

"On the contrary, you have been the best," said I. "I have been trying to catch your likeness; and, while telling your story, you have unconsciously shown me the natural expression I wanted to insure my success."

NOTE BY Mrs KERBY.

I cannot let this story end without mentioning what the chance saying was, which caused it to be told at the farmhouse the other night. Our friend, the young sailor, among his other quaint objections to sleeping on shore, declared that he particularly hated four-post beds because he never slept in one without doubting whether the top might not come down in the night and suffocate him. I thought this chance reference to the distinguishing feature of William's narrative curious enough, and my husband agreed with me. But he says it is scarcely worthwhile to mention such a trifle in anything so important as a book. I cannot venture, after this, to do more than slip these lines in modestly at the end of the story. If the printer should notice my few last words, perhaps he may not mind the trouble of putting them into some out-of-the-way corner.

L. K.

THE SCREAMING SKULL

by F. Marion Crawford

I have often heard it scream. No, I am not nervous, I am not imaginative, and I never believed in ghosts unless that thing is one. Whatever it is, it hates me almost as much as it hated Luke Pratt, and it screams at me.

If I were you, I would never tell ugly stories about ingenious ways of killing people, for you never can tell but that someone at the table may be tired of his or her nearest and dearest. I have always blamed myself for Mrs Pratt's death, and I suppose I was responsible for it in a way, though heaven knows I never wished her anything but long life and happiness. If I had not told that story, she might be alive yet. That is why the thing screams at me, I fancy.

She was a good little woman with a sweet temper, all things considered, and a nice gentle voice, but I remember hearing her shriek once when she thought her little boy was killed by a pistol that went off, though everyone was sure that it was not loaded. It was the same scream, exactly the same, with a sort of rising quaver at the end; do you know what I mean? Unmistakable.

The truth is, I had not realized that the doctor and his wife were not on good terms. They used to bicker a bit now and then when I was here, and I often noticed that little Mrs Pratt got very red and bit her lip hard to keep her temper while Luke grew pale and said the most offensive things. He was that sort when he was in the nursery, I remember, and afterwards at school. He was my cousin, you know; that is how I came by this house; after he died and his boy Charley was killed in South Africa, there were no relations left. Yes, it's a pretty little property, just the sort of thing for an old sailor like me who has taken to gardening.

One always remembers one's mistakes much more vividly than one's cleverest things, doesn't one? I've often noticed it. I was dining with the Pratts one night when I told them the story that afterwards made so much difference. It was a wet night in November, and the sea was moaning. Hush!—if you don't speak, you will hear it now.

Do you hear the tide? Gloomy sound, isn't it? Sometimes, about this time of year—hallo!—there it is! Don't be frightened, man—it won't eat you—it's only a noise, after all! But I'm glad you've heard it because there are always people who think it's the wind, or my imagination, or something. You won't hear it again tonight, I fancy, for it doesn't often come more than once. Yes—that's right. Put another stick on the fire and a little more stuff into that weak mixture you're so fond of. Do you remember old Blauklot, the carpenter, on that German ship that picked us up when the Clontarf went to the bottom? We were hove to in a howling gale one night, as snug as you please, with no land within five hundred miles, and the ship coming up and falling off as regularly as clockwork—"Biddy te boor beebles ashore tis night, poys!" old Blauklot sang out, as he went off to his quarters with the sail-maker. I often think of that now that I'm ashore for good and all.

Yes, it was on a night like this, when I was at home for a spell, waiting to take the Olympia out on her first trip—it was on the next voyage that she broke the record, you remember—but that dates it. Ninety-two was the year, early in November.

The weather was dirty, Pratt was out of temper, and the dinner was bad, very bad indeed, which didn't improve matters, and cold, which made it worse. The poor little lady was very unhappy about it and insisted on making a Welsh rarebit on the table to counteract the raw turnips and the half-boiled mutton. Pratt must have had a hard day. Perhaps he had lost a patient. At all events, he was in a nasty temper.

"My wife is trying to poison me, you see!" he said. "She'll succeed some day." I saw that she was hurt, and I made believe to laugh and said that Mrs Pratt was much too clever to get rid of her husband in such a simple way, and then I began to tell them about Japanese tricks with spun glass and chopped horsehair and the like.

Pratt was a doctor and knew a lot more than I did about such things, but that only put me on my mettle, and I told a story about a woman in Ireland who did for three husbands before anyone suspected foul play.

Did you never hear that tale? The fourth husband managed to keep them awake and caught her, and she was hanged. How did she do it? She drugged them and poured melted lead into their ears through a little horn funnel when they were asleep. No—that's the wind whistling. It's backing up southward again. I can tell by the sound. Besides, the other thing doesn't often come more than once in an evening, even at this time of year— when it happened. Yes, it was in November. Poor Mrs Pratt died suddenly in her bed not long after I dined here. I can fix the date because I got the news in New York by the steamer that followed the Olympia when I took her out on her first trip. You had the Leofric the same year? Yes, I remember. What a pair of old buffers we are coming to be, you and I. Nearly fifty years since we were apprentices together on the Clontarf. Shall you ever forget old

Blauklot? "Biddy te boor beebles ashore, poys!" Ha, ha! Take a little more, with all that water. It's the old Hulstkamp I found in the cellar when this house came to me, the same I brought Luke from Amsterdam five and five-and-twenty years ago. He had never touched a drop of it. Perhaps he's sorry now, poor fellow.

Where did I leave off? I told you that Mrs Pratt died suddenly—yes. Luke must have been lonely here after she was dead, I should think; I came to see him now and then, and he looked worn and nervous and told me that his practice was growing too heavy for him, though he wouldn't take an assistant on any account. Years went on, and his son was killed in South Africa, and after that, he began to be queer. There was something about him that made me not like other people. I believe he kept his senses in his profession to the end; there was no complaint of his having made bad mistakes in cases or anything of that sort, but he had a look about him

————

Luke was a red-headed man with a pale face when he was young, and he was never stout; in middle age, he turned a sandy grey, and after his son died he grew thinner and thinner, till his head looked like a skull with parchment stretched over it very tight, and his eyes had a sort of glare in them that was very disagreeable to look at.

He had an old dog that poor Mrs Pratt had been fond of and that used to follow her everywhere. He was a bulldog, and the sweetest-tempered beast you ever saw, though he had a way of hitching his upper lip behind one of his fangs that frightened strangers a good deal. Sometimes, on an evening, Pratt and Bumble—that was the dog's name—used to sit and look at each other a long time, thinking about old times, I suppose, when Luke's wife used to sit in that chair you've got. That was always her place, and this was the doctor's, where I'm sitting. Bumble used to climb up by the footstool—he was old and fat by that time and could not jump much, and his teeth were getting shaky. He would look steadily at Luke, and Luke looked steadily at the dog, his face growing more and more like a skull with two little coals for eyes; and after about five minutes or so, though it may have been less, old Bumble would suddenly begin to shake all over, and all on a sudden he would set up an awful howl, as if he had been shot, and tumble out of the easy-chair and trot away, and hide under the sideboard, and lie there making odd noises.

Considering Pratt's looks in those last months, the thing is not surprising, you know. I'm not nervous or imaginative, but I can quite believe he might have sent a sensitive woman into hysterics—his head looked so much like a skull in parchment.

At last, I came down one day before Christmas when my ship was in the dock, and I had three weeks off. Bumble was not about, and I said that I supposed the old dog was dead.

"Yes," Pratt answered, and I thought there was something odd in his tone even before he went on after a little pause. "I killed him," he said presently. "I could not stand it any longer."

I asked what it was that Luke could not stand, though I guessed well enough.

"He had a way of sitting in her chair and glaring at me, and then howling." Luke shivered a little. "He didn't suffer at all, poor old Bumble," he went on in a hurry as if he thought I might imagine he had been cruel. "I put dionine into his drink to make him sleep soundly, and then I chloroformed him gradually, so that he could not have felt suffocated even if he was dreaming. It's been quieter since then."

I wondered what he meant, for the words slipped out as if he could not help saying them. I've understood since. He meant that he did not hear that noise so often after the dog was out of the way. Perhaps he thought at first that it was old Bumble in the yard howling at the moon, though it's not that kind of noise, is it? Besides, I know what it is if Luke didn't. It's only a noise, after all, and a noise has never hurt anybody yet. But he was much more imaginative than I am. No doubt there really is something about this place that I don't understand, but when I don't understand a thing, I call it a phenomenon, and I don't take it for granted that it's going to kill me, as he did. I don't understand everything by long odds, nor do you, nor does any man who has been to sea. We used to talk of tidal waves, for instance, and we could not account for them; now we account for them by calling them submarine earthquakes, and we branch off into fifty theories, any one of which might make earthquakes quite comprehensible if we only knew what they are. I fell in with one of them once, and the inkstand flew straight up from the table against the ceiling of my cabin. The same thing happened to Captain Lecky—I dare say you've read about it in his "Wrinkles." Very good. If that sort of thing took place ashore, in this room, for instance, a nervous person would talk about spirits and levitation and fifty things that mean nothing instead of just quietly setting it down as a "phenomenon" that has not been explained yet. My view of that voice, you see.

Besides, what is there to prove that Luke killed his wife? I would not even suggest such a thing to anyone but you. After all, there was nothing but the coincidence that poor little Mrs Pratt died suddenly in her bed a few days after I told that story at dinner. She was not the only woman who ever died like that. Luke got the doctor over from the next parish, and they agreed that she had died of something the matter with her heart. Why not? It's common enough.

Of course, there was the ladle. I never told anybody about that, and it made me start when I found it in the cupboard in the bedroom. It was new, too—a little tinned iron ladle that had not been in the fire more than once or twice, and there was some lead in it that had been melted and stuck to the bottom of the bowl, all grey, with hardened dross on it. But that proves nothing. A country doctor is generally a handyman, who does everything for himself, and Luke may have had a dozen reasons for melting a little lead in a ladle. He was fond of sea fishing, for instance, and he may have cast a sinker for a night line; perhaps it was a weight for the hall clock or something like that. All the same, when I found it, I had a rather queer sensation because it looked so much like the thing I had described when I told them the story. Do you understand? It affected me unpleasantly, and I threw it away; it's at the bottom of the sea a mile from the Spit, and it will be jolly well rusted beyond recognising if it's ever washed up by the tide.

You see, Luke must have bought it in the village years ago, for the man sells just such ladles still. I suppose they are used in cooking. In any case, there was no reason why an inquisitive housemaid should find such a thing lying about, with lead in it, and wonder what it was, and perhaps talk to the maid who heard me tell the story at dinner—for that girl married the plumber's son in the village, and may remember the whole thing.

You understand me, don't you? Now that Luke Pratt is dead and gone and lies buried beside his wife, with an honest man's tombstone at his head, I should not care to stir up anything that could hurt his memory. They are both dead, and their son, too. There was trouble enough about Luke's death, as it was.

How? He was found dead on the beach one morning, and there was a coroner's inquest. There were marks on his throat, but he had not been robbed. The verdict was that he had come to his end "by the hands or teeth of some person or animal unknown," for half the jury thought it might have been a big dog that had thrown him down and gripped his windpipe, though the skin of his throat was not broken. No one knew at what time he had gone out nor where he had been. He was found lying on his back above the high-water mark, and an old cardboard bandbox that had belonged to his wife lay under his hand, open. The lid had fallen off. He seemed to have been carrying home a skull in the box—doctors are fond of collecting such things. It had rolled out and lay near his head, and it was a remarkably fine skull, rather small, beautifully shaped and very white, with perfect teeth. That is to say, the upper jaw was perfect, but there was no lower one at all when I first saw it.

Yes, I found it here when I came. You see, it was very white and polished, like a thing meant to be kept under a glass case, and the people did not know where it came from nor what to do with it, so they put it back into the bandbox and set it on the shelf of the cupboard in the best bedroom, and of course, they showed it to me when I took possession. I was taken down to the beach, too, to be shown the place where Luke was found, and the old fisherman explained just how he was lying and the skull beside him. The only point he could not explain was why the skull had rolled up the sloping sand toward Luke's head instead of rolling downhill to his feet. It did not seem odd to me at the time, but I have often thought of it since, for the place is rather steep. I'll take you there tomorrow if you like —I made a sort of cairn of stones there afterwards.

When he fell down or was thrown down— whichever happened—the bandbox struck the sand,

and the lid came off, and the thing came out and ought to have rolled down. But it didn't. It was close to his head, almost touching it, and he turned, with face toward it. I say it didn't strike me as odd when the man told me; but I could not help thinking about it afterwards, again and again, till I saw a picture of it all when I closed my eyes; and then I began to ask myself why the plaguey thing had rolled up instead of down, and why it had stopped near Luke's head instead of anywhere else, a yard away, for instance.

You naturally want to know what conclusion I reached, don't you? None that at all explained the rolling, at all events. But I got something else into my head after a time that made me feel downright uncomfortable.

Oh, I don't mean anything supernatural! There may be ghosts, or there may not be. If there are, I'm not inclined to believe that they can hurt living people except by frightening them, and, for my part, I would rather face any shape of a ghost than a fog in the Channel when it's crowded. No. What bothered me was just a foolish idea, that's all, and I cannot tell how it began nor what made it grow till it turned into a certainty.

I was thinking about Luke and his poor wife one evening over my pipe and a dull book when it occurred to me that the skull might possibly be hers, and I have never got rid of the thought since. You'll tell me there's no sense in it, no doubt, that Mrs Pratt was buried like a Christian and is lying in the churchyard where they put her and that it's perfectly monstrous to suppose her husband kept her skull in her old bandbox in his bedroom. All the same, in the face of reason, common sense, and probability, I'm convinced that he did. Doctors do all sorts of queer things that would make men like you and me feel creepy, and those are just the things that don't seem probable, logical, or sensible to us.

Then, don't you see?—if it really was her skull, poor woman, the only way of accounting for his having it is that he really killed her and did it in that way, as the woman killed her husbands in the story, and that he was afraid there might be an examination some day which would betray him. You see, I told that too, and I believe it had really happened some fifty or sixty years ago. They dug up the three skulls, you know, and there was a small lump of lead rattling about in each one. That was what hanged the woman. Luke remembered that I'm sure. I don't want to know what he did when he thought of it; my taste never ran in the direction of horrors, and I don't fancy you care for them either, do you? No. If you did, you might supply what is wanted in the story.

It must have been rather grim, eh? I wish I did not see the whole thing so distinctly, just as everything must have happened. He took it the night before she was buried, I'm sure after the coffin had been shut and when the servant girl was asleep. I would bet anything that when he'd got it, he put something under the sheet in its place to fill up and look like it. What do you suppose he put there, under the sheet?

I don't wonder if you take me up on what I'm saying! First, I tell you that I don't want to know what happened and that I hate to think about horrors, and then I describe the whole thing to you as if I had seen it. I'm quite sure that it was her work bag that he put there. I remember the bag very well, for she always used it of an evening; it was made of brown plush, and when it was stuffed full, it was about the size of—you understand. Yes, there I am, at it again! You may laugh at me, but you don't live here alone, where it was done, and you didn't tell Luke the story about the melted lead. I'm not nervous, I tell you, but sometimes I begin to feel that I understand why some people are. I dwell on all this when I'm alone, and I dream of it, and when that thing screams—well, frankly, I don't like the noise any more than you do, though I should be used to it by this time.

I ought not to be nervous. I've sailed in a haunted ship. There was a Man in the Top, and two-thirds of the crew died of the West Coast fever within ten days after we anchored; but I was all right, then and afterwards. I have seen some ugly sights, too, just as you have, and all the rest of us. But nothing ever stuck in my head in the way this does.

You see, I've tried to get rid of the thing, but it doesn't like that. It wants to be there in its place, in Mrs Pratt's bandbox in the cupboard in the best bedroom. It's not happy anywhere else. How do I know that? Because I've tried it. You don't suppose that I've not tried, do you? As long as it's there, it only screams now and then, generally at this time of year, but if I put it out of the house, it goes on all night, and no servant will stay here twenty-four hours. As it is, I've often been left alone and have been obliged to shift for myself for a fortnight at a time. No one from the village would ever pass a night under the roof now, and as for selling the place, or even letting it, that's out of the question. The old women say that if I stay here, I shall come to a bad end myself before long.

I'm not afraid of that. You smile at the mere idea that anyone could take such nonsense seriously. Quite right. It's utterly blatant nonsense. I agree with you. Didn't I tell you that it's only a noise after all when you started and looked round as if you expected to see a ghost standing behind your chair?

I may be all wrong about the skull, and I like to think that I am—when I can. It may be just a fine specimen that Luke got somewhere long ago, and what rattles about inside when you shake it may be nothing but a pebble, or a bit of hard clay, or anything. Skulls that have lain long in the ground generally have something inside them that rattles, don't they? No, I've never tried to get it out, whatever it is; I'm afraid it might be lead, don't you see? And if it is, I don't want to know the fact, for I'd much rather not be sure. If it really is lead, I killed her quite as much as if I had done the deed myself. Anybody must see that, I should think. As long as I don't know for certain, I have the consolation of saying that it's all utterly ridiculous nonsense, that Mrs Pratt died a natural death and that the beautiful skull belonged to Luke when he was a student in

London. But if I were quite sure, I believe I should have to leave the house; indeed, I do, most certainly. As it is, I had to give up trying to sleep in the best bedroom where the cupboard is.

You ask me why I don't throw it into the pond—yes, but please don't call it a "confounded bugbear"—it doesn't like being called names.

There! Lord, what a shriek! I told you so! You're quite pale, man. Fill up your pipe and draw your chair nearer to the fire, and take some more drink. Old Hollands never hurt anybody yet. I've seen a Dutchman in Java drink half a jug of Hulstkamp in the morning without turning a hair. I don't take much rum myself because it doesn't agree with my rheumatism, but you are not rheumatic, and it won't damage you. Besides, it's a very damp night outside. The wind is howling again, and it will soon be in the southwest; do you hear how the windows rattle? The tide must have turned, too, by the moaning.

We should not have heard the thing again if you had not said that. I'm pretty sure we should not. Oh yes, if you choose to describe it as a coincidence, you are quite welcome, but I would rather that you should not call the thing names again if you don't mind. It may be that the poor little woman hears, and perhaps it hurts her, don't you know? Ghost? No! You don't call anything a ghost that you can take in your hands and look at in broad daylight and that rattles when you shake it. Do you, now? But it's something that hears and understood; there's no doubt about that.

I tried sleeping in the best bedroom when I first came to the house, just because it was the best and the most comfortable, but I had to give it up. It was their room, and there was the big bed she died in, and the cupboard is in the thickness of the wall, near the head, on the left. That's where it likes to be kept, in its bandbox. I only used the room for a fortnight after I came, and then I turned out and took the little room downstairs, next to the surgery, where Luke used to sleep when he expected to be called to a patient during the night.

I was always a good sleeper ashore; eight hours is my dose, eleven to seven when I'm alone, and twelve to eight when I have a friend with me. But I could not sleep after three o'clock in the morning in that room—a quarter past, to be accurate—as a matter of fact, I timed it with my old pocket chronometer, which still keeps good time, and it was always at exactly seventeen minutes past three. I wonder whether that was the hour when she died.

It was not what you heard. If it had been that, I could not have stood it two nights. It was just a start and a moan and hard breathing for a few seconds in the cupboard, and it could never have waked me under ordinary circumstances, I'm sure. I suppose you are like me in that, and we are just like other people who have been to sea. No natural sounds disturb us at all. Not all the racket of a square rigger hove to in a heavy gale or rolling on her beam ends before the wind. But if a lead pencil gets adrift and rattles in the drawer of your cabin table, you are awake in a moment. Just so—you always understand. Very well, the noise in the cupboard was no louder than that, but it woke me instantly.

I said it was like a "start." I know what I mean, but it's hard to explain without seeming to talk nonsense. Of course, you cannot exactly "hear" a person "start"; at the most, you might hear the quick drawing of the breath between the parted lips and closed teeth and the almost imperceptible sound of clothing that moved suddenly though very slightly. It was like that.

You know how one feels about what a sailing vessel is going to do two or three seconds before she does it when one has the wheel. Riders say the same of a horse, but that's less strange because the horse is a live animal with feelings of its own, and only poets and landsmen talk about a ship being alive and all that. But I have always felt somehow that besides being a steaming machine or a sailing machine for carrying weights, a vessel at sea is a sensitive instrument and a means of communication between nature and man, and most particularly, the man at the wheel if she is steered by hand. She takes her impressions directly from wind and sea, tide and stream, and transmits them to the man's hand, just as the wireless telegraph picks up the interrupted currents aloft and turns them out below in the form of a message.

You see what I am driving at; I felt that something started in the cupboard, and I felt it so vividly that I heard it, though there may have been nothing to hear, and the sound inside my head waked me suddenly. But I really heard the other noise. It was as if it were muffled inside a box, as far away as if it came through a long-distance telephone, and yet I knew that it was inside the cupboard near the head of my bed. My hair did not bristle, and my blood did not run cold at that time. I simply resented being waked up by something that had no business to make a noise, any more than a pencil should rattle in the drawer of my cabin table on board ship. For I did not understand; I just supposed that the cupboard had some communication with the outside air and that the wind had got in and was moaning through it with a sort of very faint screech. I struck a light and looked at my watch, it was seventeen minutes past three. Then I turned over and went to sleep on my right ear. That's my good one; I'm pretty deaf with the other, for I struck the water with it when I was a lad in diving from the foretopsail yard. Silly thing to do, it was, but the result is very convenient when I want to go to sleep when there's a noise.

That was the first night, and the same thing happened again and several times afterwards, but not regularly, though it was always at the same time, to a second; perhaps I was sometimes sleeping on my good ear, and sometimes not. I overhauled the cupboard, and there was no way by which the wind could get in, or anything else, for the door makes a good fit, having been meant to keep out moths, I suppose; Mrs Pratt must have kept her winter things in it, for it still smells of camphor and turpentine.

After about a fortnight, I had had enough of the noises. So far, I had said to myself that it would be silly to yield to it and take the skull out of the room. Things always look differently by daylight, don't they? But the voice grew louder—I suppose one may call it a voice—and it got inside my deaf ear, too, one night. I realized that when I was wide awake, for my good ear was jammed down on the pillow, and I ought not to have heard a fog horn in that position. But I heard that, and it made me lose my temper, unless it scared me, for sometimes the two are not far apart. I struck a light and got up, and I opened the cupboard, grabbed the bandbox and threw it out of the window as far as I could.

Then my hair stood on end. The thing screamed in the air like a shell from a twelve-inch gun. It fell on the other side of the road. The night was very dark, and I could not see it fall, but I knew it fell beyond the road. The window is just over the front door, it's fifteen yards to the fence, more or less, and the road is ten yards wide. There's a quickset hedge beyond, along the glebe that belongs to the vicarage.

I did not sleep much more that night. It was not more than half an hour after I had thrown the bandbox out when I heard a shriek outside—like what we've had tonight, but worse, more despairing, I should call it, and it may have been my imagination, but I could have sworn that the screams came nearer and nearer each time. I lit a pipe and walked up and down for a bit, and then took a book and sat up reading, but I'll be hanged if I can remember what I read nor even what the book was, for every now and then a shriek came up that would have made a dead man turn in his coffin.

A little before dawn, someone knocked at the front door. There was no mistaking that for anything else, and I opened my window and looked down, for I guessed that someone wanted the doctor, supposing that the new man had taken Luke's house. It was rather a relief to hear a human knock after that awful noise.

You cannot see the door from above, owing to the little porch. The knocking came again, and I called out, asking who was there, but nobody answered, though the knock was repeated. I sang out again and said that the doctor did not live there any longer. There was no answer, but it occurred to me that it might be some old countryman who was stone-deaf. So I took my candle and went down to open the door. Upon my word, I was not thinking of the thing yet, and I had almost forgotten the other noises. I went down convinced that I should find somebody outside, on the doorstep, with a message. I set the candle on the hall table so that the wind should not blow it out when I opened it. While I was drawing the old-fashioned bolt, I heard the knocking again. It was not loud, and it had a queer, hollow sound. Now that I was close to it, I remember, but I certainly thought it was made by some person who wanted to get in.

It wasn't. There was nobody there, but as I opened the door inward, standing a little on one side so as to see out at once, something rolled across the threshold and stopped against my foot.

I drew back as I felt it, for I knew what it was before I looked down. I cannot tell you how I knew, and it seemed unreasonable, for I am still quite sure that I had thrown it across the road. It's a French window that opens wide, and I got a good swing when I flung it out. Besides, when I went out early in the morning, I found the bandbox beyond the thickset hedge.

You may think it opened when I threw it and that the skull dropped out, but that's impossible, for nobody could throw an empty cardboard box so far. It's out of the question; you might as well try to fling a ball of paper twenty-five yards or a blown bird's egg.

To go back, I shut and bolted the hall door, picked the thing up carefully, and put it on the table beside the candle. I did that mechanically, as one instinctively does the right thing in danger without thinking at all—unless one does the opposite. It may seem odd, but I believe my first thought had been that somebody might come and find me there on the threshold while it was resting against my foot, lying a little on its side, and turning one hollow eye up at my face as if it meant to accuse me. And the light and shadow from the candle played in the hollows of the eyes as it stood on the table so that they seemed to open and shut at me. Then the candle went out quite unexpectedly, though the door was fastened, and there was not the least draught, and I used up at least half a dozen matches before it would burn again.

I sat down rather suddenly, without quite knowing why. Probably I had been badly frightened, and perhaps you will admit there was no great shame in being scared. The thing had come home, and it wanted to go upstairs, back to its cupboard. I sat still and stared at it for a bit till I began to feel very cold; then I took it and carried it up and set it in its place, and I remember that I spoke to it and promised that it should have its bandbox again in the morning.

Do you want to know whether I stayed in the room till daybreak? Yes, but I kept a light burning, and sat up smoking and reading, most likely out of fright; plain, undeniable fear, and you need not call it cowardice either, for that's not the same thing. I could not have stayed alone with that thing in the cupboard; I should have been scared to death, though I'm not timider than other people. Confound it all, man, it had crossed the road alone, had got up the doorstep and had knocked to be let in.

When dawn came, I put on my boots and went out to find the bandbox. I had to go a good way round, by the gate near the high road, and I found the box open and hanging on the other side of the hedge. It had caught on the twigs by the string, and the lid had fallen off and was lying on the ground below it. That shows that it did not open till it was well over, and if it had not opened as soon as it left my hand, what was inside it must have gone beyond the road too.

That's all. I took the box upstairs to the cupboard, put the skull back and locked it up. When the girl brought me my breakfast, she said she was sorry but that she must go, and she did not care if she lost her month's wages. I looked at her, and her face was a sort of greenish, yellowish-white. I pretended to be surprised and asked what was the matter, but that was of no use, for she just turned on me and wanted to know whether I meant to stay in a haunted house, and how long I expected to live if I did, for though she noticed I was sometimes a little hard of hearing, she did not believe that even I could sleep through those screams again—and if I could, why had I been moving about the house and opening and shutting the front door, between three and four in the morning? There was no answering that, since she had heard me, so off she went, and I was left to myself. I went down to the village during the morning and found a woman who was willing to come and do the little work there is and cook my dinner, on condition that she might go home every night. As for me, I moved downstairs that day, and I have never tried to sleep in the best bedroom since. After a little while, I got a brace of middle-aged Scotch servants from London, and things were quiet enough for a long time. I began by telling them that the house was in a very exposed position and that the wind whistled around it a good deal in the autumn and winter, which had given it a bad name in the village, the Cornish people being inclined to superstition and telling ghost stories. The two hard-faced, sandy-haired sisters almost smiled, and they answered with great contempt that they had no great opinion of any Southern bogey whatever, having been in service in two English haunted houses where they had never seen so much as the Boy in Gray, whom they reckoned no very particular rarity in Forfarshire.

They stayed with me for several months, and while they were in the house, we had peace and quiet. One of them is here again now, but she went away with her sister within the year. This one—she was the cook—married the sexton, who works in my garden. That's the way of it. It's a small village, and he has not much to do, and he knows enough about flowers to help me nicely, besides doing most of the hard work; for though I'm fond of exercise, I'm getting a little stiff in the hinges. He's a sober, silent sort of fellow, who minds his own business, and he was a widower when I came here—Trehearn is his name, James Trehearn. The Scotch sisters would not admit that there was anything wrong about the house, but when November came, they gave me warning that they were going, on the ground that the chapel was such a long walk from here, being in the next parish, and that they could not possibly go to our church. But the younger one came back in the spring, and as soon as the banns could be published, she was married to James Trehearn by the vicar, and she seems to have had no scruples about hearing him preach since then. I'm quite satisfied if she is! The couple lives in a small cottage that looks over the churchyard.

I suppose you are wondering what all this has to do with what I was talking about. I'm alone so much that when an old friend comes to see me, I sometimes go on talking just for the sake of hearing my own voice. But in this case, there is really a connection of ideas. It was James Trehearn who buried poor Mrs Pratt and her husband after her in the same grave, and it's not far from the back of his cottage. That's the connection in my mind, you see.

It's plain enough. He knows something; I'm quite sure that he does, by his manner, though he's such a reticent beggar.

Yes, I'm alone in the house at night now, for Mrs Trehearn does everything herself, and when I have a friend, the sexton's niece comes in to wait on the table. He takes his wife home every evening in winter, but in summer, when there's light, she goes by herself. She's not a nervous woman, but she's less sure than she used to be that there are no bogies in England worth a Scotchwoman's notice. Isn't it amusing the idea that Scotland has a monopoly on the supernatural? Odd sort of national pride, I call that, don't you?

That's a good fire, isn't it? When driftwood gets started at last, there's nothing like it, I think. Yes, we get lots of it, for I'm sorry to say there are still a great many wrecks about here. It's a lonely coast, and you may have all the wood you want for the trouble of bringing it in. Trehearn and I borrow a cart now and then and load it between here and the Spit. I hate a coal fire when I can get wood of any sort. A log is a company, even if it's only a piece of a deck beam or timber sawn off, and the salt in it makes pretty sparks. See how they fly, like Japanese hand fireworks! Upon my word, with an old friend and a good fire and a pipe, one forgets all about that thing upstairs, especially now that the wind has moderated. It's only a lull, though, and it will blow a gale before morning.

Do you think you would like to see the skull? I've no objection. There's no reason why you shouldn't have a look at it, and you never saw a perfect one in your life, except that there are two front teeth missing in the lower jaw.

Oh yes—I had not told you about the jaw yet. Trehearn found it in the garden last spring when he was digging a pit for a new asparagus bed. You know we make asparagus beds six or eight feet deep here. Yes, yes—I had forgotten to tell you that. He was digging straight down, just as he digs a grave; if you want a good asparagus bed made, I advise you to get a sexton to make it for you. Those fellows have a wonderful knack for that sort of digging.

Trehearn had got down about three feet when he cut into a mass of white lime in the side of the trench. He had noticed that the earth was a little looser there, though he says it had not been disturbed for a number of years. I suppose he thought that even old lime might not be good for asparagus, so he broke it out and threw it up. It was pretty hard, he says, in biggish lumps, and out of sheer force of habit, he cracked the lumps with his spade as they lay outside the pit beside him; the jawbone of a skull dropped out of one of the pieces. He thinks he must have knocked out the two front teeth in breaking up the lime, but he did not see them anywhere. He's a very experienced man in such things, as you may imagine, and he said at once that the jaw had probably belonged to a young woman and that the teeth had been complete when she died. He brought it to me and asked me if I wanted to keep it; if I did not, he said he would drop it into the next grave he made in the churchyard, as he supposed it was a Christian jaw and ought to have a decent burial, wherever the rest of the body might be. I told him that doctors often put bones into quicklime to whiten them nicely and that I supposed Dr Pratt had once had a little lime pit in the garden for that purpose and had forgotten the jaw. Trehearn looked at me quietly.

"Maybe it fitted that skull that used to be in the cupboard upstairs, sir," he said. "Maybe Dr. Pratt had put the skull into the lime to clean it, or something, and when he took it out he left the lower jaw behind. There's some human hair sticking in the lime, sir."

I saw there was, and that was what Trehearn said. If he did not suspect something, why in the world should he have suggested that the jaw might fit the skull? Besides, it did. That's proof that he knows more than he cares to tell. Do you suppose he looked before she was buried? Or perhaps—when he buried Luke in the same grave——

Well, well, it's of no use to go over that, is it? I said I would keep the jaw with the skull, and I took it upstairs and fitted it into its place. There's not the slightest doubt about the two belonging together, and together they are.

Trehearn knows several things. We were talking about plastering the kitchen a while ago, and he happened to remember that it had not been done since the very week when Mrs Pratt died. He did not say that the mason must have left some lime on the place, but he thought and that it was the very same lime he had found in the asparagus pit. He knows a lot. Trehearn is one of your silent beggars who can put two and two together. That grave is very near the back of his cottage, too, and he's one of the quickest men with a spade I ever saw. If he wanted to know the truth, he could, and no one else would ever be the wiser unless he chose to tell. In a quiet village like ours, people don't go and spend the night in the churchyard to see whether the sexton potters about by himself between ten o'clock and daylight.

What is awful to think of is Luke's deliberation, if he did it; his cool certainty that no one would find him out, and above all, his nerve, for that must have been extraordinary. I sometimes think it's bad enough to live in the place where it was done if it really was done. I always put in the condition, you see, for the sake of his memory and a little bit for my own sake, too.

I'll go upstairs and fetch the box in a minute. Let me light my pipe; there's no hurry! We had supper early, and it was only half past nine o'clock. I never let a friend go to bed before twelve or with less than three glasses—you may have as many more as you like, but you shan't have less for the sake of old times.

It's breezing up again, do you hear? That was only a lull just now, and we are going to have a bad night.

A thing happened that made me start a little when I found that the jaw fitted exactly. I'm not very easily startled myself, but I had seen people make a quick movement, drawing their breath sharply when they had thought they were alone and suddenly turned and saw someone very near them. Nobody can call that fear. You wouldn't, would you? No. Well, just when I had set the jaw in its place under the skull, the teeth closed sharply on my finger. It felt as if it were biting me hard, and I confess that I jumped before I realized that I had been pressing the jaw and the skull together with my other hand. I assure you I was not at all nervous. It was broad daylight, too, and a fine day and the sun was streaming into the best bedroom. It would have been absurd to be nervous, and it was only a quick mistaken impression, but it really made me feel queer. Somehow it made me think of the funny verdict of the coroner's jury on Luke's death, "by the hand or teeth of some person or animal unknown." Ever since that, I've wished I had seen those marks on his throat, though the lower jaw was missing then.

I have often seen a man do insane things with his hands that he does not realize at all. I once saw a man hanging on by an old awning stop with one hand, leaning backwards, outboard, with all his weight on it, and he was just cutting the stop with the knife in his other hand when I got my arms around him. We were in mid-ocean, going twenty knots. He had not the smallest idea what he was doing; neither had I when I managed to pinch my finger between the teeth of that thing. I can feel it now. It was exactly as if it were alive and were trying to bite me. It would if it could, for I know it hates me, poor thing! Do you suppose that what rattles about inside is really a bit of lead? Well, I'll get the box down presently, and if whatever it happens to drop out into your hands, that's your affair. If it's only a clod of earth or a pebble, the whole matter would be off my mind, and I don't believe I should ever think of the skull again; but somehow, I cannot bring myself to shake out the bit of hard stuff myself. The mere idea that it may be lead makes me confoundedly uncomfortable, yet I've got the conviction that I shall know before long. I shall certainly know. I'm sure Trehearn knows, but he's such a silent beggar.

I'll go upstairs now and get it. What? You had better go with me. Ha, ha! do you think I'm afraid of a bandbox and noise? Nonsense!

Bother the candle. It won't light! As if the ridiculous thing understood what it wanted! Look at that—the third match. They light fast enough for my pipe. There, do you see? It's a fresh box, just out of the tin safe where I keep the supply on account of the dampness. Oh, you think the wick of the candle may be damp, do you? All right, I'll light the beastly thing in the fire. That won't go out at all events. Yes, it sputters a bit, but it will keep lighted now. It burns just like any other candle, doesn't it? The fact is, candles are not very good here. I don't know where they come from, but they have a way of burning low occasionally, with a greenish flame that spits tiny sparks, and I'm often annoyed by their going out of themselves. It cannot be helped, for it will be long before we have electricity in our village. It really is rather poor light, isn't it?

You think I had better leave you the candle and take the lamp, do you? I don't like to carry lamps about, that's the truth. I never dropped one in my life, but I have always thought I might, and it's so confoundedly dangerous if you do. Besides, I am pretty well used to these rotten candles by this time.

You may as well finish that glass while I'm getting it, for I don't mean to let you off with less than three before you go to bed. You won't have to go upstairs, either, for I've put you in the old study next to the surgery—that's where I live myself. The fact is, I never ask a friend to sleep upstairs now. The last man who did was Crackenthorpe, and he said he was kept awake all night. You remember old Crack, don't you? He stuck to the Service, and they've just made him an admiral. Yes, I'm off now —unless the candle goes out. I couldn't help asking if you remembered Crackenthorpe. If anyone had told us that the skinny little idiot he used to be was to turn out the most successful of the lot of us, we should have laughed at the idea, shouldn't we? You and I did not do badly, it's true—but I'm really going now. I don't mean to let you think that I've been putting it off by talking! As if there were anything to be afraid of! If I were scared, I should tell you so quite frankly and get you to go upstairs with me.

* * * *

Here's the box. I brought it down very carefully so as not to disturb it, poor thing. You see, if it were shaken, the jaw might get separated from it again, and I'm sure it wouldn't like that. Yes, the candle went out as I was coming downstairs, but that was the draught from the leaky window on the landing. Did you hear anything? Yes, there was another scream. Am I pale, do you say? That's nothing. My heart is a little queer sometimes, and I went upstairs too fast. In fact, that's one reason why I really prefer to live altogether on the ground floor.

Wherever that shriek came from, it was not from the skull, for I had the box in my hand when I heard the noise, and here it is now, so we have definitely proved that the screams are produced by something else. I've no doubt I shall find out someday what makes them. Some crevice in the wall, of course, or a crack in a chimney or a chink in the frame of a window. That's the way all ghost stories end in real life. Do you know, I'm jolly glad I thought of going up and bringing it down for you to see, for that last shriek settles the question. To think that I should have been so weak as to fancy that the poor skull could really cry out like a living thing!

Now I'll open the box, and we'll take it out and look at it under the bright light. It's awful to think that the poor lady used to sit there, in your chair, evening after evening, in just the same light, isn't it? But then—I've made up my mind that it's all rubbish from beginning to end and that it's just an old skull that Luke had when he was a student, and perhaps he put it into the lime merely to whiten it and could not find the jaw.

I made a seal on the string, you see after I had put the jaw in its place, and I wrote on the cover.

There's the old white label on it still, from the milliner's, addressed to Mrs Pratt when the hat was sent to her, and as there was the room, I wrote on edge: "A skull, once the property of the late Luke Pratt, M.D." I don't quite know why I wrote that unless it was with the idea of explaining how the thing happened to be in my possession. I cannot help sometimes wondering what sort of hat it was that came in the bandbox. What color was it, do you think? Was it a gay spring hat with a bobbing feather and pretty ribands? Strange that the very same box should hold the head that wore the finery —perhaps. No—we made up our minds that it just came from the hospital in London where Luke did his time. It's far better to look at it in that light, isn't it? There's no more connection between that skull and poor Mrs Pratt than there was between my story about the lead and——

Good Lord! Take the lamp—don't let it go out if you can help it—I'll have the window fastened again in a second—I say, what a gale! There, it's out! I told you so! Never mind, there's the firelight—I've got the window shut—the bolt was only half down. Was the box blown off the table? Where is the deuce? There! That won't open again, for I've put up the bar. Good dodge, an old-fashioned bar—there's nothing like it. Now, you find the bandbox while I light the lamp. Confound those wretched matches! Yes, a pipe spill is better—it must light in the fire—I hadn't thought of it—thank you—there we are again. Now, where's the box? Yes, put it back on the table, and we'll open it.

That's the first time I have ever known the wind to burst that window open, but it was partly carelessness on my part when I last shut it. Yes, of course, I heard the scream. It seemed to go all around the house before it broke in at the window. That proves that it's always been the wind and nothing else, doesn't it? When it was not the wind, it was my imagination. I've always been a very imaginative man: I must have been, though I did not know it. As we grow older, we understand ourselves better, don't you know?

I'll have a drop of the Hulstkamp neat by way of an exception since you are filling up your glass. That damp gust chilled me, and with my rheumatic tendency, I'm very much afraid of a chill, for the cold sometimes seems to stick in my joints all winter when it once gets in.

By George, that's good stuff! I'll just light a fresh pipe now that everything is snug again, and then we'll open the box. I'm so glad we heard that last scream together, with the skull here on the table between us, for a thing cannot possibly be in two places at the same time, and the noise most certainly came from outside, as any noise the wind makes must. You thought you heard it scream through the room after the window was burst open? Oh yes, so did I, but that was natural enough when everything was open. Of course, we heard the wind. What could one expect?

Look here, please. I want you to see that the seal is intact before we open the box together. Will you take my glasses? No, you have your own. All right. The seal is sound, you see, and you can read the words of the motto easily. "Sweet and low"—that's it—because the poem goes on "Wind of the Western sea," and says, "blow him again to me," and all that. Here is the seal on my watch chain, where it's hung for more than forty years. My poor little wife gave it to me when I was courting, and I never had any other. It was just like her to think of those words—she was always fond of Tennyson.

It's of no use to cut the string, for it's fastened to the box, so I'll just break the wax and untie the knot, and afterwards, we'll seal it up again. You see, I like to feel that the thing is safe in its place and that nobody can take it out. Not that I should suspect Trehearn of meddling with it, but I always feel that he knows a lot more than he tells.

You see, I've managed it without breaking the string, though when I fastened it, I never expected to open the bandbox again. The lid comes off easily enough. There! Now, look!

What? Nothing in it? Empty? It's gone, man, the skull is gone!

* * * *

No, there's nothing the matter with me. I'm only trying to collect my thoughts. It's so strange. I'm positively certain that it was inside when I put on the seal last spring. I couldn't have imagined that: it's utterly impossible. If I ever took a stiff glass with a friend now and then, I would admit that I might have made some idiotic mistake when I had taken too much. But I don't, and I never did. A pint of ale at supper and half a go of rum at bedtime was the most I ever took in my good days. I believe it's always we sober fellows who get rheumatism and gout! Yet there was my seal, and there was the empty bandbox. That's plain enough.

I say I don't half like this. It's not right. There's something wrong with it, in my opinion. You needn't talk to me about supernatural manifestations, for I don't believe in them, not a little bit! Somebody must have tampered with the seal and stolen the skull. Sometimes, when I go out to work in the garden in summer, I leave my watch and chain on the table. Trehearn must have taken the seal then and used it, for he would be quite sure that I should not come in for at least an hour.

If it was not Trehearn—oh, don't talk to me about the possibility that the thing has got out by itself! If it has, it must be somewhere about the house, in some out-of-the-way corner, waiting. We may come upon it anywhere, waiting for us, don't you know?—just waiting in the dark. Then it will scream at me; it will shriek at me in the dark, for it hates me, I tell you!

The bandbox is quite empty. We are not dreaming, either of us. There, I turn it upside down.

What's that? Something fell out as I turned it over. It's on the floor, it's near your feet, I know it is, and we must find it. Help me to find it, man. Have you got it? For God's sake, give it to me quickly!

Lead! I knew it when I heard it fall. I knew it couldn't be anything else by the little thud it made on the hearth rug. So it was lead, after all, and Luke did it.

I feel a little bit shaken up—not exactly nervous, you know, but badly shaken up, that's the fact. Anybody would, I should think. After all, you cannot say that it's fear of the thing, for I went up and brought it down—at least, I believed I was bringing it down, and that's the same thing, and by George, rather than give in to such silly nonsense, I'll take the box upstairs again and put it back in its place. It's not that. It's the certainty that the poor little woman came to her end in that way, by my fault, because I told the story. That's what is so dreadful. Somehow, I had always hoped that I should never be quite sure of it, but there is no doubting it now. Look at that!

Look at it! That little lump of lead with no particular shape. Think of what it did, man! Doesn't it make you shiver? He gave her something to make her sleep, of course, but there must have been one moment of awful agony. Think of having boiling lead poured into your brain. Think of it. She was dead before she could scream, but only think of— oh! there it is again—it's just outside—I know it's just outside—I can't keep it out of my head!—oh!— oh!

* * * *

You thought I had fainted? No, I wish I had, for it would have stopped sooner. It's all very well to say that it's only noise and that a noise never hurts anybody—you're as white as a shroud yourself. There's only one thing to be done if we hope to close an eye tonight. We must find it and put it back into its bandbox and shut it up in the cupboard, where it likes to be. I don't know how it got out, but it wants to get in again. That's why it screams so awfully tonight—it was never so bad as this—never since I first——

Bury it? Yes, if we can find it, we'll bury it if it takes us all night. We'll bury it six feet deep and ram down the earth over it so that it shall never get out again, and if it screams, we shall hardly hear it so deep down. Quick, we'll get the lantern and look for it. It cannot be far away; I'm sure it's just outside—it was coming in when I shut the window, I know it.

Yes, you're quite right. I'm losing my senses, and I must get hold of myself. Don't speak to me for a minute or two; I'll sit quite still and keep my eyes shut and repeat something I know. That's the best way.

"Add together the altitude, the latitude, and the polar distance, divide by two and subtract the altitude from the half-sum; then add the logarithm of the secant of the latitude, the cosecant of the polar distance, the cosine of the half-sum and the sine of the half-sum minus the altitude"—there! Don't say that I'm out of my senses, for my memory is all right, isn't it?

Of course, you may say that it's mechanical and that we never forget the things we learned when we were boys and have used almost every day for a lifetime. But that's the very point. When a man is going crazy, it's the mechanical part of his mind that gets out of order and won't work right; he remembers things that never happened, or he sees things that aren't real, or he hears noises when there is perfect silence. That's not what is the matter with either of us, is it?

Come, we'll get the lantern and go round the house. It's not raining—only blowing like old boots, as we used to say. The lantern is in the cupboard under the stairs in the hall, and I always keep it trimmed in case of a wreck.

No use to looking for the thing? I don't see how you can say that. It was nonsense to talk of burying it, of course, for it doesn't want to be buried; it wants to go back into its bandbox and be taken upstairs poor thing! Trehearn took it out, I know, and made the seal over again. Perhaps he took it to the churchyard, and he may have meant well. I daresay he thought that it would not scream anymore if it were quietly laid in consecrated ground, near where it belongs. But it has come home. Yes, that's it. He's not half a bad fellow, Trehearn, and rather religiously inclined, I think. Does not that sound natural, reasonable, and well-meant? He supposed it screamed because it was not decently buried—with the rest. But he was wrong. How should he know that it screams at me because it hates me and because it's my fault that there was that little lump of lead in it?

No use in looking for it, anyhow? Nonsense! I tell you, it wants to be found—Hark! what's that knocking? Do you hear it? Knock—knock—knock—three times, then a pause, and then again. It has a hollow sound, hasn't it?

It has come home. I've heard that knock before. It wants to come in and be taken upstairs in its box. It's at the front door.

Will you come with me? We'll take it in. Yes, I own that. I don't like to go alone and open the door. The thing will roll in and stop against my foot, just as it did before, and the light will go out. I'm a good deal shaken by finding that bit of lead, and, besides, my heart isn't quite right—too much strong tobacco, perhaps. Besides, I'm quite willing to own that I'm a bit nervous tonight if I never was before in my life.

That's right, come along! I'll take the box with me so as not to come back. Do you hear the knocking? It's not like any other knocking I've ever heard. If you hold this door open, I can find the lantern under the stairs by the light from this room without bringing the lamp into the hall—it would only go out.

The thing knows, we are coming—hark! It's impatient to get in. Don't shut the door till the lantern is ready, whatever you do. There will be the usual trouble with the matches, I suppose—no, the first one, by Jove! I tell you, it wants to get in, so there's no trouble. All right with that door now; shut it, please. Now come and hold the lantern, for it's blowing so hard outside that I shall have to use both hands. That's it. Hold the light low. Do you hear the knocking still? Here goes—I'll open just enough with my foot against the bottom of the door—now!

Catch it! it's only the wind that blows it across the floor, that's all—there's half a hurricane outside, I tell you! Have you got it? The bandbox is on the table. One minute and I'll have the bar up. There!

Why did you throw it into the box so roughly? It doesn't like that, you know.

What do you say? Bitten your hand? Nonsense, man! You did just what I did. You pressed the jaws together with your other hand and pinched yourself. Let me see. You don't mean to say you have drawn blood? You must have squeezed hard, by Jove, for the skin is certainly torn. I'll give you some carbolic solution for it before we go to bed, for they say a scratch from a skull's tooth may go bad and give trouble.

Come inside again and let me see it by the lamp. I'll bring the bandbox—never mind the lantern, it may just as well burn in the hall, for I shall need it presently when I go up the stairs. Yes, shut the door if you will; it makes it more cheerful and bright. Is your finger still bleeding? I'll get you the carbolic in an instant; just let me see the thing.

Ugh! There's a drop of blood on the upper jaw. It's on the eye-tooth. Ghastly, isn't it? When I saw it running along the floor of the hall, the strength almost went out of my hands, and I felt my knees bending; then, I understood that it was the gale, driving it over the smooth boards. You don't blame me? No, I should think not! We were boys together, and we've seen a thing or two, and we may just as well own to each other that we were both in a beastly funk when it slid across the floor at you. No wonder you pinched your finger picking it up after that if I did the same thing out of sheer nervousness, in broad daylight, with the sun streaming in on me.

Strange that the jaw should stick to it so closely, isn't it? I suppose it's the dampness, for it shuts like a vice—I have wiped off the drop of blood, for it was not nice to look at. I'm not going to try to open the jaws, don't be afraid! I shall not play any tricks with the poor thing, but I'll seal the box again, and we'll take it upstairs and put it away where it wants to be. The wax is on the writing table by the window. Thank you. It will be long before I leave my seal lying about again for Trehearn to use, I can tell you. Explain? I don't explain natural phenomena, but if you choose to think that Trehearn had hidden it somewhere in the bushes and that the gale blew it to the house against the door and made it knock as if it wanted to be let in, you're not thinking the impossible. I'm quite ready to agree with you.

Do you see that? You can swear that you've seen me seal it this time in case anything of the kind should occur again. The wax fastens the strings to the lid, which cannot possibly be lifted, even enough to get in one finger. You're quite satisfied, aren't you? Yes. Besides, I shall lock the cupboard and keep the key in my pocket hereafter.

Now we can take the lantern and go upstairs. Do you know? I'm very much inclined to agree with your theory that the wind blew it against the house. I'll go ahead, for I know the stairs; just hold the lantern near my feet as we go up. How the wind howls and whistles! Did you feel the sand on the floor under your shoes as we crossed the hall?

Yes—this is the door to the best bedroom. Hold up the lantern, please. This site is by the head of the bed. I left the cupboard open when I got the box. Isn't it queer how the faint odour of women's dresses will hang about an old closet for years? This is the shelf. You've seen me set the box there, and now you see me turn the key and put it into my pocket. So that's done!

* * * * *

Good-night. Are you sure you're quite comfortable? It's not much of a room, but I daresay you would as soon sleep here as upstairs tonight. If you want anything, sing out; there's only a lath and plaster partition between us. There's not so much wind on this side by half. There's the Hollands on the table if you'll have one more nightcap. No? Well, do as you please. Good night again, and don't dream about that thing if you can.

* * * * *

The following paragraph appeared in the Penraddon News, 23rd November 1906:

"Mysterious Death of a Retired Sea Captain

"The village of Tredcombe is much disturbed by the strange death of Captain Charles Braddock and all sorts of impossible stories are circulating with regard to the circumstances, which certainly seem difficult of explanation. The retired captain, who had successfully commanded in his time the largest and fastest liners belonging to one of the principal transatlantic steamship companies, was found dead in his bed on Tuesday morning in his own cottage, a quarter of a mile from the village. An examination was made at once by the local practitioner, which revealed the horrible fact that the deceased had been bitten in the throat by a human assailant with such amazing force as to crush the windpipe and cause death. The marks of the teeth of both jaws were so plainly visible on the skin that they could be counted, but the perpetrator of the deed had evidently lost the two lower middle incisors. It is hoped that this peculiarity may help to identify the murderer, who can only be a dangerous escaped maniac. The deceased, though over sixty-five years of age, is said to have been a hale man of considerable physical strength, and it is remarkable that no signs of any struggle were visible in the room, nor could it be ascertained how the murderer had entered the house. A warning has been sent to all the insane asylums in the United Kingdom, but as yet, no information has been received regarding the escape of any dangerous patient.

"The coroner's jury returned the somewhat singular verdict that Captain Braddock came to his death 'by the hands or teeth of some person unknown.' The local surgeon is said to have expressed privately the opinion that the maniac is a woman, a view he deduces from the small size of the jaws, as shown by the marks of the teeth. The whole affair is shrouded in mystery. Captain Braddock was a widower, and lived alone. He leaves no children."

[Note.—Students of ghost lore and haunted houses will find the foundation of the foregoing story in the legends about a skull which is still preserved in the farm-house called Bettiscombe Manor, situated, I believe, on the Dorsetshire coast.]

THE TRIAL FOR MURDER

by Charles Dickens

I have always noticed a prevalent want of courage, even among persons of superior intelligence and culture, as to imparting their own psychological experiences when those have been of a strange sort. Almost all men are afraid that what they could relate in such wise would find no parallel or response in a listener's internal life and might be suspected or laughed at. A truthful traveller, who should have seen some extraordinary creature in the likeness of a sea serpent, would have no fear of mentioning it; but the same traveller, having had some singular presentiment, impulse, vagary of thought, vision (so-called), dream, or another remarkable mental impression, would hesitate before he would own to it. To this reticence, I attribute much of the obscurity in which such subjects are involved. We do not habitually communicate our experiences of these subjective things as we do our experiences of objective creation. The consequence is that the general stock of experience in this regard appears exceptional and really is so, in respect of being miserably imperfect.

In what I am going to relate, I have no intention of setting up, opposing, or supporting, any theory. I know the history of the Bookseller of Berlin, I have studied the case of the wife of a late Astronomer Royal as related by Sir David Brewster, and I have followed the minutest details of a much more remarkable case of Spectral Illusion occurring within my private circle of friends. It may be necessary to state as to this last that the sufferer (a lady) was in no degree, however distant, related to me. A mistaken assumption on that head might suggest an explanation of a part of my own case—but only a part—which would be wholly without foundation. It cannot be referred to my inheritance of any developed peculiarity, nor had I ever before any at all similar experience, nor have I ever had any at all similar experience since.

It does not signify how many years ago, or how few, a certain murder was committed in England, which attracted great attention. We hear more than enough of murderers as they rise in succession to their atrocious eminence, and I would bury the memory of this particular brute if I could, as his body was buried in Newgate Jail. I purposely abstain from giving any direct clue about the criminal's individuality.

When the murder was first discovered, no suspicion fell—or I ought rather say, for I cannot be too precise in my facts, it was nowhere publicly hinted that any suspicion fell—on the man who was afterwards brought to trial. As no reference was at that time made to him in the newspapers, it is obviously impossible that any description of him can at that time has been given in the newspapers. It is essential that this fact be remembered.

Unfolding at breakfast my morning paper, containing the account of that first discovery, I found it to be deeply interesting, and I read it with close attention. I read it twice, if not three times. The discovery had been made in a bedroom, and, when I laid down the paper, I was aware of a flash —rush—flow—I do not know what to call it,—no word I can find is satisfactorily descriptive,—in which I seemed to see that bedroom passing through my room, like a picture impossibly painted on a running river. Though almost instantaneous in its passing, it was perfectly clear, so clear that I distinctly, and with a sense of relief, observed the absence of the dead body from the bed.

It was in no romantic place that I had this curious sensation, but in chambers in Piccadilly, very near to the corner of St. James's Street. It was entirely new to me. I was in my easy chair at the moment, and the sensation was accompanied by a peculiar shiver which started the chair from its position.   (But it is to be noted that the chair ran easily on castors.) I went to one of the windows (there are two in the room, and the room is on the second floor) to refresh my eyes with the moving objects down in Piccadilly. It was a bright autumn morning, and the street was sparkling and cheerful. The wind was high. As I looked out, it brought down from the Park a number of fallen leaves, which a gust took and whirled into a spiral pillar. As the pillar fell and the leaves dispersed, I saw two men on the opposite side of the way, going from West to East. They were one behind the other. The foremost man often looked back over his shoulder. The second man followed him, at a distance of some thirty paces, with his right hand menacingly raised. First, the singularity and steadiness of this threatening gesture in so public a thoroughfare attracted my attention; and next, the more remarkable circumstance that nobody heeded it. Both men threaded their way among the other passengers with a smoothness hardly consistent even with the action of walking on a pavement and no single creature that I could see gave them the place, touched them, or looked after them. In passing before my windows, they both stared up at me. I saw their two faces very distinctly, and I knew that I could recognize them anywhere. Not that I had consciously noticed anything very remarkable in either face, except that the man who went first had an unusually lowering appearance and that the face of the man who followed him was of the color of impure wax.

I am a bachelor, and my valet and his wife constitute my whole establishment. My occupation is in a certain Branch Bank, and I wish that my duties as head of a Department were as light as they are popularly supposed to be. They kept me in town that autumn when I stood in need of change. I was not ill, but I was not well. My reader is to make the most that can be reasonably made of my feeling jaded, having a depressing sense upon me of a monotonous life, and being "slightly dyspeptic." I am assured by my renowned doctor that my real state of health at that time justifies no stronger description, and I quote his own from his written answer to my request for it.

As the circumstances of the murder gradually unravelled and took stronger and stronger possession of the public mind, I kept them away from mine by knowing as little about them as was possible in the midst of the universal excitement. But I knew that a verdict of Wilful Murder had been found against the suspected murderer and that he had been committed to Newgate for trial. I also knew that his trial had been postponed over one Session of the Central Criminal Court on the ground of general prejudice and want of time for the preparation of the defence. I may further have known, but I believe I did not know when or about when the Sessions to which his trial stood postponed would come on.

My sitting room, bedroom, and dressing room are all on one floor. With the last, there is no communication but through the bedroom. True, there is a door in it, once communicating with the staircase, but a part of the fitting of my bath has been—and had then been for some years—fixed across it. At the same period, and as a part of the same arrangement—the door had been nailed up and canvased over.

I was standing in my bedroom late one night, giving some directions to my servant before he went to bed. My face was towards the only available door of communication with the dressing room, and it was closed. My servant's back was towards that door. While I was speaking to him, I saw it open, and a man looked in, who very earnestly and mysteriously beckoned to me. That man was the man who had gone second of the two along Piccadilly and whose face was of the color of impure wax.

The figure, having beckoned, drew back and closed the door. With no longer pause than was made by my crossing the bedroom, I opened the dressing room door and looked in. I had a lighted candle already in my hand. I felt no inward expectation of seeing the figure in the dressing room, and I did not see it there.

Conscious that my servant stood amazed, I turned round to him and said: "Derrick, could you believe that in my cool senses I fancied I saw a —" As I there laid my hand upon his breast, with a sudden start, he trembled violently, and said, "O Lord, yes, sir! A dead man beckoning!"

Now I do not believe that this John Derrick, my trusty and attached servant for more than twenty years, had any impression whatever of having seen any such figure until I touched him. The change in him was so startling when I touched him that I fully believe he derived his impression in some occult manner from me at that instant.

I bade John Derrick bring some brandy, and I gave him a dram and was glad to take one myself. Of what had preceded that night's phenomenon, I told him not a single word. Reflecting on it, I was absolutely certain that I had never seen that face before, except on the one occasion in Piccadilly. Comparing its expression when beckoning at the door with its expression when it had stared up at me as I stood at my window, I came to the conclusion that on the first occasion, it had sought to fasten itself upon my memory, and that on the second occasion it had made sure of being immediately remembered.

I was not very comfortable that night, though I felt a certainty, difficult to explain, that the figure would not return. At daylight, I fell into a heavy sleep, from which I was awakened by John Derrick's coming to my bedside with a paper in his hand.

This paper, it appeared, had been the subject of an altercation at the door between its bearer and my servant. It was a summons to me to serve upon a Jury at the forthcoming Sessions of the Central Criminal Court at the Old Bailey. I had never before been summoned on such a Jury as John Derrick well knew. He believed—I am not certain at this hour whether with reason or otherwise—that that class of Jurors were customarily chosen on a lower qualification than mine, and he had at first refused to accept the summons. The man who served it had taken the matter very coolly. He had said that my attendance or non-attendance was nothing to him; there the summons was, and I should deal with it at my own peril and not at his.

For a day or two, I was undecided whether to respond to this call or take no notice of it. I was not conscious of the slightest mysterious bias, influence, or attraction, one way or another. Of that, I am as strictly sure as every other statement that I make here. Ultimately I decided, as a break in the monotony of my life, that I would go.

The appointed morning was a raw morning in the month of November. There was a dense brown fog in Piccadilly, and it became positively black and, in the last degree, oppressive East of Temple Bar. I found the passages and staircases of the Court-House flaringly lit with gas and the Court itself similarly illuminated. I think that until I was conducted by officers into the Old Court and saw its crowded state, I did not know that the Murderer was to be tried that day. I think that, until I was so helped into the Old Court with considerable difficulty, I did not know into which of the two Courts sitting my summons would take me. But this must not be received as a positive assertion, for I am not completely satisfied in my mind on either point.

I took my seat in the place appropriated to Jurors in waiting, and I looked about the Court as well as I could through the cloud of fog and breath that was heavy in it. I noticed the black vapour hanging like a murky curtain outside the great windows, and I noticed the stifled sound of wheels on the straw or tan that was littered in the street;

also, the hum of the people gathered there, which a shrill whistle, or a louder song or hail than the rest, occasionally pierced. Soon afterwards, the Judges, two in number, entered and took their seats. The buzz in the Court was awfully hushed. The direction was given to put the Murderer in the bar. He appeared there. And in that same instant, I recognized in him the first of the two men who had gone down Piccadilly.

If my name had been called then, I doubt if I could have answered it audibly. But it was called about sixth or eighth in the panel, and I was by that time able to say, "Here!" Now, observe. As I stepped into the box, the prisoner, who had been looking on attentively, but with no sign of concern, became violently agitated and beckoned to his attorney. The prisoner's wish to challenge me was so manifest that it occasioned a pause, during which the attorney, with his hand upon the dock, whispered with his client and shook his head. I afterwards had it from that gentleman that the prisoner's first affrighted words to him were, "At all hazards, challenge that man!" But that, as he would give no reason for it and admitted that he had not even known my name until he heard it called and I appeared, it was not done.

Both on the ground already explained that I wish to avoid reviving the unwholesome memory of that Murderer, and also because a detailed account of his long trial is by no means indispensable to my narrative, I shall confine myself closely to such incidents in the ten days and nights during which we, the Jury, were kept together, as directly bear on my own curious personal experience. It is in that, and not in the Murderer that I seek to interest my reader. It is to that, and not to a page of the Newgate Calendar that I beg attention.

I was chosen Foreman of the Jury. On the second morning of the trial, after evidence had been taken for two hours (I heard the church clocks strike), happening to cast my eyes over my brother's jurymen, I found an inexplicable difficulty in counting them. I counted them several times, yet always with the same difficulty. In short, I made them one too many.

I touched the brother jurymen whose place was next to me, and I whispered to him, "Oblige me by counting us." He looked surprised by the request but turned his head and counted. "Why," says he, suddenly, "we are Thirt—; but no, it's not possible. No. We are twelve."

According to my counting that day, we were always right in detail, but in the gross, we were always one too many. There was no appearance— no figure—to account for it, but I had now an inward foreshadowing of the figure that was surely coming.

The Jury were housed at the London Tavern. We all slept in one large room on separate tables, and we were constantly in charge and under the eye of the officer sworn to hold us in safekeeping. I see no reason for suppressing the real name of that officer. He was intelligent, highly polite, obliging, and (I was glad to hear) much respected in the City. He had an agreeable presence, good eyes, enviable black whiskers, and a fine sonorous voice. His name was Mr Harker.

When we turned into our twelve beds at night, Mr Harker's bed was drawn across the door. On the night of the second day, not being disposed to lie down and seeing Mr Harker sitting on his bed, I went and sat beside him and offered him a pinch of snuff. As Mr Harker's hand touched mine in taking it from my box, a peculiar shiver crossed him, and he said, "Who is this?"

Following Mr Harker's eyes and looking along the room, I saw again the figure I expected—the second of the two men who had gone down Piccadilly. I rose and advanced a few steps, then stopped and looked around at Mr Harker. He was quite unconcerned, laughed, and said in a pleasant way, "I thought for a moment we had a thirteenth juryman, without a bed. But I see it is the moonlight."

Making no revelation to Mr Harker but inviting him to take a walk with me to the end of the room, I watched what the figure did. It stood for a few moments by the bedside of each of my eleven brother jurymen, close to the pillow. It always went to the right-hand side of the bed and always passed out, crossing the foot of the next bed. It seemed, from the action of the head, merely to look down pensively at each recumbent figure. It took no notice of me or of my bed, which was that nearest to Mr Harker's. It seemed to go out where the moonlight came in, through a high window, as by an aërial flight of stairs.

The next morning at breakfast, it appeared that everybody present had dreamed of the murdered man last night except myself and Mr Harker.

I now felt as convinced that the second man who had gone down Piccadilly was the murdered man (so to speak), as if it had been borne into my comprehension by his immediate testimony.   But even this took place, and in a manner for which I was not at all prepared.

On the fifth day of the trial, when the case for the prosecution was drawing to a close, a miniature of the murdered man, missing from his bedroom upon the discovery of the deed, and afterwards found in a hiding place where the Murderer had been seen digging, was put in evidence.   Having been identified by the witness under examination, it was handed up to the Bench and thence handed down to be inspected by the Jury.   As an officer in a black gown was making his way with it across to me, the figure of the second man who had gone down Piccadilly impetuously started from the crowd, caught the miniature from the officer, and gave it to me with his own hands, at the same time saying, in a low and hollow tone,—before I saw the miniature, which was in a locket,—"I was younger then, and my face was not then drained of blood." It also came between the brother juryman to whom I would have given the miniature and me, and between him and the brother juryman to whom he would have given it, and so passed it on through the whole of our number and back into my possession.   Not one of them, however, detected this.

At the table and generally, when we were shut up together in Mr Harker's custody, we had from the first naturally discussed the day's proceedings a good deal. On that fifth day, the case for the prosecution was closed, and we had that side of the question in complete shape before us. Our discussion was more animated and serious. Among our number was a vestryman,—the densest idiot I have ever seen at large,—who met the plainest evidence with the most preposterous objections and who was sided with by two flabby parochial parasites; all the three impanelled from a district so delivered over to Fever that they ought to have been upon their own trial for five hundred Murders. When these mischievous blockheads were at their loudest, which was towards midnight, while some of us were already preparing for bed, I again saw the murdered man. He stood grimly behind them, beckoning to me. On my going towards them and striking into the conversation, he immediately retired. This was the beginning of a separate series of appearances, confined to that long room in which we were confined. Whenever a knot of my brother jurymen laid their heads together, I saw the head of the murdered man among theirs. Whenever their comparison of notes was going against him, he would solemnly and irresistibly beckon to me.

It will be borne in mind that down to the production of the miniature, on the fifth day of the trial, I had never seen the Appearance in Court. Three changes occurred now that we entered the case for the defence. Two of them I will mention the two together first. The figure was now in Court continually, and it never there addressed itself to me but always to the person who was speaking at the time. For instance: the throat of the murdered man had been cut straight across. In the opening speech for the defence, it was suggested that the deceased might have cut his own throat. At that very moment, the figure, with its throat in the dreadful condition referred to (this it had concealed before), stood at the speaker's elbow, motioning across and across its windpipe, now with the right hand, now with the left, vigorously suggesting to the speaker himself the impossibility of such a wound having been self-inflicted by either hand. For another instance: a witness to character a woman, deposed to the prisoner's being the most amiable of humankind. The figure, at that instant, stood on the floor before her, looking her full in the face, and pointing out the prisoner's evil countenance with an extended arm and an outstretched finger.

The third change now to be added impressed me strongly as the most marked and striking of all. I do not theorise upon it; I accurately state it and there leave it. Although the Appearance was not itself perceived by those whom it addressed, its coming close to such persons was invariably attended by some trepidation or disturbance on their part. It seemed to me as if it were prevented, by laws to which I was not amenable, from fully revealing itself to others, and yet as if it could invisibly, dumbly, and darkly overshadow their minds. When the leading counsel for the defence suggested that hypothesis of suicide, and the figure stood at the learned gentleman's elbow, frightfully sawing at its severed throat, it is undeniable that the counsel faltered in his speech, lost for a few seconds the thread of his ingenious discourse, wiped his forehead with his handkerchief, and turned extremely pale. When the witness to character was confronted by the Appearance, her eyes most certainly did follow the direction of its pointed finger, and rest in great hesitation and trouble upon the prisoner's face. Two additional illustrations will suffice. On the eighth day of the trial, after the pause which was made every day early in the afternoon for a few minutes of rest and refreshment, I came back into Court with the rest of the Jury some little time before the return of the Judges. Standing up in the box and looking about me, I thought the figure was not there, until, chancing to raise my eyes to the gallery, I saw it bending forward and leaning over a very decent woman as if to assure itself whether the Judges had resumed their seats or not. Immediately afterwards, that woman screamed, fainted, and was carried out. So with the venerable, sagacious, and patient Judge who conducted the trial. When the case was over, and he settled himself and his papers, to sum up, the murdered man, entering by the Judges' door, advanced to his Lordship's desk and looked eagerly over his shoulder at the pages of his notes which he was turning. A change came over his Lordship's face; his hand stopped; the peculiar shiver, that I knew so well, passed over him; he faltered, "Excuse me, gentlemen, for a few moments. I am somewhat oppressed by the vitiated air;" and did not recover until he had drunk a glass of water.

Through all the monotony of six of those interminable ten days,—the same Judges and others on the bench, the same Murderer in the dock, the same lawyers at the table, the same tones of question and answer rising to the roof of the court, the same scratching of the Judge's pen, the same ushers going in and out, the same lights kindled at the same hour when there had been any natural light of day, the same foggy curtain outside the great windows when it was foggy, the same rain pattering and dripping when it was rainy, the same footmarks of turnkeys and prisoner day after day on the same sawdust, the same keys locking and unlocking the same heavy doors,—through all the wearisome monotony which made me feel as if I had been Foreman of the Jury for a vast period of time, and Piccadilly had flourished coevally with Babylon, the murdered man never lost one trace of his distinctness in my eyes, nor was he at any moment less distinct than anybody else. I must not omit, as a matter of fact, that I never once saw the Appearance which I call by the name of the murdered man look at the Murderer. Again and again, I wondered, "Why does he not?" But he never did.

Nor did he look at me after the production of the miniature until the last closing minutes of the trial arrived. We retired to consider, at seven minutes before ten at night. The idiotic vestryman and his two parochial parasites gave us so much trouble that we twice returned to Court to beg to have certain extracts from the Judge's notes re-read. Nine of us had not the smallest doubt about those passages, neither, I believe, had anyone in the Court;

the dunder-headed triumvirate, having no idea but obstruction, disputed them for that very reason. At length, we prevailed, and finally, the Jury returned to Court at ten minutes past twelve.

The murdered man at that time stood directly opposite the Jury-box, on the other side of the Court. As I took my place, his eyes rested on me with great attention; he seemed satisfied and slowly shook a great grey veil, which he carried on his arm for the first time, over his head and whole form. As I gave in our verdict, "Guilty," the veil collapsed, all was gone, and his place was empty.

The Murderer, being asked by the Judge, according to usage, whether he had anything to say before, a sentence of Death should be passed upon him, indistinctly muttered something which was described in the leading newspapers of the following day as "a few rambling, incoherent, and half-audible words, in which he was understood to complain that he had not had a fair trial, because the Foreman of the Jury was prepossessed against him." The remarkable declaration that he really made was this: "My Lord, I knew I was a doomed man, when the Foreman of my Jury came into the box. My Lord, I knew he would never let me off, because, before I was taken, he somehow got to my bedside in the night, woke me, and put a rope round my neck."

THE PHANTOM COACH

by Amelia B. Edwards

The circumstances I am about to relate to you have truth to recommend them. They happened to me, and my recollection of them is as vivid as if they had taken place only yesterday. Twenty years, however, have gone by since that night. During those twenty years, I have told the story to but one other person. I tell it now with a reluctance which I find difficult to overcome. All I entreat, meanwhile, is that you will abstain from forcing your own conclusions upon me. I want nothing explained away. I desire no arguments. My mind on this subject is quite made up, and, having the testimony of my own senses to rely upon, I prefer to abide by it.

Well! It was just twenty years ago and within a day or two of the end of the grouse season. I had been out all day with my gun and had had no sport to speak of. The wind was due east; the month, December; the place, a bleak wide moor in the far north of England. And I had lost my way. It was not a pleasant place in which to lose one's way, with the first feathery flakes of a coming snowstorm just fluttering down upon the heather and the leaden evening closing in all around. I shaded my eyes with my hand and stared anxiously into the gathering darkness, where the purple moorland melted into a range of low hills, some ten or twelve miles distant. Not the faintest smoke wreath, not the tiniest cultivated patch, or fence, or sheep track, met my eyes in any direction. There was nothing for it but to walk on and take my chance of finding what shelter I could, by the way. So I shouldered my gun again and pushed wearily forward; for I had been on foot since an hour after daybreak and had eaten nothing since breakfast.

Meanwhile, the snow began to come down with ominous steadiness, and the wind fell. After this, the cold became more intense, and the night came rapidly up. As for me, my prospects darkened with the darkening sky, and my heart grew heavy as I thought how my young wife was already watching for me through the window of our little inn parlour and thought of all the suffering in store for her throughout this weary night. We had been married four months and, having spent our autumn in the Highlands, were now lodging in a remote little village situated just on the verge of the great English moorlands. We were very much in love and, of course, very happy. This morning, when we parted, she had implored me to return before dusk, and I had promised her that I would. What would I not have given to have kept my word?

Even now, weary as I was, I felt that with a supper, an hour's rest, and a guide, I might still get back to her before midnight if only a guide and shelter could be found.

And all this time, the snow fell and the night thickened. I stopped and shouted every now and then, but my shouts seemed only to make the silence deeper. Then a vague sense of uneasiness came upon me, and I began to remember stories of travellers who had walked on and on in the falling snow until, wearied out, they were fain to lie down and sleep their lives away. Would it be possible, I asked myself, to keep on thus through all the long dark night? Would there not come a time when my limbs must fail, and my resolution give way? When I, too, must sleep the sleep of death. Death! I shuddered. How hard to die just now when life lay all so bright before me! How hard for my darling, whose whole loving heart but that thought was not to be borne! To banish it, I shouted again, louder and longer, and then listened eagerly. Was my shout answered, or did I only fancy that I heard a far-off cry? I halloed again, and again the echo followed. Then a wavering speck of light came suddenly out of the dark, shifting, disappearing, growing momentarily nearer and brighter. Running towards it at full speed, I found myself, to my great joy, face to face with an old man and a lantern.

"Thank God!" was the exclamation that burst involuntarily from my lips.

Blinking and frowning, he lifted his lantern and peered into my face.

"What for?" he growled sulkily.

"Well—for you. I began to fear I should be lost in the snow."

"Eh, then, folks do get cast away hereabouts fra' time to time, an' what's to hinder you from bein' cast away likewise, if the Lord's so minded?"

"If the Lord is so minded that you and I shall be lost together, friend, we must submit," I replied, "but I don't mean to be lost without you. How far am I now from Dwolding?"

"A gude twenty mile, more or less."

"And the nearest village?"

"The nearest village is Wyke, an' that's twelve mile t'other side."

"Where do you live, then?"

"Out yonder," said he, with a vague jerk of the lantern.

"You're going home, I presume?"

"Maybe I am."

"Then I'm going with you."

The older man shook his head and rubbed his nose reflectively with the handle of the lantern.

"It ain't o' no use," growled he. "He 'ont let you in—not he."

"We'll see about that," I replied briskly. "Who is He?"

"The master."

"Who is the master?"

"That's nowt to you," was the unceremonious reply.

"Well, well; you lead the way, and I'll engage that the master shall give me shelter and a supper to-night."

"Eh, you can try him!" muttered my reluctant guide and still shaking his head, he hobbled, gnome-like, away through the falling snow. A large mass loomed up presently out of the darkness, and a huge dog rushed out, barking furiously.

"Is this the house?" I asked.

"Ay, it's the house. Down, Bey!" And he fumbled in his pocket for the key.

I drew up close behind him, prepared to lose no chance of entrance, and saw in the little circle of light shed by the lantern that the door was heavily studded with iron nails, like the door of a prison. In another minute, he had turned the key, and I had pushed past him into the house.

Once inside, I looked round with curiosity and found myself in a great raftered hall, which served, apparently, a variety of uses. One end was piled to the roof with corn, like a barn. The other was stored with flour sacks, agricultural implements, casks, and all kinds of miscellaneous lumber, while from the beams overhead hung rows of hams, flitches, and bunches of dried herbs for winter use. In the centre of the floor stood some huge object gauntly dressed in a dingy wrapping cloth and reaching halfway to the rafters. Lifting a corner of this cloth, I saw, to my surprise, a telescope of very considerable size mounted on a rude movable platform with four small wheels. The tube was made of painted wood, bound round with bands of metal rudely fashioned; the speculum, so far as I could estimate its size in the dim light, measured at least fifteen inches in diameter. While I was yet examining the instrument and asking myself whether it was not the work of some self-taught optician, a bell rang sharply.

"That's for you," said my guide with a malicious grin. "Yonder's his room."

He pointed to a low black door at the opposite side of the hall. I crossed over, rapped somewhat loudly, and went in without waiting for an invitation. A huge, white-haired old man rose from a table covered with books and papers and confronted me sternly.

"Who are you?" said he. "How came you here? What do you want?"

"James Murray, barrister-at-law. On foot across the moor. Meat, drink, and sleep."

He bent his bushy brows into a portentous frown.

"Mine is not a house of entertainment," he said haughtily. "Jacob, how dared you admit this stranger?"

"I didn't admit him," grumbled the old man. "He followed me over the muir, and shouldered his way in before me. I'm no match for six foot two."

"And pray, sir, by what right have you forced an entrance into my house?"

"The same by which I should have clung to your boat, if I were drowning. The right of self-preservation."

"Self-preservation?"

"There's an inch of snow on the ground already," I replied briefly, "and it would be deep enough to cover my body before daybreak."

He strode to the window, pulled aside a heavy black curtain, and looked out.

"It is true," he said. "You can stay, if you choose, till morning. Jacob, serve the supper."

With this, he waved me to a seat, resumed his own, and became absorbed in the studies from which I had disturbed him.

I placed my gun in a corner, drew a chair to the hearth, and examined my quarters at leisure. Smaller and less incongruous in its arrangements than the hall, this room contained, nevertheless, much to awaken my curiosity. The floor was carpetless. The whitewashed walls were, in parts, scrawled over with strange diagrams and, in others, covered with shelves crowded with philosophical instruments, the uses of many of which were unknown to me. On one side of the fireplace stood a bookcase filled with dingy folios; on the other, a small organ, fantastically decorated with painted carvings of mediæval saints and devils. Through the half-opened door of a cupboard at the further end of the room, I saw a long array of geological specimens, surgical preparations, crucibles, retorts, and jars of chemicals; while on the mantelshelf beside me, amid a number of small objects, stood a model of the solar system, a small galvanic battery, and a microscope. Every chair had its burden. Every corner was heaped high with books. The very floor was littered over with maps, casts, papers, tracings, and learned lumber of all conceivable kinds.

I stared about me with amazement increased by every fresh object upon which my eyes chanced to rest. So strange a room I had never seen, yet seemed it, stranger, still, to find such a room in a lone farmhouse amid those wild and solitary moors! Over and over again, I looked from my host to his surroundings and from his surroundings back to my host, asking myself who and what he could be. His head was singularly fine, but it was more the head of a poet than of a philosopher. Broad in the temples, prominent over the eyes, and clothed with a rough profusion of perfectly white hair, it had all the ideality and much of the ruggedness that characterises the head of Louis von Beethoven.

There were the same deep lines about the mouth and the same stern furrows in the brow. There was the same concentration of expression. While I was yet observing him, the door opened, and Jacob brought in the supper. His master then closed his book, rose, and with more courtesy of manner than he had yet shown, invited me to the table.

A dish of ham and eggs, a loaf of brown bread, and a bottle of admirable sherry were placed before me.

"I have but the homeliest farmhouse fare to offer you, sir," said my entertainer. "Your appetite, I trust, will make up for the deficiencies of our larder."

I had already fallen upon the viands and now protested, with the enthusiasm of a starving sportsman, that I had never eaten anything so delicious.

He bowed stiffly and sat down to his own supper, which consisted, primitively, of a jug of milk and a basin of porridge. We ate in silence, and when we had done, Jacob removed the tray. I then drew my chair back to the fireside. My host, somewhat to my surprise, did the same and, turning abruptly towards me, said:

"Sir, I have lived here in strict retirement for three-and-twenty years. During that time, I have not seen as many strange faces, and I have not read a single newspaper. You are the first stranger who has crossed my threshold for more than four years. Will you favour me with a few words of information respecting that outer world from which I have parted company so long?"

"Pray interrogate me," I replied. "I am heartily at your service."

He bent his head in acknowledgement; leaned forward, with his elbows resting on his knees and his chin supported in the palms of his hands; stared fixedly into the fire; and proceeded to question me.

His inquiries related chiefly to scientific matters, with the later progress of which, as applied to the practical purposes of life, he was almost wholly unacquainted. No student of science myself, I replied as well as my slight information permitted; but the task was far from easy, and I was much relieved when, passing from interrogation to discussion, he began pouring forth his own conclusions upon the facts which I had been attempting to place before him. He talked, and I listened spellbound. He talked till I believe he almost forgot my presence and only thought aloud. I had never heard anything like it then; I have never heard anything like it since. Familiar with all systems of all philosophies, subtle in analysis, bold in generalisation, he poured forth his thoughts in an uninterrupted stream and, still leaning forward in the same moody attitude with his eyes fixed upon the fire, wandered from topic to topic, from speculation to speculation, like an inspired dreamer. From practical science to mental philosophy; from electricity in the wire to electricity in the nerve; from Watts to Mesmer, from Mesmer to Reichenbach, from Reichenbach to Swedenborg, Spinoza,

Condillac, Descartes, Berkeley, Aristotle, Plato, and the Magi and mystics of the East, were transitions which, however bewildering in their variety and scope, seemed easy and harmonious upon his lips as sequences in music. By and by—I forget now by what link of conjecture or illustration—he passed on to that field which lies beyond the boundary line of even conjectural philosophy and reaches no man knows whither. He spoke of the soul and its aspirations; of the spirit and its powers; of second sight; of prophecy; of those phenomena which, under the names of ghosts, spectres, and supernatural appearances, have been denied by the sceptics and attested by the credulous, of all ages.

"The world," he said, "grows hourly more and more sceptical of all that lies beyond its own narrow radius; and our men of science foster the fatal tendency. They condemn as fable all that resists experiment. They reject as false all that cannot be brought to the test of the laboratory or the dissecting-room. Against what superstition have they waged so long and obstinate a war, as against the belief in apparitions? And yet what superstition has maintained its hold upon the minds of men so long and so firmly? Show me any fact in physics, in history, in archæology, which is supported by testimony so wide and so various. Attested by all races of men, in all ages, and in all climates, by the soberest sages of antiquity, by the rudest savage of to-day, by the Christian, the Pagan, the Pantheist, the Materialist, this phenomenon is treated as a nursery tale by the philosophers of our century. Circumstantial evidence weighs with them as a feather in the balance. The comparison of causes with effects, however valuable in physical science, is put aside as worthless and unreliable. The evidence of competent witnesses, however conclusive in a court of justice, counts for nothing. He who pauses before he pronounces, is condemned as a trifler. He who believes, is a dreamer or a fool."

He spoke with bitterness and, having said thus, relapsed for some minutes into silence. Presently he raised his head from his hands and added, with an altered voice and manner, "I, sir, paused, investigated, believed, and was not ashamed to state my convictions to the world. I, too, was branded as a visionary, held up to ridicule by my contemporaries, and hooted from that field of science in which I had laboured with honour during all the best years of my life. These things happened just three-and-twenty years ago. Since then, I have lived as you see me living now, and the world has forgotten me, as I have forgot—ten the world. You have my history."

"It is a very sad one," I murmured, scarcely knowing what to answer.

"It is a very common one," he replied. "I have only suffered for the truth, as many a better and wiser man has suffered before me."

He rose, as if desirous of ending the conversation, and went over to the window.

"It has ceased snowing," he observed as he dropped the curtain and came back to the fireside.

"Ceased!" I exclaimed, starting eagerly to my feet. "Oh, if it were only possible—but no! it is hopeless. Even if I could find my way across the moor, I could not walk twenty miles to-night."

"Walk twenty miles to-night!" repeated my host. "What are you thinking of?"

"Of my wife," I replied impatiently. "Of my young wife, who does not know that I have lost my way, and who is at this moment breaking her heart with suspense and terror."

"Where is she?"

"At Dwolding, twenty miles away."

"At Dwolding," he echoed thoughtfully. "Yes, the distance, it is true, is twenty miles; but—are you so very anxious to save the next six or eight hours?"

"So very, very anxious, that I would give ten guineas at this moment for a guide and a horse."

"Your wish can be gratified at a less costly rate," said he, smiling. "The night mail from the north, which changes horses at Dwolding, passes within five miles of this spot, and will be due at a certain cross-road in about an hour and a quarter. If Jacob were to go with you across the moor, and put you into the old coach-road, you could find your way, I suppose, to where it joins the new one?"

"Easily—gladly."

He smiled again, rang the bell, gave the old servant his directions, and, taking a bottle of whisky and a wineglass from the cupboard in which he kept his chemicals, said:

"The snow lies deep, and it will be difficult walking to-night on the moor. A glass of usquebaugh before you start?"

I would have declined the spirit, but he pressed it on me, and I drank it. It went down my throat like a liquid flame and almost took my breath away.

"It is strong," he said, "but it will help to keep out the cold. And now you have no moments to spare. Good night!"

I thanked him for his hospitality and would have shaken hands, but he had turned away before I could finish my sentence. In another minute, I had traversed the hall, Jacob had locked the outer door behind me, and we were out on the wide white moor.

Although the wind had fallen, it was still bitterly cold. Not a star glimmered in the black vault overhead. Not a sound, save the rapid crunching of the snow beneath our feet, disturbed the heavy stillness of the night. Jacob, not too well pleased with his mission, shambled on before in sullen silence, his lantern in his hand and his shadow at his feet. I followed, with my gun over my shoulder, as little inclined for conversation as himself. My thoughts were full of my late host. His voice yet rang in my ears. His eloquence yet held my imagination captive. I remember to this day, with surprise, how my over-excited brain retained whole sentences and parts of sentences, troops of brilliant images, and fragments of splendid reasoning in the very words in which he had uttered them. Musing thus over what I had heard and striving to recall a lost link here and there, I strode on at the heels of my guide, absorbed and unobservant. Presently—at the end, as it seemed to me, of only a few minutes—he came to a sudden halt and said:

"Yon's your road. Keep the stone fence to your right hand, and you can't fail of the way."

"This, then, is the old coach-road?"

"Ay, 'tis the old coach-road."

"And how far do I go, before I reach the cross-roads?"

"Nigh upon three mile."

I pulled out my purse, and he became more communicative.

"The road's a fair road enough," said he, "for foot passengers; but 'twas over steep and narrow for the northern traffic. You'll mind where the parapet's broken away, close again the sign-post. It's never been mended since the accident."

"What accident?"

"Eh, the night mail pitched right over into the valley below—a gude fifty feet an' more—just at the worst bit o' road in the whole county."

"Horrible! Were many lives lost?"

"All. Four were found dead, and t'other two died next morning."

"How long is it since this happened?"

"Just nine year."

"Near the sign-post, you say? I will bear it in mind. Good night."

"Gude night, sir, and thankee." Jacob pocketed his half-crown, made a faint pretence of touching his hat, and trudged back by the way he had come.

I watched the light of his lantern till it quite disappeared and then turned to pursue my way alone. This was no longer a matter of the slightest difficulty, for, despite the dead darkness overhead, the line of stone fence showed distinctly enough against the pale gleam of the snow. How silent it seemed now, with only my footsteps to listen to; how silent and how solitary! A strange disagreeable sense of loneliness stole over me. I walked faster. I hummed a fragment of a tune. I cast up enormous sums in my head and accumulated them at compound interest. I did my best, in short, to forget the startling speculations to which I had but just been listening, and, to some extent, I succeeded.

Meanwhile, the night air seemed to become colder and colder, and though I walked fast, I found it impossible to keep myself warm. My feet were like ice. I lost sensation in my hands and grasped my gun mechanically. I even breathed with difficulty, as though, instead of traversing a quiet north country highway, I were scaling the uppermost heights of some gigantic Alp. This last symptom became presently so distressing that I was forced to stop for a few minutes and lean against the stone fence. As I did so, I chanced to look back up the road, and there, to my infinite relief, I saw a distant point of light, like the gleam of an approaching lantern. I at first concluded that Jacob had retraced his steps and followed me, but even as the conjecture presented itself, a second light flashed into sight—a light evidently parallels with the first and approaching at the same rate of motion. It needed no second thought to show me that these must be the carriage lamps of some private vehicle, though it seemed strange that any private vehicle should take a road professedly disused and dangerous.

There could be no doubt, however, of the fact, for the lamps grew larger and brighter every moment, and I even fancied I could already see the dark outline of the carriage between them. It was coming up very fast and quite noiselessly, the snow being nearly a foot deep under the wheels.

And now the body of the vehicle became distinctly visible behind the lamps. It looked strangely lofty. A sudden suspicion flashed upon me. Was it possible that I had passed the crossroads in the dark without observing the signpost, and could this be the very coach which I had come to meet?

No need to ask me that question a second time, for here it came round the bend of the road, guard and driver, one outside passenger, and four steaming greys, all wrapped in a soft haze of light, through which the lamps blazed out, like a pair of fiery meteors.

I jumped forward, waved my hat, and shouted. The mail came down at full speed and passed me. For a moment, I feared that I had not been seen or heard, but it was only for a moment. The coachman pulled up; the guard, muffled to the eyes in capes and comforters and apparently sound asleep in the rumble, neither answered my hail nor made the slightest effort to dismount; the outside passenger did not even turn his head. I opened the door for myself and looked in. There were but three travellers inside, so I stepped in, shut the door, slipped into the vacant corner, and congratulated myself on my good fortune.

The atmosphere of the coach seemed, if possible, colder than that of the outer air, and was pervaded by a singularly damp and disagreeable smell. I looked around at my fellow passengers. They were all three, men and all silent. They did not seem to be asleep, but each leaned back in his corner of the vehicle as if absorbed in his own reflections. I attempted to open a conversation.

"How intensely cold it is to-night," I said, addressing my opposite neighbour.

He lifted his head and looked at me but made no reply.

"The winter," I added, "seems to have begun in earnest."

Although the corner in which he sat was so dim that I could distinguish none of his features very clearly, I saw that his eyes were still turned full upon me. And yet he answered never a word.

At any other time, I should have felt, and perhaps expressed, some annoyance, but at the moment, I felt too ill to do either. The icy coldness of the night air had struck a chill to my very marrow, and the strange smell inside the coach was affecting me with intolerable nausea. I shivered from head to foot and, turning to my left-hand neighbour, asked if he had any objection to an open window.

He neither spoke nor stirred.

I repeated the question somewhat more loudly but with the same result. Then I lost patience and let the sash down. As I did so, the leather strap broke in my hand, and I observed that the glass was covered with a thick coat of mildew, the accumulation, apparently, of years. My attention being thus drawn to the condition of the coach, I examined it more narrowly and saw by the uncertain light of the outer lamps that it was in the last stage of dilapidation. Every part of it was not only out of repair but in a condition of decay. The sashes splintered at a touch. The leather fittings were crusted over with mould, and literally rotting from the woodwork. The floor was almost breaking away beneath my feet. The whole machine, in short, was foul with damp and had evidently been dragged from some outhouse in which it had been mouldering away for years to do another day or two of duty on the road.

I turned to the third passenger, whom I had not yet addressed, and hazarded one more remark.

"This coach," I said, "is in a deplorable condition. The regular mail, I suppose, is under repair?"

He moved his head slowly and looked me in the face without speaking a word. I shall never forget that look while I live. I turned cold at heart under it. I turn cold at heart even now when I recall it. His eyes glowed with a fiery unnatural lustre. His face was livid as the face of a corpse. His bloodless lips were drawn back as if in the agony of death and showed the gleaming teeth between.

The words that I was about to utter died upon my lips, and a strange horror—a dreadful horror—came upon me. My sight had by this time become used to the gloom of the coach, and I could see with tolerable distinctness. I turned to my opposite neighbour. He, too, was looking at me with the same startling pallor on his face and the same stony glitter in his eyes. I passed my hand across my brow. I turned to the passenger on the seat beside my own and saw—oh, Heaven! How shall I describe what I saw? I saw that he was no living man—that none of them was a living man like myself! A pale phosphorescent light—the light of putrefaction—played upon their awful faces; upon their hair, dank with the dews of the grave; upon their clothes, earth-stained and dropping to pieces; upon their hands, which were as the hands of corpses long buried. Only their eyes, their terrible eyes, were living; and those eyes were all turned menacingly upon me!

A shriek of terror, a wild unintelligible cry for help and mercy, burst from my lips as I flung myself against the door and strove in vain to open it.

In that single instant, brief and vivid as a landscape beheld in the flash of summer lightning, I saw the moon shining down through a rift of stormy cloud—the ghastly sign-post rearing its warning finger by the wayside—the broken parapet—the plunging horses—the black gulf below. Then, the coach reeled like a ship at sea. Then came a mighty crash—a sense of crushing pain—and then, darkness.

It seemed as if years had gone by when I awoke one morning from a deep sleep and found my wife watching I will pass over the scene that ensued and give you, in half a dozen words, the tale she told me with tears of thanksgiving. I had fallen over a precipice, close against the junction of the old coach road and the new, and had only been saved from certain death by lighting upon a deep snowdrift that had accumulated at the foot of the rock beneath. In this snowdrift, I was discovered at daybreak by a couple of shepherds, who carried me to the nearest shelter, and brought a surgeon to my aid. The surgeon found me in a state of raving delirium, with a broken arm and a compound fracture of the skull. The letters in my pocketbook showed my name and address; my wife was summoned to nurse me; and, thanks to youth and a fine constitution, I came out of danger at last. The place of my fall, I need scarcely say, was precisely that at which a frightful accident had happened to the north mail nine years before.

I never told my wife the fearful events which I have just related to you. I told the surgeon who attended me, but he treated the whole adventure as a mere dream born of the fever in my brain. We discussed the question over and over again until we found that we could discuss it with temper no longer, and then we dropped it. Others may form what conclusions they please—I know that twenty years ago, I was the fourth inside passenger in that Phantom Coach.

THE OLD NURSE'S STORY

by Elizabeth Gaskell

You know, my dears, that your mother was an orphan and an only child and I dare say you have heard that your grandfather was a clergyman up in Westmoreland, where I come from. I was just a girl in the village school when, one day, your grandmother came in to ask the mistress if there was any scholar there who would do for a nurse-maid; and mighty proud I was, I can tell ye when the mistress called me up and spoke to my being a good girl at my needle, and a steady, honest girl, and one whose parents were very respectable, though they might be poor. I thought I should like nothing better than to serve the pretty young lady, who was blushing as deep as I was, as she spoke of the coming baby, and what I should have to do with it. However, I see you don't care so much for this part of my story as for what you think is to come, so I'll tell you at once. I was engaged and settled at the parsonage before Miss Rosamond (that was the baby who is now your mother) was born. To be sure, I had little enough to do with her when she came, for she was never out of her mother's arms and slept by her all night long; and proud enough was I sometimes when missis trusted her to me. There never was such a baby before or since, though you've all of you been fine enough in your turns, for sweet, winning ways, you've none of you come up to your mother. She took after her mother, who was a real lady born; a Miss Furnivall, a grand-daughter of Lord Furnivall's, in Northumberland. I believe she had neither brother nor sister and had been brought up in my lord's family till she had married your grandfather, who was just a curate, son to a shopkeeper in Carlisle—but a clever, fine gentleman as ever was—and one who was a right-down hard worker in his parish, which was very wide, and scattered all abroad over the Westmoreland Fells. When your mother, little Miss Rosamond, was about four or five years old, both her parents died in a fortnight—one after the other. Ah! that was a sad time. My pretty young mistress and I were looking for another baby when my master came home from one of his long rides, wet and tired, and took the fever he died of; and then she never held up her head again but just lived to see her dead baby, and have it laid on her breast before she sighed away her life. My mistress had asked me, on her deathbed, never to leave Miss Rosamond, but if she had never spoken a word, I would have gone with the little child to the end of the world.

The next thing, and before we had well stilled our sobs, the executors and guardians came to settle the affairs. They were my poor young mistress's own cousin, Lord Furnivall, and Mr Esthwaite, my master's brother, a shopkeeper in Manchester; not so well-to-do then as he was afterwards and with a large family rising about him. Well! I don't know if it were their settling, or because of a letter my mistress wrote on her death-bed to her cousin, my lord; but somehow it was settled that Miss Rosamond and I were to go to Furnivall Manor House in Northumberland, and my lord spoke as if it had been her mother's wish that she should live with his family, and as if he had no objections, for that one or two more or less could make no difference in so grand a household. So, though that was not the way in which I should have wished the coming of my bright and pretty pet to have been looked at—who was like a sunbeam in any family, be it never so grand—I was well pleased that all the folks in the Dale should stare and admire when they heard I was going to be young lady's maid at my Lord Furnivall's at Furnivall Manor.

But I made a mistake in thinking we were to go and live where my lord did. It turned out that the family had left Furnivall Manor House fifty years or more. I could not hear that my poor young mistress had ever been there, though she had been brought up in the family, and I was sorry for that, for I should have liked Miss Rosamond's youth to have passed where her mother's had been.

My lord's gentleman, from whom I asked as many questions as I durst, said that the Manor House was at the foot of the Cumberland Fells, and a very grand place; that an old Miss Furnivall, a great-aunt of my lord's, lived there, with only a few servants; but that it was a very healthy place, and my lord had thought that it would suit Miss Rosamond very well for a few years and that her being there might perhaps amuse his old aunt.

I was bidden by my lord to have Miss Rosamond's things ready by a certain day. He was a stern, proud man, as they say, all the Lords Furnivall were, and he never spoke a word more than was necessary. Folk did say he had loved my young mistress; but that, because she knew that his father would object, she would never listen to him and married Mr Esthwaite; but I don't know. He never married, at any rate. But he never took much notice of Miss Rosamond, which I thought he might have done if he had cared for her dead mother. He sent his gentleman with us to the Manor House, telling him to join him at Newcastle that same evening, so there was no great length of time for him to make us known to all the strangers before he, too, shook us off, and we were left, two lonely young things (I was not eighteen) in the great old Manor House. It seems like yesterday that we drove there. We had left our own dear parsonage very early, and we had both cried as if our hearts would break, though we were travelling in my lord's carriage, which I thought so much of once. And now it was long past noon on a September day, and we stopped to change horses for the last time at a little smoky town, all full of colliers and miners. Miss Rosamond had fallen asleep, but Mr Henry told me to wake her, that she might see the park and the Manor House as we drove up. I thought it rather a pity, but I did what he bade me for fear he should complain of me to my lord. We had left all signs of a town, or even a village, and were then inside the gates of a large wild park—not like the parks here in the south, but with rocks, the noise of running water, and gnarled thorn trees and old oaks, all white and peeled with age.

The road went up about two miles, and then we saw a great and stately house, with many trees close around it, so close that in some places their branches dragged against the walls when the wind blew, and some hung broken down; for no one seemed to take much charge of the place;—to lop the wood, or to keep the moss-covered carriage-way in order. Only in front of the house was all clear. The great oval drive was without a weed; and neither tree nor creeper was allowed to grow over the long, many-windowed front; at both sides of which a wing projected, which were each the ends of other side fronts; for the house, although it was so desolate, was even grander than I expected. Behind it rose the Fells, which seemed unenclosed and bare enough and on the left hand of the house, as you stood facing it, was a little, old-fashioned flower garden, as I found out afterwards. A door opened out upon it from the west front; it had been scooped out of the thick, dark wood for some old Lady Furnivall, but the branches of the great forest trees had grown and overshadowed it again, and there were very few flowers that would live there at that time.

When we drove up to the great front entrance and went into the hall, I thought we should be lost —it was so large, vast, and grand. There was a chandelier, all of bronze, hung down from the middle of the ceiling, and I had never seen one before and looked at it all in amazement. Then, at one end of the hall, was a great fireplace, as large as the sides of the houses in my country, with massy andirons and dogs to hold the wood; and by it were heavy old-fashioned sofas. At the opposite end of the hall, to the left, as you went in—on the western side—was an organ built into the wall, and so large that it filled up the best part of that end. Beyond it, on the same side, was a door; and opposite, on each side of the fireplace, were also doors leading to the east front; but those I never went through as long as I stayed in the house, so I can't tell you what lay beyond.

The afternoon was closing in, and the hall, which had no fire lighted in it, looked dark and gloomy; but we did not stay there a moment. The old servant, who had opened the door for us, bowed to Mr Henry, took us in through the door at the further side of the great organ, and led us through several smaller halls and passages into the west drawing room, where he said that Miss Furnivall was sitting. Poor little Miss Rosamond held very tight to me as if she were scared and lost in that great place, and as for myself, I was not much better. The west drawing-room was very cheerful-looking, with a warm fire in it and plenty of good, comfortable furniture about. Miss Furnivall was an old lady not far from eighty, I should think, but I do not know. She was thin and tall and had a face as full of fine wrinkles as if they had been drawn all over it with a needle's point. Her eyes were very watchful to makeup, I suppose, for her being so deaf as to be obliged to use a trumpet. Sitting with her, working at the same great piece of tapestry, was Mrs Stark, her maid and companion, and almost as old as she was. She had lived with Miss Furnivall ever since they both were young, and now she seemed more like a friend than a servant; she looked so cold, grey, and stony as if she had never loved or cared for anyone, and I don't suppose she did care for anyone, except her mistress; and, owing to the great deafness of the latter, Mrs Stark treated her very much as if she were a child. Mr Henry gave some message from my lord, and then he bowed goodbye to us all—taking no notice of my sweet little Miss Rosamond's outstretched hand—and left us standing there, being looked at by the two old ladies through their spectacles.

I was right glad when they rang for the old footman who had shown us in at first and told him to take us to our rooms. So we went out of that great drawing room, and into another sitting room, and out of that, and then up a great flight of stairs, and along a broad gallery—which was something like a library, having books all down one side, and windows and writing-tables all down the other—till we came to our rooms, which I was not sorry to hear were just over the kitchens; for I began to think I should be lost in that wilderness of a house. There was an old nursery that had been used for all the little lords and ladies long ago, with a pleasant fire burning in the grate and the kettle boiling on the hob, and tea things spread out on the table; and out of that room was the night-nursery, with a little crib for Miss Rosamond close to my bed. And old James called up Dorothy, his wife, to bid us welcome; and both he and she were so hospitable and kind, that by and by Miss Rosamond and I felt quite at home; and by the time tea was over, she was sitting on Dorothy's knee, and chattering away as fast as her little tongue could go. I soon found out that Dorothy was from Westmoreland, and that bound her and me together, as it were, and I would never wish to meet with kinder people than were old James and his wife. James had lived pretty nearly all his life in my lord's family and thought there was no one so grand as they. He even looked down a little on his wife; because, till he had married her, she had never lived in any but a farmer's household. But he was very fond of her, as well, he might be. They had one servant under them to do all the rough work. Agnes, they called her; and she and me, and James and Dorothy, with Miss Furnivall and Mrs Stark, made up the family, always remembering my sweet little Miss Rosamond! I used to wonder what they had done before she came. They thought so much of her now. Kitchen and drawing-room, it was all the same. The hard, sad Miss Furnivall, and the cold Mrs Stark, looked pleased when she came fluttering in like a bird, playing and pranking hither and thither with a continual murmur and pretty prattle of gladness. I am sure they were sorry many a time when she flitted away into the kitchen, though they were too proud to ask her to stay with them and were a little surprised at her taste; though to be sure, as Mrs Stark said, it was not to be wondered at, remembering what stock her father had come off. The great, old rambling house was a famous place for little Miss Rosamond. She made expeditions all over it, with me at her heels: all, except the east wing, which was never opened, and whither we never thought of going. But in the western and northern part was many a pleasant room, full of things that were curiosities to us, though they might not have been to people who had seen more. The windows were darkened by the sweeping boughs of the trees, and the ivy which had overgrown them; but, in the green gloom, we could manage to see old china jars and carved ivory boxes, great heavy books, and, above all, the old pictures!

Once, I remember, my darling would have Dorothy go with us to tell us who they all were; for they were all portraits of some of my lord's family, though Dorothy could not tell us the names of everyone. We had gone through most of the rooms when we came to the old state drawing-room over the hall, and there was a picture of Miss Furnivall, or, as she was called in those days, Miss Grace, for she was the younger sister. Such a beauty she must have been! but with such a set, proud look and such scorn looking out of her handsome eyes, with her eyebrows just a little raised, as if she wondered how anyone could have the impertinence to look at her, and her lip curled at us as we stood there gazing. She had a dress on, the like of which I had never seen before, but it was all the fashion when she was young: a hat of some soft white stuff like beaver pulled a little over her brows and a beautiful plume of feathers sweeping round it on one side, and her gown of blue satin was open in front to a quilted white stomacher.

"Well, to be sure!" said I when I had gazed my fill. "Flesh is grass, they do say; but who would have thought that Miss Furnivall had been such an out-and-out beauty, to see her now?"

"Yes," said Dorothy. "Folks change sadly. But if what my master's father used to say was true, Miss Furnivall, the elder sister, was handsomer than Miss Grace. Her picture is here somewhere; but, if I show it you, you must never let on, even to James, that you have seen it Can the little lady hold her tongue, think you?" asked she.

I was not so sure, for she was such a little sweet, bold, open-spoken child, so I set her to hide herself, and then I helped Dorothy to turn a great picture that leaned with its face towards the wall and was not hung up as the others were. To be sure, it beat Miss Grace for beauty; and, I think, for scornful pride, too, though in that matter, it might be hard to choose. I could have looked at it an hour, but Dorothy seemed half frightened at having shown it to me, and hurried it back again, and bade me run and find Miss Rosamond, for that there were some ugly places about the house, where she should like ill for the child to go. I was a brave, high-spirited girl, and thought little of what the old woman said, for I liked hide-and-seek as well as any child in the parish, so off I ran to find my little one.

As winter drew on and the days grew shorter, I was sometimes almost certain that I heard a noise as if someone was playing on the great organ in the hall. I did not hear it every evening, but certainly, I did very often, usually when I was sitting with Miss Rosamond after I had put her to bed and keeping quite still and silent in the bedroom. Then I used to hear it booming and swelling away in the distance. The first night, when I went down to my supper, I asked Dorothy who had been playing music, and James said very shortly that I was a gowk to take the wind soughing among the trees for music; but I saw Dorothy look at him very fearfully, and Bessy, the kitchen-maid, said something beneath her breath and went quite white. I saw they did not like my question, so I held my peace till I was with Dorothy alone, when I knew I could get a good deal out of her. So, the next day, I watched my time, and I coaxed and asked her who it was that played the organ; for I knew that it was the organ and not the wind well enough, for all I had kept silent before James. But Dorothy had had her lesson. I'll warrant, and never a word could I get from her. So then I tried Bessy, though I had always held my head rather above her, as I was evened to James and Dorothy, and she was little better than their servant. So she said I must never, never tell, and if ever told, I was never to say she had told me; but it was a very strange noise, and she had heard it many a time, but most of all on winter nights, and before storms; and folks did say it was the old lord playing on the great organ in the hall, just as he used to do when he was alive; but who the old lord was, or why he played, and why he played on stormy winter evenings, in particular, she either could not or would not tell me.

Well! I told you I had a brave heart, and I thought it was rather pleasant to have that grand music rolling about the house, let who would be the player; for now, it rose above the great gusts of wind and wailed and triumphed just like a living creature, and then it fell to a softness most complete, only it was always music, and tunes, so it was nonsense to call it the wind. I thought at first, that it might be Miss Furnivall who played, unknown to Bessy; but one day, when I was in the hall by myself, I opened the organ and peeped all about it and around it, as I had done to the organ in Crosthwaite Church once before, and I saw it was all broken and destroyed inside, though it looked so brave and fine; and then, though it was noon-day, my flesh began to creep a little, and I shut it up, and run away pretty quickly to my own bright nursery; and I did not like hearing the music for some time after that, any more than James and Dorothy did. All this time, Miss Rosamond was making herself more and more beloved. The old ladies liked her to dine with them at their early dinner. James stood behind Miss Furnivall's chair, and I behind Miss Rosamond's all in the state; and, after dinner, she would play about in the corner of the great drawing-room as still as any mouse while Miss Furnivall slept, and I had my dinner in the kitchen. But she was glad enough to come to me in the nursery afterwards; for, as she said, Miss Furnivall was so sad, and Mrs Stark so dull; but she and were merry enough; and, by-and-by, I got not to care for that weird rolling music, which did one no harm, if we did not know where it came from.

That winter was very cold. In the middle of October, the frosts began and lasted many, many weeks. I remember one day, at dinner, Miss Furnivall lifted up her sad, heavy eyes and said to Mrs Stark, "I am afraid we shall have a terrible winter," in a strange kind of meaningful way But Mrs Stark pretended not to hear and talked very loud of something else. My little lady and I did not care for the frost, not we? As long as it was dry, we climbed up the steep brows behind the house and went up on the Fells, which were bleak and bare enough, and there we ran races in the fresh, sharp air; and once we came down by a new path, that took us past the two old gnarled holly-trees, which grew about half-way down by the east side of the house. But the days grew shorter and shorter, and the old lord, if it was he, played away, more and more stormily and sadly, on the great organ. One Sunday afternoon—it must have been towards the end of November—I asked Dorothy to take charge of little missy when she came out of the drawing room after Miss Furnivall had had her nap; for it was too cold to take her with me to church, and yet I wanted to go, And Dorothy was glad enough to promise and was so fond of the child, that all seemed well; and Bessy and I set off very briskly, though the sky hung heavy and black over the white earth as if the night had never fully gone away, and the air, though still, was very biting.

"We shall have a fall of snow," said Bessy to me. And sure enough, even while we were in church, it came down thick, in great large flakes—so thick, it almost darkened the windows. It had stopped snowing before we came out, but it lay soft, thick, and deep beneath our feet as we tramped home. Before we got to the hall, the moon rose, and I think it was lighter than—what with the moon, and what with the dazzling white snow—than it had been when we went to the church between two and three o'clock. I have not told you that Miss Furnivall and Mrs Stark never went to church; they used to read the prayers together in their quiet, gloomy way; they seemed to feel the Sunday very long without their tapestry work to be busy at. So when I went to Dorothy in the kitchen to fetch Miss Rosamond and take her upstairs with me, I did not know many wonders when the old woman told me that the ladies had kept the child with them and that she had never come to the kitchen, as I had bidden her when she was tired of behaving pretty in the drawing-room. So I took off my things and went to find her and bring her to her supper in the nursery. But when I went into the best drawing room, there sat the two old ladies, very still and quiet, dropping out a word now and then but looking as if nothing so bright and merry as Miss Rosamond had ever been near them. Still, I thought she might be hiding from me; it was one of her pretty ways—and that she had persuaded them to look as if they knew nothing about her, so I went softly peeping under this sofa and behind that chair, making believe I was sadly frightened at not finding her.

"What's the matter, Hester?" said Mrs Stark sharply. I don't know if Miss Furnivall had seen me for, as I told you, she was very deaf, and she sat quite still, idly staring into the fire, with her hopeless face. "I'm only looking for my little Rosy

Posy," replied I, still thinking that the child was there and near me, though I could not see her.

"Miss Rosamond is not here," said Mrs Stark. "She went away, more than an hour ago, to find Dorothy." And she, too, turned and went on looking into the fire.

My heart sank at this, and I began to wish I had never left my darling. I went back to Dorothy and told her. James was gone out for the day, but she, me, and Bessy took lights and went up into the nursery first, and then we roamed over the great, large house, calling and entreating Miss Rosamond to come out of her hiding place, and not frighten us to death in that way. But there was no answer, no sound.

"Oh!" said I, at last, "can she have got into the east wing and hidden there?"

But Dorothy said it was not possible, for that she herself had never been in there; that the doors were always locked, and my lord's steward had the keys, she believed; at any rate, neither she nor James had ever seen them: so I said I would go back, and see if, after all, she was not hidden in the drawing-room, unknown to the old ladies; and if I found her there, I said, I would whip her well for the fright she had given me; but I never meant to do it. Well, I went back to the west drawing room, and I told Mrs Stark we could not find her anywhere and asked for leave to look all about the furniture there, for I thought now that she might have fallen asleep in some warm, hidden corner; but no! we looked— Miss Furnivall got up and looked, trembling all over

—and she was nowhere there; then we set off again, everyone in the house, and looked in all the places we had searched before, but we could not find her. Miss Furnivall shivered and shook so much that Mrs Stark took her back into the warm drawing room, but not before they had made me promise to bring her to them when she was found. Well-a-day! I began to think she never would be found when I bethought me to look into the great front court, all covered with snow. I was upstairs when I looked out, but, it was such clear moonlight, I could see, quite plain, two little footprints, which might be traced from the hall door and around the corner of the east wing. I don't know how I got down, but I tugged open the great stiff hall door, and, throwing the skirt of my gown over my head for a cloak, I ran out. I turned the east corner, and there a black shadow fell on the snow, but when I came again into the moonlight, there were the little footmarks going up—up to the Fells. It was bitter cold; so cold that the air almost took the skin off my face as I ran; but I ran on, crying to think how my poor little darling must be perished and frightened. I was within sight of the holly trees when I saw a shepherd coming down the hill, bearing something in his arms, wrapped in his maud. He shouted to me and asked me if I had lost a bairn; and, when I could not speak for crying, he bore towards me, and I saw my wee bairnie, lying still, and white, and stiff in his arms, as if she had been dead. He told me he had been up the Fells to gather in his sheep before the deep cold of the night came on and that under the holly trees (black marks on the hill-side, where no other bush was for miles around) he had found my little lady— my lamb—my queen—my darling—stiff and cold in the terrible sleep which is frost-begotten. Oh! the joy and the tears of having her in my arms once again I, for I would not let him carry her, but took her, maud and all, into my own arms, and held her near my own warm neck and heart, and felt the life stealing slowly back again into her little gentle limbs. But she was still insensible when we reached the hall, and I had no breath for speech. We went in by the kitchen door.

"Bring the warming-pan," said I, and I carried her upstairs and began undressing her by the nursery fire, which Bessy had kept up. I called my little Lammie all the sweet and playful names I could think of,—even while my eyes were blinded by my tears; and at last, oh! at length she opened her large blue eyes. Then I put her into her warm bed and sent Dorothy down to tell Miss Furnivall that all was well, and I made up my mind to sit by my darling's bedside the live-long night. She fell away into a soft sleep as soon as her pretty head had touched the pillow, and I watched by her till morning light; when she wakened up bright and clear—or so I thought at first—and, my dears, so I think now.

She said that she had fancied that she should like to go to Dorothy, for that both the old ladies were asleep, and it was very dull in the drawing room, and that, as she was going through the west lobby, she saw the snow through the high window falling—falling—soft and steady; but she wanted to see it lying pretty and white on the ground; so she made her way into the great hall: and then, going to the window, she saw it bright and soft upon the drive; but while she stood there, she saw a little girl, not so old as she was, "but so pretty," said my darling; "and this little girl beckoned to me to come out; and oh, she was so pretty and so sweet, I could not choose but go." And then this other little girl had taken her by the hand, and side by side the two had gone round the east corner.

"Now you are a naughty little girl, and telling stories," said I. "What would your good mamma, that is in heaven, and never told a story in her life, say to her little Rosamond, if she heard her—and I dare say she does—telling stories!"

"Indeed, Hester," sobbed out my child, "I'm telling you true. Indeed I am."

"Don't tell me!" said I, very stern. "I tracked you by your foot-marks through the snow; there were only yours to be seen: and if you had had a little girl to go hand-in-hand with you up the hill, don't you think the footprints would have gone along with yours?"

"I can't help it, dear, dear Hester," said she, crying, "if they did not; I never looked at her feet, but she held my hand fast and tight in her little one, and it was very, very cold. She took me up the Fell-path, up to the holly-trees; and there I saw a lady weeping and crying; but when she saw me, she hushed her weeping, and smiled very proud and grand, and took me on her knee, and began to lull me to sleep, and that's all, Hester—but that is true; and my dear mamma knows it is," said she, crying. So I thought the child was in a fever and pretended to believe her as she went over her story—over and over again, and always the same. At last, Dorothy knocked at the door with Miss Rosamond's breakfast; and she told me the old ladies were down in the eating parlour and that they wanted to speak to me. They had both been in the night nursery the evening before, but it was after Miss Rosamond was asleep, so they had only looked at her—not asked me any questions.

"I shall catch it," thought I to myself as I went along the north gallery. "And yet," I thought, taking courage, "it was in their charge I left her; and it's they that's to blame for letting her steal away unknown and unwatched." So I went in boldly and told my story. I told it all to Miss Furnivall, shouting it close to her ear, but when I came to the mention of the other little girl out in the snow, coaxing and tempting her out and wiling her up to the grand and beautiful lady by the holly-tree, she threw her arms up—her old and withered arms—and cried aloud, "Oh! Heaven forgive! Have mercy!"

Mrs Stark took hold of her; roughly enough, I thought; but she was past Mrs Stark's management and spoke to me in a kind of wild warning and authority.

"Hester! keep her from that child! It will lure her to her death! That evil child! Tell her it is a wicked, naughty child." Then, Mrs Stark hurried me out of the room; where, indeed, I was glad enough to go; but Miss Furnivall kept shrieking out, "Oh, have mercy! Wilt Thou never forgive! It is many a long year ago"—

I was very uneasy in my mind after that. I durst never leave Miss Rosamond, night or day, for fear lest she might slip off again, after some fancy or other; and all the more, because I thought I could make out that Miss Furnivall was crazy, from their odd ways about her; and I was afraid lest something of the same kind (which might be in the family, you know) hung over my darling. And the great frost never ceased all this time, and whenever it was a more stormy night than usual, between the gusts and through the wind, we heard the old lord playing on the great organ. But, old lord or not, wherever Miss Rosamond went, there I followed; for my love for her, pretty, helpless orphan, was stronger than my fear for the grand and terrible sound. Besides, it rested with me to keep her cheerful and merry, as beseemed her age. So we played together, and wandered together, here and there, and everywhere; for I never dared to lose sight of her again in that large and rambling house. And so it happened, that one afternoon, not long before Christmas day, we were playing together on the billiard table in the great hall (not that we knew the right way of playing, but she liked to roll the smooth ivory balls with her pretty hands, and I liked to do whatever she did); and, by-and-by, without our noticing it, it grew dusk indoors, though it was still light in the open air, and I was thinking of taking her back into the nursery, when, all of a sudden, she cried out—

"Look, Hester! look! there is my poor little girl out in the snow!"

I turned towards the long narrow windows, and there, sure enough, I saw a little girl, less than my Miss Rosamond—dressed all unfit to be out-of-doors such a bitter night—crying, and beating against the window panes, as if she wanted to be let in. She seemed to sob and wail, till Miss Rosamond could bear it no longer, and was flying to the door to open it, when, all of a sudden, and close upon us, the great organ pealed out so loud and thundering, it fairly made me tremble; and all the more, when I remembered me that, even in the stillness of that dead-cold weather, I had heard no sound of little battering hands upon the window-glass, although the phantom child had seemed to put forth all its force; and, although I had seen it wail and cry, no faintest touch of sound had fallen upon my ears. Whether I remembered all this at the very moment, I do not know; the great organ sound had so stunned me into terror; but this I know, I caught up with Miss Rosamond before she got the hall door opened, and clutched her, and carried her away, kicking and screaming, into the large, bright kitchen, where Dorothy and Agnes were busy with their mince-pies.

"What is the matter with my sweet one?" cried Dorothy as I bore in Miss Rosamond, who was sobbing as if her heart would break.

"She won't let me open the door for my little girl to come in; and she'll die if she is out on the Fells all night. Cruel, naughty Hester," she said, slapping me; but she might have struck harder, for I had seen a look of ghastly terror on Dorothy's face, which made my very blood run cold.

"Shut the back-kitchen door fast, and bolt it well," said she to Agues. She said no more; she gave me raisins and almonds to quiet Miss Rosamond, but she sobbed about the little girl in the snow and would not touch any of the good things. I was thankful when she cried herself to sleep in the bed. Then I stole down to the kitchen and told Dorothy I had made up my mind. I would carry my darling back to my father's house in Applethwaite, where, if we lived humbly, we lived at peace. I said I had been frightened enough with the old lord's organ playing, but now that I had seen for myself this little moaning child, all decked out as no child in the neighbourhood could be, beating and battering to get in, yet always without any sound or noise—with the dark wound on its right shoulder; and that Miss Rosamond had known it again for the phantom that had nearly lured her to death (which Dorothy knew was true); I would stand it no longer.

I saw Dorothy change color once or twice. When I had done, she told me she did not think I could take Miss Rosamond with me, for that she was my lord's ward, and I had no right over her; and she asked me if I would leave the child that I was so fond of just for sounds and sights that could do me no harm; and that they had all had to get used to in their turns? I was all in a hot, trembling passion, and I said it was very well for her to talk, that knew what these sights and noises betokened, and that had, perhaps, had something to do with the spectre child while it was alive. And I taunted her so that she told me all she knew at last, and then I wished I had never been told, for it only made me more afraid than ever.

She said she had heard the tale from old neighbours that were alive when she was first married when folks used to come to the hall sometimes before it had got such a bad name in the countryside: it might not be true, or it might, what she had been told.

The old lord was Miss Furnivall's father—Miss Grace, as Dorothy called her, for Miss Maude was the elder, and Miss Furnivall by lights. The old lord was eaten up with pride. Such a proud man was never seen or heard of, and his daughters were like him. No one was good enough to wed them, although they had choice enough; for they were the great beauties of their day, as I had seen by their portraits, where they hung in the state drawing room. But, as the old saying is, "Pride will have a fall;" and these two haughty beauties fell in love with the same man, and he was no better than a foreign musician, whom their father had down from London to play music with him at the Manor House. For, above all things, next to his pride, the old lord loved music. He could play on nearly every instrument that ever was heard of, and it was a strange thing it did not soften him; but he was a fierce, dour old man and had broken his poor wife's heart with his cruelty, they said. He was mad after music and would pay any money for it. So he got this foreigner to come, who made such beautiful music that they said the very birds on the trees stopped their singing to listen. And, by degrees, this foreign gentleman got such a hold over the old lord that nothing would serve him but that he must come every year; and it was he that had the great organ brought from Holland and built up in the hall, where it stood now. He taught the old lord to play on it, but many and many a time, when Lord Furnivall was thinking of nothing but his fine organ, and his finer music, the dark foreigner was walking abroad in the woods with one of the young ladies: now Miss Maude, and then Miss Grace.

Miss Maude won the day and carried off the prize, such as it was; and he and she were married, all unknown to anyone; and, before he made his next yearly visit, she had been confined of a little girl at a farm-house on the Moors, while her father and Miss Grace thought she was away at Doncaster Races. But though she was a wife and a mother, she was not a bit softened but as haughty and as passionate as ever; and perhaps more so, for she was jealous of Miss Grace, to whom her foreign husband paid a deal of court—by way of blinding her—as he told his wife. But Miss Grace triumphed over Miss Maude, and Miss Maude grew fiercer and fiercer, both with her husband and with her sister; and the former—who could easily shake off what was disagreeable and hide in foreign countries—went away a month before his usual time that summer, and half-threatened that he would never come back again. Meanwhile, the little girl was left at the farmhouse, and her mother used to have her horse saddled and gallop wildly over the hills to see her once every week, at the very least; for where she loved, she loved, and where she hated she hated. And the old lord went on playing—playing on his organ, and the servants thought the sweet music he made had soothed down his awful temper, of which (Dorothy said) some terrible tales could be told. He grew infirm too and had to walk with a crutch; and his son—that was the present Lord Furnivall's father —was with the army in America, and the other son at sea; so Miss Maude had it pretty much her own way, and she and Miss Grace grew colder and bitterer to each other every day; till at last they hardly ever spoke, except when the old lord was by. The foreign musician came again the next summer, but it was for the last time; for they led him such a life with their jealousy and their passions that he grew weary, went away, and never was heard of again. And Miss Maude, who had always meant to have her marriage acknowledged when her father should be dead, was left now a deserted wife, whom nobody knew to have been married, with a child that she dared not own, although she loved it to distraction living with a father whom she feared, and a sister whom she hated. When the next summer passed over, and the dark foreigner never came, both Miss Maude and Miss Grace grew gloomy and sad; they had a haggard look about them, though they looked handsome as ever. But, by and by, Miss Maude brightened for her father grew more and more infirm and more than ever carried away by his music, and she and Miss Grace lived almost entirely apart, having separate rooms, the one on the west side, Miss Maude on the east— those very rooms which were now shut up. So she thought she might have her little girl with her, and no one need ever know except those who dared not speak about it and were bound to believe that it was, as she said, a cottager's child she had taken a fancy to. All this, Dorothy said, was pretty well known; but what came afterwards no one knew, except Miss Grace and Mrs Stark, who was even then her maid, and much more of a friend to her than ever her sister had been. But the servants supposed, from words that were dropped, that Miss Maude had triumphed over Miss Grace and told her that all the time, the dark foreigner had been mocking her with pretended love—he was her own husband. The color left Miss Grace's cheek and lips every day forever, and she was heard to say many a time that sooner or later she would have her revenge, and Mrs Stark was forever spying about the east rooms.

One fearful night, just after the New Year had come in, when the snow was lying thick and deep; and the flakes were still falling—fast enough to blind anyone who might be out and abroad—there was a great and violent noise heard, and the old lord's voice above all, cursing and swearing awfully, and the cries of a little child, and the proud defiance of a fierce woman, and the sound of a blow, and a dead stillness, and moans and wailings, dying away on the hill-side! Then the old lord summoned all his servants and told them, with terrible oaths and words more terrible, that his daughter had disgraced herself, and that he had turned her out of doors—her and her child—and that if ever they gave her help, or food, or shelter, he prayed that they might never enter heaven. And, all the while, Miss Grace stood by him, white and still as any stone; and, when he had ended, she heaved a great sigh, as much as to say her work was done, and her end was accomplished. But the old lord never touched his organ again and died within the year, and no wonder I for, on the morrow of that wild and fearful night, the shepherds, coming down the Fell side, found Miss Maude sitting, all crazy and smiling, under the holly-trees, nursing a dead child, with a terrible mark on its right shoulder. "But that was not what killed it," said Dorothy: "it was the frost and the cold. Every wild creature was in its hole, and every beast in its fold, while the child and its mother were turned out to wander on the Fells! And now you know all! and I wonder if you are less frightened now?"

I was more frightened than ever, but I said I was not. I wished Miss Rosamond and myself well out of that dreadful house forever, but I would not leave her, and I dared not take her away. But oh, how I watched her and guarded her! We bolted the doors, and shut the window-shutters fast, an hour or more before dark, rather than leave them open five minutes too late. But my little lady still heard the weird child crying and mourning, and not all we could do or say could keep her from wanting to go to her and let her in from the cruel wind and snow. All this time, I kept away from Miss Furnivall and Mrs Stark as much as ever I could; for I feared them —I knew no good could be about them, with their grey, hard faces and their dreamy eyes, looking back into the ghastly years that were gone. But, even in my fear, I had a kind of pity for Miss Furnivall, at least. Those gone down to the pit can hardly have a more hopeless look than that which was ever on her face. At last, I even got so sorry for her—who never said a word but what was quite forced from her— that I prayed for her, and I taught Miss Rosamond to pray for one who had done a deadly sin; but often, when she came to those words, she would listen, and start-up from her knees, and say, "I hear my little girl plaining and crying, very sad,—oh, let her in, or she will die!"

One night—just after New Year's Day had come at last, and the long winter had taken a turn, as I hoped—I heard the west drawing-room bell ring three times, which was the signal for me. I would not leave Miss Rosamond alone, for all she was asleep—for the old lord had been playing wilder than ever—and I feared lest my darling should waken to hear the spectre child; see her I knew she could not. I had fastened the windows too well for that. So I took her out of her bed, and wrapped her up in such outer clothes as were most handy, and carried her down to the drawing room, where the old ladies sat at their tapestry work as usual. They looked up when I came in, and Mrs Stark asked, quite astounded, "Why did I bring Miss Rosamond there, out of her warm bed?" I had begun to whisper, "Because I was afraid of her being tempted out while I was away, by the wild child in the snow," when she stopped me shortly (with a glance at Miss Furnivall), and said Miss Furnivall wanted me to undo some work she had done wrong, and which neither of them could see to unpick. So I laid my pretty dear on the sofa, sat down on a stool by them, and hardened my heart against them as I heard the wind rising and howling.

Miss Rosamond slept on sound, for all the wind blew so, and Miss Furnivall never said a word nor looked round when the gusts shook the windows. All at once she started up to her full height and put up one hand as if to bid us listen.

"I hear voices!" said she. "I hear terrible screams—I hear my father's voice!"

Just at that moment, my darling wakened with a sudden start: "My little girl is crying, oh, how she is crying!" and she tried to get up and go to her, but she got her feet entangled in the blanket, and I caught her up; for my flesh had begun to creep at these noises, which they heard while we could catch no sound. In a minute or two, the noises came and gathered fast and filled our ears; we, too, heard voices and screams and no longer heard the winter's wind that raged abroad. Mrs Stark looked at me, and I at her, but we dared not speak. Suddenly Miss Furnivall went towards the door, out into the ante-room, through the west lobby, and opened the door into the great hall. Mrs Stark followed, and I durst not be left, though my heart almost stopped beating for fear. I wrapped my darling tight in my arms and went out with them. In the hall, the screams were louder than ever; they seemed to come from the east wing—nearer and nearer—close on the other side of the locked-up doors—close behind them. Then I noticed that the great bronze chandelier seemed all alight, though the hall was dim, and that a fire was blazing in the vast hearth-place, though it gave no heat, and I shuddered up with terror and folded my darling closer to me. But as I did so, the east door shook, and she, suddenly struggling to get free from me, cried, "Hester! I must go. My little girl is there I hear her; she is coming! Hester, I must go!"

I held her tight with all my strength; with a set will, I held her. If I had died, my hands would have grasped her still I was so resolved in my mind. Miss

Furnivall stood listening and paid no regard to my darling, who had got down to the ground, and whom I, upon my knees now, was holding with both my arms clasped around her neck; she still striving and crying to get free.

All at once, the east door gave way with a thundering crash, as if torn open in a violent passion, and there came into that broad and mysterious light the figure of a tall old man with grey hair and gleaming eyes. He drove before him, with many a relentless gesture of abhorrence, a stern and beautiful woman with a little child clinging to her dress.

"O Hester! Hester!" cried Miss Rosamond; "it's the lady! the lady below the holly-trees; and my little girl is with her. Hester! Hester! let me go to her; they are drawing me to them. I feel them—I feel them. I must go!"

Again she was almost convulsed by her efforts to get away, but I held her tighter and tighter till I feared I should do her hurt, but rather that than let her go towards those terrible phantoms. They passed along towards the great hall door, where the winds howled and ravened for their prey; but before they reached that, the lady turned, and I could see that she defied the old man with a fierce and proud defiance, but then she quailed—and then she threw up her arms wildly and piteously to save her child—her little child—from a blow from his uplifted crutch.

And Miss Rosamond was torn as by a power stronger than mine, and writhed in my arms, and sobbed (for by this time, the poor darling was growing faint).

"They want me to go with them on to the Fells —they are drawing me to them. Oh, my little girl! I would come, but cruel, wicked Hester holds me very tight." But when she saw the uplifted crutch, she swooned away, and I thanked God for it. Just at this moment—when the tall old man, his hair streaming as in the blast of a furnace, was going to strike the shrinking little child—Miss Furnivall, the old woman by my side, cried out, "O father! father! spare the little innocent child!" But just then, I saw— we all saw—another phantom shape itself, and it grew to clear out of the blue and misty light that filled the hall; we had not seen her till now, for it was another lady who stood by the old man, with a look of relentless hate and triumphant scorn. That figure was very beautiful to look upon, with a soft, white hat drawn down over the proud brows and a red and curling lip. It was dressed in an open robe of blue satin. I had seen that figure before. It was the likeness of Miss Furnivall in her youth, and the terrible phantoms moved on, regardless of old Miss Furnivall's wild entreaty—and the uplifted crutch fell on the right shoulder of the little child, and the younger sister looked on, stony, and deadly serene. But at that moment, the dim lights, and the fire that gave no heat, went out of themselves, and Miss Furnivall lay at our feet, stricken down by the palsy —death-stricken.

Yes! she was carried to her bed that night, never to rise again. She lay with her face to the wall, muttering low but always muttering: "Alas! alas!

what is done in youth can never be undone in age!
What is done in youth can never be undone in age!"

EACH MAN KILLS

by Victoria Glad

Now that it's all over, it seems like a bad dream. But when I look at Maria's picture on my desk, I realize it couldn't have been a dream. Actually, it was only six months ago that I sat at this same desk, looking at her picture, wondering what could have happened to her. It had been six weeks since there had been any word from her, and she had promised to write as soon as she arrived in Europe. Considering that my future rested in her small hands, I had every right to be apprehensive.

We had grown up together, had lost our folks within a few years of each other and had been fond of each other the way kids are apt to be. Then the change came: It seemed I loved her, and she was still just "fond" of me. During our early college days, I sort of let things ride, but once we went on to graduate school, I began to crowd her.

The next thing I knew, she had signed up for a student tour destined for Central Europe and told me she would give me my answer when she returned. I had to be content with that, but I couldn't help worrying. Maria was a strange girl—withdrawn, dreamy and soft-hearted. Knowing the section, she was going to. I was inclined to be uneasy since it is the realm of gypsies, fortune tellers and the like. It is also the birthplace of many strange legends, and Maria claimed to be strongly psychic. As a matter of fact, she had foretold one or two things which were probably coincidental, like the death of our parents, and which even made an impression on me—and you'd hardly call me a "believer."

This so-called talent of hers led her into trouble on more than one occasion. I remember in her senior year at college she fell under the spell of a short, fat, greasy spook-reader with a strictly phony accent and all but gave her eye teeth away, until I realized something was amiss, got to the bottom of it, and dispatched friend spook-reader pronto. If she should meet some unscrupulous person now, with no one around to get her out of the scrape—but I didn't want to think of that. I was sure this time everything would be all right.

When she didn't write at first, I let it go that she was busy. Finally, six weeks of silent treatment aroused my curiosity. It also aroused my nasty temper, and the next thing I knew, I was on a plane bound for the Continent. Within two hours after landing, I found her at a little inn in Transylvania, a quaint little place that looked as if it were made of gingerbread and was surrounded by the huge, craggy Transylvania Mountain range. I also found Tod Hunter.

"What's wrong, Maria? Why didn't you write?" I asked.

Her usually gay, shining brown eyes flashed angrily. "Why couldn't you leave me alone? I told you not to come after me. I came here so I could think this out. For God's sake, Bill, can't you see I wanted to think? To be by myself?"

"But you promised to write," I persisted, wondering at this change in her, this impatience. Wondered, too, at her wraithlike slimness. She'd always been curved in the right places.

"Maria has been studying much too diligently," Tod said slowly. "She's always tired lately. She hasn't been too well, either. Her throat bothers her."

I wanted to punch his head in. For some reason, I didn't like him. Not because I sensed his rivalry; I was above that. God knows I wanted her to be happy, above everything. It was just something about him that irritated me. An attitude. Not supercilious; I could have coped with that. Rather, it was a calm imperturbability that seemed to speak his faith in his eventual success, regardless of any effort on my part.

I don't know how to fight that sort of strategy. I look like I am: blunt and obvious. Suddenly I didn't care if he was there.

"Maria. Ria, darling. This guy's no good for you, can't you see that? What do you know about him?"

She looked at me, her eyes surprised and a little hurt. Then she looked at him, seemed to be looking through him and into herself if you know what I mean. A slow flush spread from the base of her throat, that thin, almost transparent throat.

"All I have to know," she said softly. "I love him."

She looked out the window. "I'm going up into Konigstein Mountain, to a small sanitarium for my health shortly; the doctor has told me I must go away, and Tod has suggested this place. There Tod and I shall be married."

I knew then how it felt to be on the receiving end of a monkey punch. That she had come to this decision because of my objections, I had not the slightest doubt. She was going to marry someone about whom she knew absolutely nothing. She was much more ill than she knew. Hunter was undoubtedly after her money; she was considerably well-off. Obviously she was once more being influenced in the wrong direction.

"I won't let you!" I warned. "Give it some more time, if for nothing else, then for old times' sake."

"How about me, Morris?" Tod interrupted. "You haven't asked me my feelings on the subject. I happen to love Maria dearly. Have I no say just because you're a childhood friend of hers?"

"Childhood friend! I was her whole family for years before she ever heard of you! I'll see you in hell before I let her marry you!" I shouted. Looking back, I'm sure that had he said anything else, I would have killed him if Ria hadn't come between us.

"That's enough, Bill Morris! I've heard all I want to from you. I'm twenty-three, and if I choose to marry Tod, I'll do so and there's nothing you can do about it. Now, please go."

"Okay, Ria," I said, "if that's the way you want it. But I'm not through. If you won't protect yourself, I'll do it for you. I'd like to know more about the mysterious Mr Tod Hunter, American, and I do wish, for your own sake, you'd do the same. I wouldn't care if you married King Tut, so long as you knew all about him. People just don't marry strangers; not if they're smart. For God's sake, ask him about himself!"

"All right, Bill," she replied, smiling patiently. "I'll ask him. Now, do stop being childish."

"Okay, darling," I said sheepishly. "But do me one more favor. Don't marry him until I get back.

Only a little while; give me a week. Just wait a little longer."

As I closed the door, I could still feel his smile, mocking—yet a little sad.

But Maria didn't wait. I was gone for a week. I had walked my legs off trying to track down the elusive Mister Hunter and discovered exactly— nothing. All his landlady could tell me was that he was an American who had come to this climate for his health and that he slept late mornings. I was licked, and I knew it. If I had been a pup, I would have fitted my tail neatly between my legs and made for home. But I wasn't a pup, so I headed straight for Ria's flat to face the music.

They were waiting for me, she and Tod. When I saw her, I wished I were dead.

She lay in Tod's arms, her body a mere whisper of a body. White and cold she was, like frozen milk on a cold winter's day. They were both dead.

You know how it is when at a wake, someone views the deceased and says kindly, "She's beautiful," and "she" isn't beautiful at all, just a made-up, lifeless handful of clay. Dead as dead and frightening. Well, it wasn't that way this time. Their fair skins were faintly pink-tinted, and their blonde heads, hers ashen and his a reddish cast, gleamed brightly. And they sat so close on the sofa before the fire, his head resting in the hollow of her throat. They looked—peaceful; no line marred their faces. I almost fancied I saw them breathe. And on her third finger, the left hand, was the ring—a thin, platinum band. He had won, and in winning, somehow, he had lost. How they had died and why they found each other and death at the same time, I would probably never know. I only knew one thing: I had to get away from there—quickly. I almost ran the distance to my flat. Stumbled into the place and poured a triple Scotch which I could scarcely hold. The Scotch seared my throat and tasted bitter; someone must have poured salt in it. Then I realized that it was tears—my tears. I, Bill Morris, who hadn't cried since my fifth birthday—was sobbing like a baby.

I didn't call the police. That would mean I would have to go back and watch them cover that lovely body, carry it away and submit it to untold indignities in order to ascertain the cause of death. The cleaning girl would find them in the morning and would notify the police.

But it wasn't so simple as that. In the morning, I found I couldn't shake off the guilt which possessed me. Even two bottles of Scotch hadn't helped me to forget. I was dead drunk and cold sober at the same time.

I phoned Ria's landlady and told her I had failed to reach the Hunters by phone, that I was sure something was amiss. Would she please go to their flat and see if anything was wrong?

She was amused. "Really, Mr Morris, you must be mistaken. Miss Maria went out just an hour ago with her new husband. Surely you are jesting. Why she has never looked better. So happy. They have left for Konigstein. They have also left you a note.

I told her I would be right over, and hopped a cab. I began to think I was losing my mind. I had seen them both—dead. The landlady had seen them this morning—alive!"

When I arrived, the landlady looked at me for a long moment, taking in my rough, dark-blue complexion, unpressed clothes, and red-rimmed eyes, then wagged a finger playfully.

"You are playing a joke, no? A wedding joke, maybe. Here, too, we haze newlyweds. But of course I understood. Who could help loving Miss Maria? Be of good heart, young man. For you there will be another, some day. But I talk too much. Here is your letter."

I went where I would be undisturbed, to the reading room of the library on the same street as my flat. To the musty, oblong, dimly lit room whose threshold sunshine and fresh air dared not cross. Without the saving warmth of sunlight or the fresh, clean relief of sweet-smelling air, I read. Read, inhaling the pungent, sour smell of the Scotch I had consumed during the long, sleepless night. Read and then doubted that I had read at all—but the blue ink on the white paper forced me to acknowledge its actuality. It had been written by Hunter in a neat, scholar's script.

Dear Morris: (It began)

Why should I not have wanted Maria? You did; others doubtless did. Why, then, should she not be mine? There are many things worse than being married to me; she might have married a man who beat her!

With her, I have known the two happiest days of my life. I want no more than that. I have no right to ask for more. Have we, any of us, a right to endless bliss on this earth? Hardly.

You thought of her welfare above all; for that, I owe you some explanation. You must be patient, you must believe, and in the end, you must do as I ask. You must.

You wanted to know about me—of my life before Maria. Before Maria? It seems strange to think about it. There is no life without Maria. Still, there was a time when for me she didn't exist. I have constantly been going forward to the day when I would meet her, yet there was a time when I didn't know where I would find her or even what her name would be!

It was chance that brought us together. For me, good chance; for you, possibly ill chance; for Maria? Only she can say. Some three years ago, I was studying in England under a Rhodes Scholarship. The future held great things for me. I was a Yank like yourself and damn proud of it. Life in England seemed strange and slow and sometimes utterly dismal under Austerity. Then, little by little, I slipped into their slower ways, growing to love the people for their spunk and finally coming to feel I was one of them, so to speak.

I have said everything slowed down: but I was wrong. Studying intensified for me. The folklore of the British Isles intrigued me. I delved into the Black Welsh tales, the mischievous fancies of the Irish, and the English legends of the prowling werewolf. For me, it was a relief from political science, which suddenly palled and which smacked of treason in the light of current events. My extracurricular research consumed the better part of my evenings. My books were and always have been a part of me, and as was to be expected, I overdid it. I studied too hard with too little let-up. Sometimes it seemed to me there was more truth to what I read than a myth. It became somewhat of an obsession. Suddenly, one night, everything blacked out.

I came to a sanatorium. I didn't know how I got there, and when they explained it to me, I laughed. I thought they were joking. When I tried to get up to walk, I collapsed. Then I knew how bad it had been. I knew, too, I would have to go slowly.

It was there I met Eve. She was beautiful. Not like Maria, who is like a fragile, fair, spun-sugar angel. Eve was more earthy, with skin like ivory, creamy and rich and pale. Her blue-black hair she wore long and gathered in the back. She looked about twenty-five, but a streak of pure white ran back from each of her temples. She was the most striking woman I have ever met. I had never known anyone like her, nor have I since I saw her last.

You know how it is: the air of mystery about a woman makes a man like a kid again. She reminded me of a sleek, black cat with large hazel eyes. I bumped into her one day on the verandah and spent every day with her after that.

The doctors wanted me to take exercise—short walks and the like, and Eve went with me, struggling to keep up with me. The slightest effort tired her. She suffered from a rather nasty case of anemia. She seldom smiled; the effort was probably too much for her. I saw her really smile only once.

We had been on one of our short hikes in the woods close to the grounds. She stumbled over a twig or a branch. I'm not sure which. Suddenly she was in my arms. Have you ever held a cloud in your arms, Morris? So light she was, although she was almost as tall as I. Warm and pulsating. Her eyes held mine; it was almost uncanny. I have never been affected like that by a woman. Then I was kissing her; then a sharp sting, and I winced. There was the warm, salty taste of blood on my lips. I never knew how it happened. But she was smiling. Her full mouth parted in the strangest smile I have ever seen. And those small white teeth gleamed, and in her eyes, which were all black pupils now, with the iris quite hidden, was desire—or something beyond desire. I couldn't define it then; now, I think I can. Her small, pink tongue darted over her lips, tasting, seeming to savor.

I was frightened for some indefinable reason. I wanted to get away from her, from the woods, from myself. I grasped her arm roughly, and we started back for the grounds. We never mentioned the episode again, but neither of us ever forgot. She intrigued me now more than ever. The doctors were able to satisfy my curiosity somewhat. They told me she had been a patient for some four years. Some days she was better. Some days are worse. She needed rest—much rest. Most days, she slept past noon with their approval. Some days there was a faint flush beneath that ivory skin; other days, it was pale and cool.

Just when we became lovers, I scarcely remember. Things were happening so fast I could barely keep pace with them. There was a magnetism about Eve which compelled me. I couldn't have resisted if I'd wanted to—and I didn't.

I began to have long periods of lassitude, times when I would black out and remember nothing afterwards. And the dreams began. I would dream I was stroking a large, velvety-black cat, a cat with shining yellow eyes that looked at me as if it knew my every thought. I would stroke it continuously, and it would nip me playfully. Then, one night the dream intensified: I was playing with the creature, caressing it gently, when of a sudden, its lips drew back in a snarl, and without warning, it sprang at my throat and buried its fangs deep! I thought I could feel the life being drawn from me; I screamed.

The doctors told me afterwards that I was semi-conscious for days and that I had to be restrained.

When I was well again, Eve came to see me. She was gentle—soothing. She held me close to her, and oh! It was good to be alive and to belong to someone.

I remember to this day what she wore. Black velvet lounging slacks, a low-necked amber satin blouse, caught at the "V" by a curiously wrought antique silver pin. It was round about four inches in diameter. In its center was the carved figure of a serpent coiled to strike. Its eyes were deep amber topazes, and its darting tongue was raised and set with a blood-red ruby.

"What an unusual pin, Eve," I said. "I've never seen it before, have I?"

"No," she replied. "It belongs to the deep, dark, seldom discussed skeleton in the Orcaczy closet, Tod. You see, my great-great grandmother was quite a wicked lady, to hear tell. Went in for Witches' masses and the like. They say she poisoned her husband, a rather elderly and very childish man, for her lover, whom she subsequently married. Together they did away with relatives who stood in the way of their accumulating more money. This pin was the instrument of death."

Her slim fingers pressed the ruby tongue, and the pin opened, revealing a space large enough to secrete powder.

"It's like those employed by the infamous Borgias, as you can see," she continued, shrugging. "Perhaps it was fate then, that her devoted new husband tired of her once her fortune was assured him, took a young mistress for himself, and disposed of the unfortunate wife, using her own pin to perpetrate her murder. She was excommunicated by her church, too, which must have made it most unpleasant for her, poor old dear." The slim shoulders straightened. "But let's not discuss such unpleasant things, my dear. The important thing now is for you to get well quickly. I've missed you terribly, you know."

It was then I asked her to marry me. I knew I didn't really love her, but there seemed nothing to prevent our marriage. And she had gotten under my skin. It was as elemental as that. She said she thought we should wait until I fully recovered.

"Don't say any more, darling," she said. "Rest your poor, sore throat."

She bent over me solicitously, and I reached up to stroke that smooth black hair. It had a familiar feel to it that I couldn't quite place. Of course, I had stroked it hundreds of times before, but it wasn't that. Then she looked straight at me, those large, glowing hazel eyes boring into mine, and I knew. Knew and disbelieved at the same time. I froze where I lay, paralyzed by my fear, unable to make a sound.

"So you know," she whispered. "It is well. I have marked you for my own these many months. Now that you know, you will not fight. You know what I am, or at least you can guess. This pin you admired so—it was mine three hundred years ago and it will always be mine!"

Her lips were on mine. She had never kissed me like this. It was like the touch of hot ice, freezing, then searing. Unendurable. I lay inert; I couldn't have moved if I wanted to. I could scarcely breathe. Then I felt the blood within me pounding, pulsing, beginning to answer in spite of myself. I tasted once more the warm, salty fluid on my lips. Eve's body was liquid in my arms; warm, heady, narcotizing. Once again, I felt the agonizing, dagger-sharp pain in my throat and—darkness.

Have you ever wakened to a bright, sunny afternoon and heard yourself pronounced dead? They spoke in low, hushed tones. How unfortunate. Young fellow, only thirty, dying so far away from his homeland. No family. Good thing he was well-set in life. This sudden anemia was most extraordinary; fellow showed no signs of it previously. All he really needed was rest. If he had recovered, that lovely Eve Orcaczy might have made both their lives happier and richer. A sad ending to what might have been an idyll. Good of her to claim the body. She said she was going to enter it in the family vault in Konigstein Mountain in Transylvania.

I heard them distinctly. I wanted to shout that I wasn't dead; I wanted to wake up from this horrible nightmare. I was as alive as they. I knew I had to get out of there, some way; to get away from Eve, whom I now feared. They left to make arrangements.

The lassitude crept through me without warning; I dozed in spite of myself. And I dreamed again. I was a cat running, leaping through windows, loping over the countryside, stopping for no one. I panted with my exertions. Towns and cities flew by; I had to get someplace and quickly. Then the dream ended.

"Tod," she said, "Get up, my dear." I heard Her, and I hated Her. Hated Her while I was drawn to Her. There was a white mist before my eyes. I reached up to brush it away. It was not a mist; it was a cloth. I shivered.

"I must wake up," I whispered hoarsely, "I must! I'm going mad!"

There was a creaking sound, and daylight descended upon me. When I saw where I was, I covered my face with my hands and sobbed. I tried to pray, but the words froze on my lips. I was sitting in a coffin in a mausoleum! I had been buried alive!

"What am I?" I shrieked. "Where am I and what have You done? I'm out of my mind; stark, staring mad!"

Eve's lips parted, showing the even white teeth—those slightly pointed teeth.

"You're quite sane, my dear," She said calmly. "You are now one of us; a revenant, even as I, and to live you must feed on the living."

"It's not true!" I shouted. "This is all a crazy nightmare, part of my illness! You're not real! Nothing is real!"

"I'm quite real, Tod. To be trite, I am what I am, and have accepted it calmly, as you shall in time. I have told you of my life. You have been a student of legends. Legends are often—more often than you think—reality. When one has been murdered, if one has lived a so-called wicked life, he is doomed to walk the earth battening on the living. My fate was sealed as I lay in my coffin. But that wasn't enough. As I lay there, my pet cat, Suma, slunk into the room and leapt over me. That was a double insurance of my life after death. Those whom I mark for my own must, too, live on. Accept it, my dear. You have no other choice."

"No!" I cried. "I'm an American! Things like this don't happen to us! It's only in stories, and then to foreigners!"

She chuckled drily. "I'm afraid these things do happen, and in this case, you're it, my dear. Make the best of it."

But I wouldn't; I refused to—for a while. I would not feast on the blood of the living. Something within me fought for a time.

Then, the awful hunger began. The tearing pangs of hunger that ordinary food wouldn't arrest. I fought it as long as I could. I lost.

First, it was small animals, animals that I loved. It was my life or theirs. Then there was a little girl, a dear little creature who might have been my child under different circumstances.

After the episode of the little girl, Eve left me. She had no further use for me; she had wanted the child, too, and I had got it. I was now competition to be shunned. I was alone once again alone and thoroughly miserable. I couldn't understand myself and my motives, so how could I expect someone else to understand?

I only knew what I was, nor could I rationalize why I had become this way. I could only presume it had happened to others equally as innocent as myself of wrongdoing. In the daytime, when I was like others, I reproached myself; goodness knows I loathed myself and what I had to do in order to "live." I wished I might really die, for I was tired—so frightfully tired and sick of it all. But I knew of no way to accomplish this, so I had to bear it all, fasting until my voracious, disgusting appetites got the better of me.

I decided there must be some information on my kind, particularly in this area where vampire legends are rife, so I took to haunting reading rooms. It was there I met Maria. She told me, after we knew each other better, that she was doing graduate work in regional superstitions and had decided that her thesis would treat the history of vampirism. She found it terribly amusing but at the same time frightening: Didn't I? I fear I saw nothing laughable about it, but I held my peace. Why I could have done a thesis for her that would have driven some mild-mannered prof completely out of his mind! I kept my knowledge to myself, though; I didn't want to scare Maria.

She was like a flash of sunshine in a darkened room. She made each day worth living. For the first time, the hunger pangs ceased. Ceased for one week, then two. I was certain I was cured. Perhaps, I thought, the whole thing was just a dream, and I was finally awake.

I felt then I had the right to tell her of my love. She looked infinitely sad. She wasn't certain, she said. She knew she was awfully fond of me, but she was confused. She had just come away from the States, trying to make up her mind about someone dear, whom she didn't want to hurt, and she wanted a breather. I said I would wait up to and through eternity if she wished.

Things went along peacefully then. We would walk for hours together, walking in complete silence and understanding. My strength seemed to be returning more day by day. We went far afield in search of material for her thesis. She would track down the most minute speck of hearsay to get authenticity.

One day, in our wanderings, I thoughtlessly let myself be led too near my resting place. One of the locals mentioned a "place of horror" nearby, and Maria wanted to investigate. I had no choice. We poked amid the still fustiness of the deserted mausoleum I knew so well. She thought it odd that the door was unlocked. I said, yes, wasn't it? Then she saw the box, that gleaming copper box that Eve had so thoughtfully provided. She stroked it gently, commenting on its beauty, and before I could prevent it or divert her attention, she lifted the heavy lid exposing the disarranged shroud, the remains of one or two hapless small creatures, the horrible blood-stained satin lining. She screamed and dropped the lid, somehow pinching her finger. She hopped on one foot, as one usually does to fight down sudden pain. Then she was clinging to me, thoroughly frightened.

"What does it mean, Tod?"

I quieted her with the usual platitudes. Then I was kissing that poor, red little finger. Without warning to myself or her, I nipped it affectionately. A warm glow spread through me; there was a taste more delightful than fine old brandy or vintage wine, and I knew irrevocably that I was not cured; no, nor ever should be! And I knew, too, that I wanted Maria—not just as a man longs for the woman he loves—but to drink of the fountain of her life, that warm, intoxicating fountain, greedily, joyously. She never knew what went through my mind at that moment. If I could have killed myself then, I would have, and with no compunction. But there is more to killing a revenant than that. The Church knows the procedure. I hurried Maria home as fast as I could and told her I had to go away for a week on business. She believed me and said she would miss me. But I didn't go away. That night I fought a losing battle with myself, and then and every night thereafter, I returned to her, partook of her and slunk away, loathing myself. I knew that I must soon kill the one being I loved above all others, kill, too, her immortal soul, and there was nothing I could do to prevent it.

She began to fade visibly. When I "returned" in a week, she was so ill that a few steps tired her. Her appetite all but vanished. She seemed genuinely glad to see me. She was beset by nightmares, she said. Could I help her get some rest? I took her to a physician who sagely prescribed a change in climate, rest and a diet rich in blood and iron, gave her a prescription for sedatives and called it a day.

You know how she looked when you saw her. The day was approaching when she would have no more blood when life as you know it would stop, and she would become like me. Somehow I couldn't take her with me without some warning, but I didn't know how to do it. You see since I was an innocent victim myself. I could speak, could warn my intended victim because although my soul had all but died, there was still a spark that evil hadn't touched. I knew she would think it a joke if I told her about myself without warning.

Then, happily, for me, you came along. I knew you would sense something amiss, and I didn't care. I was almost certain of her love, and I decided to seize the few minutes left. I and the devil take the hindmost! When you told her to confront me, you gave me the happiest days of my life. For this, I thank you sincerely. For what I have done and will ask you to do, forgive me!

Maria asked me directly, as you had known she would. I replied frankly, sparing her nothing. I told her that the fact that this life had been wished on me, as it were, gave me some rights and that I could tell her how to rid herself of me if she wished. Then she turned to me, her large, lovely eyes thoughtful.

"Tod, dearest," she said softly, "I must die some day, really die, so what difference does it make when? I only know that I love you. Why wait until I'm decrepit and alone, with only a few memories to look back on? Why not now, with you, where life doesn't really stop? With all I've read about this, don't you think I could free myself if I wished?"

I still wonder if she really believed me. We were married three days later. I never told her what her life with me would be like—that one day I would desert her, fearing and hating her rivalry for the very source of my life, and the ghastly chain would continue. I couldn't. I loved her so, Morris, can you understand that? I couldn't betray her then, and I can't now.

On the second night of our marriage, she died, as you know it, in my arms. I don't think she knows it yet. But it won't be long until she does discover it. We were quite alive when you found us; she was in a hypnotic state induced by her condition. She heard and saw nothing. But I knew. And I must keep my faith. I must, and you are the only one who can help me.

If you show this to a priest, he will gladly accompany you to the place in Konigstein, where we rest during the morning in a new "bed" I had specially constructed for us. I couldn't bring Maria to that other bed of corruption. A map of how to get there is enclosed. There you will perform the ancient, effective rites, and you will lay us to rest together, as we wish. That is all I ask.

When I had finished reading, I stared at nothing, trying to force myself to think. This was "all", he asked. In substance, he wished me to murder the girl I loved. I could refuse; I could ignore his request. I could even doubt the verity of his statements. He might be a madman. But I didn't doubt it. I believed every word, and I knew I would do as he asked.

That she had gone willingly, I didn't doubt. I no longer hated him so much; rather, I pitied him, the hapless victim of a horrible chain of circumstances.

I found the priest, a venerable, gentle soul, after much searching. The younger men had looked at me searchingly, laughed and told me to read the Good Book for consolation and to lay off the bottle. Father Kalman was understanding, with the wisdom of the very old.

"Yes, my son," he said, "I will go. Many might doubt, but I believe. Lucifer roams the earth in many guises and must be recognized and exorcised."

It was five o'clock in the morning when we approached the mausoleum. The Good Father explained that the "creatures of darkness" had to be back in their resting places before the cock crew. At night they drew sustenance; during the morning, they slept.

There was a gleaming copper casket. Tod had not lied. We approached it warily. In it was nothing but grisly remains, bloodstains and dust. We drew back, fearful. Then we saw the other, newer casket in the richest mahogany, almost twice the width of the copper box: Their bridal bed!

They lay together, his arm about her. She wore a gown of the palest blue, but oh, that mockery of a gown! Stained, it was with fresh blood which had seeped onto it from him. Obviously, she had not taken to prowling yet. His mouth was dark, rich with blood, slightly open in a half-smile. His hand pressed her fair head close to his chest. She lay trustingly within the circle of his arm, like a small child. The priest crossed himself. The bodies twitched slightly.

"You know what you must do," Father Kalman whispered.

I nodded, the pit of my stomach churning madly. I couldn't do it! Not Maria, the lovely. But I knew I would; I had to. She must not wake again to see that blood-stained gown or to wonder at her husband's gory lips. She should know rest, eternal rest.

Father Kalman circled the box several times, ringing his small bell, and at one point laid a crucifix upon each of their chests. Their faces writhed, and I felt my skin creep.

Then, chanting in a low, firm voice, the priest gave me the signal. Together we drove two long stakes, dipped first in Holy Water, home, piercing their hearts simultaneously.

The bodies leapt forward in the box, straining against the stake, and a horrible, drawn-out wail shattered the stillness of the tomb. The priest dropped to his knees, and I clapped my hands over my ears, but the dreadful shriek penetrated. My stomach turned over, and I retched. The Good Father followed suit. We were no supermen, and our bodies and our very souls revolted against this monstrous thing.

"Let us finish, my son," the priest said slowly, after a time, his face the color of ashes. "We must bury these dead, that they may sleep in consecrated ground."

I couldn't. I had to see her again before it was done. She lay, small and fragile as ever, her face calm, only there was no trace of life now. She was still and white, as only the dead—the truly dead—are. Tod's arm was flung across her chest as if to protect her. I made myself move the arm, resting her head upon his shoulder, where it belonged. Then, as I looked, there was just Maria. Tod was gone, and only a handful of dust lay piled up around the stake. It was enough. I slammed the lid shut.

Looking back now, I can see it was all for the best. Ria was different—apart from other women. A dreamer, a mystic, too easily influenced by the bizarre and un-normal. I, on the other hand, am practical, almost to a fault. Had she married me, I might have crushed in her the very thing that drew me to her. In time she might have grown to hate me.

Hunter, on the other hand, was a student. Introspective, given to romanticizing. Susceptible to suggestion. Had I been confronted with an Eve, I should have run like hell. To him, though, she was cloaked in mystery; hence, more desirable. What better choice for him ultimately than Ria? That Ria had to die to achieve her happiness is of no real importance. Life is a transitory thing, anyway.

Sometimes, though, when I look at Ria's picture, it's hard to be practical. She was everything I shall ever want.

I had never been to Europe before the summer of 1947. I went to find Maria, to marry her. Instead, I found and murdered her, and I will never go back again.

THE TOLL HOUSE

by W. W. Jacobs

It's all nonsense," said Jack Barnes. "Of course people have died in the house; people die in every house. As for the noises—wind in the chimney and rats in the wainscot are very convincing to a nervous man. Give me another cup of tea, Meagle."

"Lester and White are first," said Meagle, who was presiding at the tea table of the Three Feathers Inn. "You've had two."

Lester and White finished their cups with irritating slowness, pausing between sips to sniff the aroma and to discover the sex and dates of arrival of the "strangers", which floated in some numbers in the beverage. Mr Meagle served them to the brim and then, turning to the grimly expectant Mr Barnes, blandly requested him to ring for hot water.

"We'll try and keep your nerves in their present healthy condition," he remarked. "For my part I have a sort of half-and-half belief in the super-natural."

"All sensible people have," said Lester. "An aunt of mine saw a ghost once."

White nodded.

"I had an uncle that saw one," he said.

"It always is somebody else that sees them," said Barnes.

"Well, there is a house," said Meagle, "a large house at an absurdly low rent, and nobody will take it. It has taken toll of at least one life of every family that has lived there—however short the time—and since it has stood empty caretaker after care-taker has died there. The last caretaker died fifteen years ago."

"Exactly," said Barnes. "Long enough ago for legends to accumulate."

"I'll bet you a sovereign you won't spend the night there alone, for all your talk," said White suddenly.

"And I," said Lester.

"No," said Barnes slowly. "I don't believe in ghosts nor in any supernatural things whatever; all the same I admit that I should not care to pass a night there alone."

"But why not?" inquired White.

"Wind in the chimney," said Meagle with a grin.

"Rats in the wainscot," chimed in Lester. "As you like," said Barnes, coloring.

"Suppose we all go," said Meagle. "Start after supper, and get there about eleven. We have been walking for ten days now without an adventure—except Barnes's discovery that ditchwater smells longest. It will be a novelty, at any rate, and, if we break the spell by all surviving, the grateful owner ought to come down handsome."

"Let's see what the landlord has to say about it first," said Lester. "There is no fun in passing a night in an ordinary empty house. Let us make sure that it is haunted."

He rang the bell and, sending for the landlord, appealed to him in the name of our common humanity not to let them waste a night watching in a house in which spectres and hobgoblins had no part. The reply was more than reassuring, and the landlord, after describing with considerable art the exact appearance of a head which had been seen hanging out of a window in the moonlight, wound up with a polite but urgent request that they would settle his bill before they went.

"It's all very well for you young gentlemen to have your fun," he said indulgently, "but supposing as how you are all found dead in the morning, what about me? It ain't called the Toll-House for nothing, you know."

"Who died there last?" inquired Barnes, with an air of polite derision.

"A tramp," was the reply. "He went there for the sake of half a crown, and they found him next morning hanging from the balusters, dead."

"Suicide," said Barnes. "Unsound mind."

The landlord nodded. "That's what the jury brought it in," he said slowly, "but his mind was sound enough when he went in there. I'd known him, off and on, for years. I'm a poor man, but I wouldn't spend the night in that house for a hundred pounds."

He repeated this remark as they started on their expedition a few hours later. They left as the inn was closing for the night; bolts shot noisily behind them, and as the regular customers trudged slowly homewards, they set off at a brisk pace in the direction of the house. Most of the cottages were already in darkness, and lights in others went out as they passed.

"It seems rather hard that we have got to lose a night's rest in order to convince Barnes of the existence of ghosts," said White.

"It's in a good cause," said Meagle. "A most worthy object; and something seems to tell me that we shall succeed. You didn't forget the candles, Lester?"

"I have brought two," was the reply, "all the old man could spare."

There was but a little moon, and the night was cloudy. The road between high hedges was dark and in one place, where it ran through a wood, so black that they twice stumbled on the uneven ground at the side of it.

"Fancy leaving our comfortable beds for this!" said White again. "Let me see; this desirable residential sepulchre lies to the right, doesn't it?"

"Farther on," said Meagle.

They walked on for some time in silence, broken only by White's tribute to the softness, the cleanliness, and the comfort of the bed, which was receding farther and farther into the distance. Under Meagle's guidance, they turned oft at last to the right and, after a walk of a quarter of a mile, saw the gates of the house before them.

The lodge was almost hidden by overgrown shrubs and the drive was choked with rank growths. Meagle leading, they pushed through it until the dark pile of the house loomed above them.

"There is a window at the back where we can get in, so the landlord says," said Lester as they stood before the hall door.

"Window?" said Meagle. "Nonsense. Let's do the thing properly. Where's the knocker?"

He felt for it in the darkness and gave a thundering rat-tat-tat at the door.

"Don't play the fool," said Barnes crossly.

"Ghostly servants are all asleep," said Meagle gravely, "but I'll wake them up before I've done with them. It's scandalous keeping us out here in the dark."

He plied the knocker again, and the noise volleyed in the emptiness beyond. Then with a sudden exclamation, he put out his hands and stumbled forward.

"Why, it was open all the time," he said, with an odd catch in his voice. "Come on."

"I don't believe it was open," said Lester, hanging back. "Somebody is playing us a trick."

"Nonsense," said Meagle sharply. "Give me a candle. Thanks. Who's got a match?"

Barnes produced a box and struck one, and Meagle, shielding the candle with his hand, led the way forward to the foot of the stairs. "Shut the door, somebody," he said, "there's too much draught."

"It is shut," said White, glancing behind him.

Meagle fingered his chin. "Who shut it?" he inquired, looking from one to the other. "Who came in last?"

"I did," said Lester, "but I don't remember shutting it—perhaps I did, though."

Meagle, about to speak, thought better of it and, still carefully guarding the flame, began to explore the house with the others close behind. Shadows danced on the walls and lurked in the corners as they proceeded. At the end of the passage, they found a second staircase and, ascending it, slowly gained the first floor.

"Careful!" said Meagle as they gained the landing.

He held the candle forward and showed where the balusters had broken away. Then he peered curiously into the void beneath.

"This is where the tramp hanged himself, I suppose," he said thoughtfully.

"You've got an unwholesome mind," said White as they walked on. "This place is qutie creepy enough without your remembering that. Now let's find a comfortable room and have a little nip of whiskey apiece and a pipe. How will this do?"

He opened a door at the end of the passage and revealed a small square room. Meagle led the way with the candle and, first melting a drop or two of tallow, stuck it on the mantelpiece. The others seated themselves on the floor and watched pleasantly as White drew from his pocket a small bottle of whiskey and a tin cup.

"H'm! I've forgotten the water," he exclaimed. "I'll soon get some," said Meagle.

He tugged violently at the bell handle, and the rusty jangling of a bell sounded from a distant kitchen. He rang again.

"Don't play the fool," said Barnes roughly.

Meagle laughed. "I only wanted to convince you," he said kindly. "There ought to be, at any rate, one ghost in the servants' hall."

Barnes held up his hand for silence.

"Yes?" said Meagle with a grin at the other two. "Is anybody coming?"

"Suppose we drop this game and go back," said Barnes suddenly. "I don't believe in spirits, but nerves are outside anybody's command. You may laugh as you like, but it really seemed to me that I heard a door open below and steps on the stairs."

His voice was drowned in a roar of laughter.

"He is coming round," said Meagle with a smirk. "By the time I have done with him he will be a confirmed believer. Well, who will go and get some water? Will you, Barnes?"

"No," was the reply.

"If there is any it might not be safe to drink after all these years," said Lester. "We must do without it."

Meagle nodded and, taking a seat on the floor, held out his hand for the cup. Pipes were lit, and the clean, wholesome smell of tobacco filled the room.

White produced a pack of cards; talk and laughter rang through the room and died away reluctantly in distant corridors.

"Empty rooms always delude me into the belief that I possess a deep voice," said Meagle. "To-morrow——"

He started up with a smothered exclamation as the light went out suddenly, and something struck him on the head. The others sprang to their feet. Then Meagle laughed.

"It's the candle," he exclaimed. "I didn't stick it enough."

Barnes struck a match and, relighting the candle, stuck it on the mantelpiece and, sitting down, took up his cards again.

"What was I going to say?" said Meagle. "Oh, I know; to-morrow I——"

"Listen!" said White, laying his hand on the other's sleeve. "Upon my word I really thought I heard a laugh."

"Look here!" said Barnes. "What do you say to going back? I've had enough of this. I keep fancying that I hear things too; sounds of something moving about in the passage outside. I know it's only fancy, but it's uncomfortable."

"You go if you want to," said Meagle, "and we will play dummy. Or you might ask the tramp to take your hand for you, as you go downstairs."

Barnes shivered and exclaimed angrily. He got up and, walking to the half-closed door, listened.

"Go outside," said Meagle, winking at the other two. "I'll dare you to go down to the hall door and back by yourself."

Barnes came back and, bending forward, lit his pipe at the candle.

"I am nervous but rational," he said, blowing out a thin cloud of smoke. "My nerves tell me that there is something prowling up and down the long passage outside; my reason tells me that it is all nonsense. Where are my cards?"

He sat down again and, taking up his hand, looked through it carefully and led.

"Your play, White," he said after a pause. White made no sign.

"Why, he is asleep," said Meagle. "Wake up, old man. Wake up and play."

Lester, who was sitting next to him, took the sleeping man by the arm and shook him gently at first and then with some roughness; but White, with his back against the wall and his head bowed, made no sign. Meagle bawled in his ear and then turned a puzzled face to the others.

"He sleeps like the dead," he said, grimacing. "Well, there are still three of us to keep each other company."

"Yes," said Lester, nodding. "Unless—Good Lord! suppose——"

He broke off and eyed them trembling.

"Suppose what?" inquired Meagle.

"Nothing," stammered Lester. "Let's wake him. Try him again. White! White!"

"It's no good," said Meagle seriously; "there's something wrong about that sleep."

"That's what I meant," said Lester, "and if he goes to sleep like that, why shouldn't——"

Meagle sprang to his feet. "Nonsense," he said roughly. "He's tired out; that's all. Still, let's take him up and clear out. You take his legs and Barnes will lead the way with the candle. Yes? Who's that?"

He looked up quickly towards the door. "Thought I heard somebody tap," he said with a shamefaced laugh. "Now, Lester, up with him. One, two— Lester! Lester!"

He sprang forward too late; Lester, with his face buried in his arms, had rolled over on the floor fast asleep, and his utmost efforts failed to awaken him.

"He—is—asleep," he stammered. "'Asleep!"

Barnes, who had taken the candle from the mantelpiece, stood peering at the sleepers in silence and dropping tallow over the floor.

"We must get out of this," said Meagle. "Quick!" Barnes hesitated. "We can't leave them here —" he began.

"We must," said Meagle in strident tones. "If you go to sleep I shall go—Quick! Come."

He seized the other by the arm and strove to drag him to the door. Barnes shook him off and, putting the candle back on the mantelpiece, tried again to arouse the sleepers.

"It's no good," he said at last and, turning from them, watched Meagle. "Don't you go to sleep," he said anxiously.

Meagle shook his head, and they stood for some time in uneasy silence. "May as well shut the door," said Barnes at last.

He crossed over and closed it gently. Then at a scuffling noise behind him, he turned and saw Meagle in a heap on the hearthstone.

With a sharp catch in his breath, he stood motionless. Inside the room, the candle, fluttering in the draught, showed the grotesque attitudes of the sleepers dimly. Beyond the door, there seemed to his over-wrought imagination a strange and stealthy unrest. He tried to whistle, but his lips were parched, and in a mechanical fashion, he stooped and began to pick up the cards which littered the floor.

He stopped once or twice and stood with bent head listening. The unrest outside seemed to increase; a loud creaking sounded from the stairs.

"Who is there?" he cried loudly.

The creaking ceased. He crossed to the door and, flinging it open, strode out into the corridor. As he walked, his fears left him suddenly.

"Come on!" he cried with a low laugh. "All of you! All of you! Show your faces—your infernal ugly faces! Don't skulk!"

He laughed again and walked on, and the heap in the fireplace put out his head tortoise fashion and listened in horror to the retreating footsteps. Not until they had become inaudible in the distance did the listeners' features relax.

"Good Lord, Lester, we've driven him mad," he said in a frightened whisper. "We must go after him."

There was no reply. Meagle sprung to his feet. "Do you hear?" he cried. "Stop your fooling now; this is serious. White! Lester! Do you hear?"

He bent and surveyed them in angry bewilderment. "All right," he said in a trembling voice. "You won't frighten me, you know."

He turned away and walked with exaggerated carelessness in the direction of the door. He even went outside and peeped through the crack, but the sleepers did not stir. He glanced into the blackness behind and then came hastily into the room again.

He stood for a few seconds regarding them. The stillness in the house was horrible; he could not even hear them breathe. With a sudden resolution, he snatched the candle from the Mantelpiece and held the flame to White's finger. Then as he reeled back stupefied, the footsteps again became audible.

He stood with the candle in his shaking hand, listening. He heard them ascending the farther staircase, but they stopped suddenly as he went to the door. He walked a little way along the passage, and they went scurrying down the stairs and then at a jog-trot along the corridor below. He went back to the main staircase, and they ceased again.

For a time, he hung over the balusters, listening and trying to pierce the blackness below; then, slowly, step by step, he made his way downstairs and, holding the candle above his head, peered about him.

"Barnes!" he called. "Where are you?" Shaking with fright, he made his way along the passage and, summoning up all his courage, pushed open doors and gazed fearfully into empty rooms. Then, quite suddenly, he heard footsteps in front of him.

He followed slowly for fear of extinguishing the candle until they led him at last into a vast bare kitchen with damp walls and a broken floor. In front of him, a door leading into an inside room had just closed. He ran towards it and flung it open, and cold air blew out the candle. He stood aghast.

"Barnes!" he cried again. "Don't be afraid! It is I —Meagle!"

There was no answer. He stood gazing into the darkness, and all the time, the idea of something close at hand watching was upon him. Then suddenly, the steps broke out overhead again.

He drew back hastily and, passing through the kitchen, groped his way along the narrow passages. He could now see better in the darkness and, finding himself at last at the foot of the staircase, began to ascend it noiselessly. He reached the landing just in time to see a figure disappear around the angle of a wall. Still careful to make no noise, he followed the sound of the steps until they led him to the top floor, and he cornered the chase at the end of a short passage.

"Barnes!" he whispered. "Barnes!"

Something stirred in the darkness. A small circular window at the end of the passage just softened the blackness and revealed the dim outlines of a motionless figure. Meagle, in place of advancing, stood almost as still as a sudden horrible doubt took possession of him. With his eyes fixed on the shape in front, he fell back slowly and, as it advanced upon him, burst into a terrible cry.

"Barnes! For God's sake! Is it you?"

The echoes of his voice left the air quivering, but the figure before him paid no heed. For a moment, he tried to brace his courage up to endure its approach, then with a smothered cry, he turned and fled.

The passages wound like a maze, and he threaded them blindly in a vain search for the stairs. If he could get down and open the hall door——

He caught his breath in a sob; the steps had begun again. At a lumbering trot, they clattered up and down the bare passages, in and out, up and down, as though in search of him. He stood appalled and then, as they drew near, entered a small room and stood behind the door as they rushed by. He came out and ran swiftly and noiselessly in the other direction, and in a moment, the steps were after him. He found the long corridor and raced along it at top speed. The stairs he knew were at the end, and with the steps close behind, he descended them in blind haste. The steps gained on him, and he shrank to the side to let them pass, still continuing his headlong flight. Then suddenly, he seemed to slip off the earth into space.

Lester awoke in the morning to find the sunshine streaming into the room and White sitting up and regarding with some perplexity a badly blistered finger.

"Where are the others?" inquired Lester. "Gone, I suppose," said White. "We must have been asleep."

Lester arose and, stretching his stiffened limbs, dusted his clothes with his hands and went out into the corridor. White followed. At the noise of their approach, a figure which had been lying asleep at the other end sat up and revealed the face of Barnes. "Why, I've been asleep," he said in surprise. "I don't remember coming here. How did I get here?"

"Nice place to come for a nap," said Lester, severely as he pointed to the gap in the balusters. "Look there! Another yard and where would you have been?"

He walked carelessly to the edge and looked over. In response to his startled cry, the others drew near, and all three stood gazing at the dead man below.

A WARNING TO THE CURIOUS

by M.R. James

The place on the east coast that the reader is asked to consider is Seaburgh. It is not very different now from what I remember it to have been when I was a child. Marshes intersected by dykes to the south, recalling the early chapters of Great Expectations; flat fields to the north, merging into heath; heath, fir woods, and, above all, gorse, inland. A long sea-front and a street: behind that, a spacious church of flint, with a broad, solid western tower and a peal of six bells. How well I remember their sound on a hot Sunday in August as our party went slowly up the white, dusty slope of the road towards them, for the church stands at the top of a short, steep incline. They rang with a flat clacking sort of sound on those hot days, but when the air was softer, they were mellower too. The railway ran down to its little terminus farther along the same road. There was a gay white windmill just before you came to the station, another down near the shingle at the south end of the town, and others on higher ground to the north. There were cottages of bright red brick with slate roofs, but why do I encumber you with these commonplace details? The fact is that they come crowding to the point of the pencil when it begins to write of Seaburgh. I should like to be sure that I allowed the right ones to get onto the paper. But I forgot. I have not quite done with the word-painting business yet.

Walk away from the sea and the town, pass the station, and turn up the road on the right. It is a sandy road parallel to the railway, and if you follow it, it climbs to somewhat higher ground. On your left (you are now going northward) is heath. On your right (the side towards the sea) is a belt of old firs, wind-beaten, thick at the top, with the slope that old seaside trees have; seen on the skyline from the train, they would tell you in an instant if you did not know it, that you were approaching a windy coast. Well, at the top of my little hill, a line of these firs strikes out and runs towards the sea, for there is a ridge that goes that way; and the ridge ends in a rather well-defined mound commanding the level fields of rough grass, and a little knot of fir trees crowns it. And here you may sit on a hot spring day, very well content to look at the blue sea, white windmills, red cottages, bright green grass, church tower, and distant martello tower on the south.

As I have said, I began to know Seaburgh as a child; but a gap of a good many years separates my early knowledge from that which is more recent. Still, it keeps its place in my affections, and any tales of it that I pick up have an interest for me. One such tale is this: it came to me in a place very remote from Seaburgh and quite accidentally, from a man whom I had been able to oblige—enough in his opinion to justify his making me his confidant to this extent.

I know all that country more or less, (he said). I used to go to Seaburgh pretty regularly for golf in the spring. I generally put up at the "Bear," with a friend—Henry Long it was, you knew him perhaps —("Slightly," I said) and we used to take a sitting room and be very happy there. Since he died, I haven't cared to go there. And I don't know that I should anyhow after the particular thing that happened on our last visit.

It was on April 19—we were there, and by some chance, we were almost the only people in the hotel. So the ordinary public rooms were practically empty, and we were the more surprised when, after dinner, our sitting-room door opened, and a young man put his head in. We were aware of this young man. He was rather a rabbity anæmic subject—light hair and light eyes—but not unpleasing. So when he said: "I beg your pardon, is this a private room?" we did not growl and said: "Yes, it is," but Long said, or I did—no matter which: "Please come in." "Oh, may I?" he said and seemed relieved. Of course, it was obvious that he wanted company; and as he was a reasonable kind of person—not the sort to bestow his whole family history on you—we urged him to make himself at home. "I dare say you find the other rooms rather bleak," I said. Yes, he did: but it was really too good of us, and so on. That being got over, he made some pretence of reading a book. Long was playing Patience, and I was writing. It became plain to me after a few minutes that this visitor of ours was in rather a state of fidgets or nerves, which communicated itself to me, and so I put away my writing and turned to engaging him in talk.

After some remarks, which I forget, he became rather confidential. "You'll think it very odd of me," (this was the sort of way he began), "but the fact is I've had something of a shock." Well, I recommended a drink of some cheering kind, and we had it. The waiter coming in made an interruption (and I thought our young man seemed very jumpy when the door opened), but after a while, he got back to his woes again. There was nobody he knew in the place, and he did happen to know who we both were (it turned out there was some common acquaintance in town), and really he did want a word of advice if we didn't mind. Of course, we both said: "By all means," or "Not at all," and Long put away his cards. And we settled down to hear what his difficulty was.

"It began," he said, "more than a week ago, when I bicycled over to Froston, only about five or six miles, to see the church—I'm very much interested in architecture, and it's got one of those pretty porches with niches and shields. I took a photograph of it, and then an old man who was tidying up in the churchyard came and asked if I'd care to look into the church. I said yes, and he produced a key and let me in. There wasn't much inside, but I told him it was a nice little church, and he kept it very clean, 'but,' I said, 'the porch is the best part of it.' We were just outside the porch then, and he said, 'Ah, yes, that is a nice porch; and do you know, sir, what's the meanin' of that coat of arms there?'

"It was the one with the three crowns, and though I'm not much of a herald, I was able to say yes. I thought it was the old arms of the kingdom of East Anglia.

"'That's right, sir,' he said, 'and do you know the meanin' of them three crowns that's on it?'

"I said I'd no doubt it was known, but I couldn't recollect having heard it myself.

"'Well, then,' he said, 'for all, you're a scholard. I can tell you something you don't know. Them's the three 'oly crowns what was buried in the ground nearby the coast to keep the Germans from landing—ah, I can see you don't believe that. But I tell you, if it hadn't have been for one of them 'oly crowns bein' there still, them Germans would a landed here time and again, they would. Landed with their ships and killed men, women and children in their beds. Now then, that's the truth what I'm telling you, that is; and if you don't believe me, you ast the rector. There he comes: you ast him, I says.'

"I looked around, and there was the rector, a nice-looking old man, coming up the path; and before I could begin assuring my old man, who was getting quite excited, that I didn't disbelieve him, the rector struck in, and said: 'What's all this about, John? Good day to you, sir. Have you been looking at our little church?'

"So then there was a little talk which allowed the old man to calm down, and then the rector asked him again what was the matter.

"'Oh,' he said, 'it warn't nothink, only I was telling this gentleman he'd ought to ast you about them 'oly crowns.'

"'Ah, yes, to be sure,' said the rector, 'that's a very curious matter, isn't it? But I don't know whether the gentleman is interested in our old stories, eh?'

"'Oh, he'll be interested fast enough,' says the old man, 'he'll put his confidence in what you tells him, sir; why, you knew William Ager yourself, father and son too.'

"Then I put in a word to say how much I should like to hear all about it, and before many minutes I was walking up the village street with the rector who had one or two words to say to parishioners and then to the rectory, where he took me into his study. He had made out, on the way, that I really was capable of taking an intelligent interest in a piece of folklore and not quite the ordinary tripper. So he was very willing to talk, and it is rather surprising to me that the particular legend he told me has not made its way into print before. His account of it was this: 'There has always been a belief in these parts in the three holy crowns. The old people say they were buried in different places near the coast to keep off the Danes or the French, or the Germans. And they say that one of the three was dug up a long time ago, and another has disappeared by the encroaching of the sea, and one's still left doing its work, keeping off invaders. Well, now, if you have read the ordinary guides and histories of this county, you will remember perhaps that in 1687 a crown, which was said to be the crown of Redwald, King of the East Angles, was dug up at Rendlesham, and alas! alas! melted down before it was even properly described or drawn. Well, Rendlesham isn't on the coast, but it isn't so very far inland, and it's on a very important line of access. And I believe that is the crown which the people mean when they say that one has been dug up. Then on the south, you don't want me to tell you where there was a Saxon royal palace which is now under the sea, eh? Well, there was the second crown, I take it. And between these two, they say, lies the third.'

"'Do they say where it is?' of course, I asked.

"He said, 'Yes, indeed, they do, but they don't tell,' and his manner did not encourage me to put the obvious question. Instead of that I waited a moment and said: 'What did the old man mean when he said you knew William Ager as if that had something to do with the crowns?'

"'To be sure,' he said, 'now that's another curious story. These Agers—it's a very old name in these parts, but I can't find that they were ever people of quality or big owners—these Agers say, or said, that their branch of the family were the guardians of the last crown. A certain old Nathaniel Ager was the first one I knew—I was born and brought up quite near here—and he, I believe, camped out at the place during the whole of the war of 1870. William, his son, did the same, I know, during the South African War. And young William, his son, who has only died fairly recently, took lodgings at the cottage nearest the spot, and I've no doubt hastened his end, for he was a consumptive by exposure and night watching. And he was the last of that branch. It was a dreadful grief to him to think that he was the last, but he could do nothing. The only relations at all near to him were in the colonies. I wrote letters for him to them imploring them to come over on business very important to the family, but there has been no[149] answer. So the last of the holy crowns, if it's there, has no guardian now.'

"That was what the rector told me, and you can fancy how interesting I found it. The only thing I could think of when I left him was how to hit upon the spot where the crown was supposed to be. I wish I'd left it alone.

"But there was a sort of fate in it, for as I bicycled back past the churchyard wall, my eye caught a fairly new gravestone, and on it was the name of William Ager. Of course, I got off and read it. It said, 'of this parish, died at Seaburgh, 19—, aged 28.' There it was, you see. A little judicious questioning in the right place, and I should at least find the cottage nearest the spot. Only I didn't quite know what was the right spot to begin my questioning at. Again there was fate: it took me to the curiosity shop down that way—you know—and I turned over some old books, and, if you please, one was a prayer book of 1740 odd, in a rather handsome binding—I'll just go and get it, it's in my room."

He left us in a state of some surprise, but we had hardly time to exchange any remarks when he was back, panting, and handed us the book opened at the fly-leaf, on which was, in a straggly hand:

"Nathaniel Ager is my name, and England is my nation,

Seaburgh is my dwelling-place, and Christ is my Salvation,

When I am dead and in my Grave, and all my bones are rotton,

I hope the Lord will think on me when I am quite forgotton."

This poem was dated 1754, and there were many more entries of Agers, Nathaniel, Frederick, William, and so on, ending with William, 19—.

"You see," he said, "anybody would call it the greatest bit of luck. I did, but I don't know. Of course, I asked the shopman about William Ager, and of course, he happened to remember that he lodged in a cottage in the North Field and died there. This was just chalking the road for me. I knew which the cottage must be: there is only one sizable one about there. The next thing was to scrape some sort of acquaintance with the people, and I took a walk that way at once. A dog did the business for me: he made at me so fiercely that they had to run out and beat him off, and then naturally begged my pardon, and we got into the talk. I had only to bring up Ager's name and pretend I knew or thought I knew something of him, and then the woman said how sad it was him dying so young, and she was sure it came of him spending the night out of doors in the cold weather. Then I had to say: 'Did he go out on the sea at night?' and she said: 'Oh, no, it was on the hillock yonder with the trees on it.' And there I was.

"I know something about digging in these barrows: I've opened many of them in the down country. But that was with owner's leave, and in broad daylight and with men to help. I had to prospect very carefully here before I put a spade in: I couldn't trench across the mound, and with those old firs growing there, I knew there would be awkward tree roots. Still the soil was very light and sandy and easy, and there was a rabbit hole or so that might be developed into a sort of tunnel. The going out and coming back at odd hours to the hotel was going to be the awkward part. When I made up my mind about the way to excavate I told the people that I was called away for a night, and I spent it out there. I made my tunnel: I won't bore you with the details of how I supported it and filled it in when I'd done, but the main thing is that I got the crown."

Naturally, we both broke out into exclamations of surprise and interest. I, for one, had long known about the finding of the crown at Rendlesham and had often lamented its fate. No one had ever seen an Anglo-Saxon crown—at least, no one had. But our man gazed at us with a rueful eye. "Yes," he said, "and the worst of it is I don't know how to put it back."

"Put it back?" we cried out. "Why, my dear sir, you've made one of the most exciting finds ever heard of in this country. Of course, it ought to go to the Jewel House at the Tower. What's your difficulty? If you're thinking about the owner of the land and treasure trove and all that, we can certainly help you through. Nobody's going to make a fuss about technicalities in a case of this kind."

Probably more was said, but all he did was put his face in his hands and mutter: "I don't know how to put it back."

At last, Long said: "You'll forgive me, I hope if I seem impertinent, but are you quite sure you've got it?" I wanted to ask the same question myself, for, of course, the story did seem like a lunatic's dream when one thought over it. But I hadn't quite dared to say what might hurt the poor young man's feelings. However, he took it quite calmly—really, with the calm of despair, you might say. He sat up and said: "Oh yes, there's no doubt of that: I have it here, in my room, locked up in my bag. You can come and look at it if you like: I won't offer to bring it here."

We were not likely to let the chance slip. We went with him; his room was only a few doors off. The boots were just collecting shoes in the passage: or so we thought: afterwards, we were not sure. Our visitor—his name was Paxton—was in a worse state of shivers than before, and went hurriedly into the room, beckoned us after him, turned on the light, and shut the door carefully. Then he unlocked his kit-bag, and produced a bundle of clean pocket handkerchiefs in which something was wrapped, laid it on the bed, and undid it. I can now say I have seen an actual Anglo-Saxon crown. It was of silver— as the Rendlesham one is always said to have been —it was set with some gems, mostly antique intaglios and cameos, and was of rather plain, almost rough workmanship. In fact, it was like those you see on the coins and in the manuscripts. I found no reason to think it was later than the ninth century. I was intensely interested, of course, and I wanted to turn it over in my hands, but Paxton prevented me. "Don't you touch it," he said, "I'll do that." And with a sigh that was, I declare to you, dreadful to hear, he took it up and turned it about so that we could see every part of it. "Seen enough?" he said at last, and we nodded. He wrapped it up and locked it in his bag, and stood looking at us dumbly. "Come back to our room," Long said, "and tell us what the trouble is." He thanked us and said: "Will you go first and see if—if the coast is clear?"

That wasn't very intelligible, for our proceedings hadn't been, after all, very suspicious, and the hotel, as I said, was practically empty. However, we were beginning to have inklings of—we didn't know what, and anyhow nerves are infectious. So we did go, first peering out as we opened the door and fancying (I found we both had the fancy) that a shadow, or more than a shadow—but it made no sound—passed from before us to one side as we came out into the passage. "It's all right," we whispered to Paxton—whispering seemed the proper tone—and we went, with him between us, back to our sitting room. I was preparing, when we got there, to be ecstatic about the unique interest of what we had seen, but when I looked at Paxton, I saw that would be terribly out of place, and I left it to him to begin.

"What is to be done?" was his opening. Long thought it right (as he explained to me afterwards) to be obtuse and said: "Why not find out who the owner of the land is, and inform——" "Oh, no, no!" Paxton broke in impatiently, "I beg your pardon: you've been very kind, but don't you see it's got to go back, and I daren't be there at night, and daytime's impossible. Perhaps, though, you don't see: well, then, the truth is that I've never been alone since I touched it." I was beginning some fairly stupid comment, but Long caught my eye, and I stopped. Long said: "I think I do see, perhaps: but wouldn't it be—a relief—to tell us a little more clearly what the situation is?"

Then it all came out: Paxton looked over his shoulder and beckoned to us to come nearer to him and began speaking in a low voice: we listened most intently, of course, and compared notes afterwards, and I wrote down our version, so I am confident I have what he told us almost word for word. He said: "It began when I was first prospecting and put me off again and again. There was always somebody—a man—standing by one of the firs. This was in daylight, you know. He was never in front of me. I always saw him with the tail of my eye on the left or the right, and he was never there when I looked straight for him. I would lie down for quite a long time and take careful observations, and make sure there was no one, and then when I got up and began prospecting again, there he was. And he began to give me hints, besides; for wherever I put that prayer-book—short of locking it up, which I did at last—when I came back to my room it was always out on my table open at the fly leaf where the names are, and one of my razors across it to keep it open. I'm sure he just can't open my bag, or something more would have happened. You see, he's light and weak, but all the same I daren't face him. Well, then, when I was making the tunnel, of course it was worse, and if I hadn't been so keen I should have dropped the whole thing and run. It was like someone scraping at my back all the time: I thought for a long time it was only soil dropping on me, but as I got nearer the—the crown, it was unmistakable. And when I actually laid it bare and got my fingers into the ring of it and pulled it out, there came a sort of cry behind me—Oh, I can't tell you how desolate it was! And horribly threatening too. It spoilt all my pleasure in my find—cut it off that moment. And if I hadn't been the wretched fool I am, I should have put the thing back and left it.

But I didn't. The rest of the time was just awful. I had hours to get through before I could decently come back to the hotel. First I spent time filling up my tunnel and covering my tracks, and all the while he was there trying to thwart me. Sometimes, you know, you see him, and sometimes you don't, just as he pleases, I think: he's there, but he has some power over your eyes. Well, I wasn't off the spot very long before sunrise, and then I had to get to the junction for Seaburgh, and take a train back. And though it was daylight fairly soon, I don't know if that made it much better. There were always hedges, or gorse-bushes, or park fences along the road—some sort of cover, I mean—and I was never easy for a second. And then when I began to meet people going to work, they always looked behind me very strangely: it might have been that they were surprised at seeing anyone so early; but I didn't think it was only that, and I don't now: they didn't look exactly at me. And the porter at the train was like that too. And the guard held open the door after I'd got into the carriage—just as he would if there was somebody else coming, you know. Oh, you may be very sure it isn't my fancy," he said with a dull sort of laugh. Then he went on: "And even if I do get it put back, he won't forgive me: I can tell that. And I was so happy a fortnight ago." He dropped into a chair, and I believe he began to cry.

We didn't know what to say, but we felt we must come to the rescue somehow, and so—it really seemed the only thing—we said if he was so set on putting the crown back in its place, we would help him. And I must say that after what we had heard, it did seem the right thing. If these horrid consequences had come on this poor man, might there not really be something in the original idea of the crown having some curious power bound up with it to guard the coast? At least, that was my feeling, and I think it was Long's too. Our offer was very welcome to Paxton, anyhow. When could we do it? It was nearing half-past ten. Could we contrive to make a late walk plausible to the hotel people that very night? We looked out of the window: there was a brilliant full moon—the Paschal moon. Long undertook to tackle the boots and propitiate him. He was to say that we should not be much over the hour, and if we did find it so pleasant that we stopped out a bit longer, we would see that he didn't lose by sitting up. Well, we were pretty regular customers of the hotel, and did not give much trouble, and were considered by the servants to be not under the mark in the way of tips; and so the boots were propitiated, and let us out on to the sea-front, and remained, as we heard later, looking after us. Paxton had a large coat over his arm, under which was the wrapped-up crown.

So we were off on this strange errand before we had time to think how very much out of the way it was. I have told this part quite shortly on purpose, for it really does represent the haste with which we settled our plan and took action. "The shortest way is up the hill and through the churchyard," Paxton said, as we stood a moment before the hotel looking up and down the front. There was nobody about— nobody at all. Seaburgh out of season is an early, quiet place. "We can't go along the dyke by the cottage because of the dog," Paxton also said when I pointed to what I thought was a shorter way along the front and across two fields. The reason he gave was good enough. We went up the road to the church and turned in at the churchyard gate. I confess to having thought that there might be someone lying there who might be conscious of our business: but if it was so, they were also conscious that one who was on their side, so to say, had us under surveillance, and we saw no sign of them. But under observation, we felt we were, as I have never felt it at another time. Especially was it so when we passed out of the churchyard into a narrow path with close high hedges, through which we hurried as Christian did through that Valley; and so got out into open fields. Then along hedges, though I would sooner have been in the open, where I could see if anyone was visible behind me; over a gate or two, and then a swerve to the left, taking us up onto the ridge which ended in that mound.

As we neared it, Henry Long felt, and I felt too, that there were what I can only call dim presences waiting for us, as well as a far more actual one attending us. Of Paxton's agitation all this time, I can give you no adequate picture: he breathed like a hunted beast, and we could not either of us look at his face. How he would manage when we got to the very place we had not troubled to think: he had seemed so sure that that would not be difficult. Nor was it. I never saw anything like the dash with which he flung himself at a particular spot in the side of the mound and tore at it so that in a very few minutes, the greater part of his body was out of sight. We stood holding the coat and that bundle of handkerchiefs and looking very fearfully, I must admit, about us. There was nothing to be seen: a line of dark firs behind us made one skyline, more trees and the church tower half-a-mile off on the right, cottages and a windmill on the horizon on the left, calm sea dead in front, faint barking of a dog at a cottage on a gleaming dyke between us and it: full moon making that path we know across the sea: the eternal whisper of the Scotch firs just above us and of the sea in front. Yet, in all this quiet, an acute, acrid consciousness of a restrained hostility very near us, like a dog on a leash that might be let go at any moment.

Paxton pulled himself out of the hole and stretched a hand back to us. "Give it to me," he whispered, "unwrapped." We pulled off the handkerchiefs, and he took the crown. The moonlight just fell on it as he snatched it. We had not touched that bit of metal, and I have thought since that it was just as well. In another moment, Paxton was out of the hole again and busy shovelling back the soil with hands that were already bleeding. He would have none of our help, though. It was much the longest part of the job to get the place to look undisturbed: yet—I don't know how—he made a wonderful success of it. At last, he was satisfied, and we turned back.

We were a couple of hundred yards from the hill when Long suddenly said to him: "I say, you've left your coat there. That won't do. See?" And I certainly did see it—the long dark overcoat lying where the tunnel had been. Paxton had not stopped, however: he only shook his head and held up the coat on his arm. And when we joined him, he said, without any excitement, but as if nothing mattered any more: "That wasn't my coat." And, indeed, when we looked back again, that dark thing was not to be seen.

Well, we got out onto the road and came rapidly back that way. It was well before twelve when we got in, trying to put a good face on it and saying—Long and I—what a lovely night it was for a walk. The boots were on the lookout for us, and we made remarks like that for his edification as we entered the hotel. He gave another look up and down the seafront before he locked the front door and said: "You didn't meet many people about, I s'pose, sir?" "No, indeed, not a soul," I said, at which I remember Paxton looked oddly at me. "Only I thought I see someone turn up the station road after you gentlemen," said the boots. "Still, you was three together, and I don't suppose he meant mischief." I didn't know what to say; Long merely said "Good-night," and we went off upstairs, promising to turn out all lights and to go to bed in a few minutes.

Back in our room, we did our very best to make Paxton take a cheerful view. "There's the crown safe back," we said, "very likely you'd have done better not to touch it" (and he heavily assented to that), "but no real harm has been done, and we shall never give this away to anyone who would be so mad as to go near it. Besides, don't you feel better yourself? I don't mind confessing," I said, "that on the way there I was very much inclined to take your view about—well, about being followed; but going back, it wasn't at all the same thing, was it?" No, it wouldn't do: "You've nothing to trouble yourselves about," he said, "but I'm not forgiven. I've got to pay for that miserable sacrilege still. I know what you are going to say. The Church might help. Yes, but it's the body that has to suffer. It's true I'm not feeling that he's waiting outside for me just now. But——" then he stopped. Then he turned to thank us, and we put him off as soon as we could. And naturally, we pressed him to use our sitting room the next day and said we should be glad to go out with him. Or did he play golf, perhaps? Yes, he did, but he didn't think he should care about that tomorrow. Well, we recommended he get up late and sit in our room in the morning while we were playing, and we would have a walk later in the day. He was very submissive and piano about it all: ready to do just what we thought best but clearly quite certain in his own mind that what was coming could not be averted or palliated. You'll wonder why we didn't insist on accompanying him to his home and seeing him safe in the care of brothers or someone. The fact was he had nobody. He had had a flat in town, but lately, he had made up his mind to settle for a time in Sweden, and he had dismantled his flat and shipped off his belongings and was whiling away a fortnight or three weeks before he made a start. Anyhow, we didn't see what we could do better than sleep on it—or not sleep very much, as was my case—and see what we felt like tomorrow morning.

We felt very different, Long and I, on as beautiful an April morning as you could desire, and Paxton also looked very different when we saw him at breakfast. "The first approach to a decent night I seem ever to have had," was what he said. But he was going to do as we had settled: stay in probably all morning, and come out with us later. We went to the links; we met some other men and played with them in the morning and had lunch there rather early so as not to be late back. All the same, the snares of death overtook him.

Whether it could have been prevented, I don't know. I think he would have been got at somehow, do what we might. Anyhow, this is what happened.

We went straight up to our room. Paxton was there, reading quite peaceably. "Ready to come out shortly?" said Long, "say in half-an-hour's time?" "Certainly," he said: and I said we would change first and perhaps have baths and call for him in half an hour. I had my bath first, went and lay down on my bed, and slept for about ten minutes. We came out of our rooms at the same time and went together to the sitting room. Paxton wasn't there—only his book. Nor was he in his room nor in the downstair rooms. We shouted for him. A servant came out and said: "Why, I thought you gentlemen was gone out already, and so did the other gentleman. He heard you a-calling from the path there, and run out in a hurry, and I looked out of the coffee-room window, but I didn't see you. 'Owever, he run off down the beach that way."

Without a word, we ran that way, too—it was the opposite direction to that of last night's expedition. It wasn't quite four o'clock, and the day was fair, though not so fair as it had been, so there was really no reason, you'd say, for anxiety: with people about, surely a man couldn't come to much harm.

But something in our look as we ran out must have struck the servant, for she came out on the steps, pointed, and said, "Yes, that's the way he went." We ran on as far as the top of the shingle bank and there pulled up. There was a choice of ways: past the houses on the sea-front or along the sand at the bottom of the beach, which, the tide being now out, was fairly broad. Or, of course, we might keep along the shingle between these two tracks and have some view of both of them; only that was heavy going. We chose the sand, for that was the loneliest, and someone might come to harm there without being seen from the public path.

Long said he saw Paxton some distance ahead, running and waving his stick as if he wanted to signal to people who were ahead of him. I couldn't be sure: one of these sea mists was coming up very quickly from the south. There was someone, that's all I could say. And there were tracks on the sand as of someone running who wore shoes, and there were other tracks made before those—for the shoes sometimes trod in them and interfered with them— of someone not in shoes. Oh, of course, it's only my word you've got to take for all this: Long's dead. We had no time or means to make sketches or take casts, and the next tide washed everything away. All we could do was notice these marks as we hurried on. But there they were over and over again, and we had no doubt whatever that what we saw was the track of a barefoot, and one that showed more bones than flesh.

The notion of Paxton running after—after anything like this, and supposing it to be the friends he was looking for, was very dreadful to us. You can guess what we fancied: how the thing he was following might stop suddenly and turn round on him, and what sort of face it would show, half-seen at first in the mist—which all the while was getting thicker and thicker. And as I ran on wondering how the poor wretch could have been lured into mistaking that other thing for us, I remembered his saying, "He has some power over your eyes." And then I wondered what the end would be, for I had no hope now that the end could be averted, and—well, there is no need to tell all the dismal and horrid thoughts that flitted through my head as we ran on into the mist. It was uncanny, too, that the sun should still be bright in the sky, and we could see nothing. We could only tell that we were now past the houses and had reached that gap there is between them and the old martello tower. When you are past the tower, you know, there is nothing but shingle for a long way—not a house, not a human creature, just that spit of land, or rather shingle, with the river on your right and the sea on your left.

But just before that, just by the martello tower, you remember there is the old battery, close to the sea. I believe there are only a few blocks of concrete left now: the rest has all been washed away, but at this time, there was a lot more, though the place was a ruin. Well, when we got there, we clambered to the top as quickly as we could to take a breath and look over the shingle in front if, by chance, the mist would let us see anything. But a moment's rest we must have. We had run a mile at least. Nothing whatever was visible ahead of us, and we were just turning by common consent to get down and run hopelessly on when we heard what I can only call a laugh: and if you can understand what I mean by a breathless, lungless laugh, you have it; but I don't suppose you can. It came from below and swerved away into the mist. That was enough. We bent over the wall. Paxton was there at the bottom.

You don't need to be told that he was dead. His tracks showed that he had run along the side of the battery, had turned sharp round the corner of it, and, small doubt of it, must have dashed straight into the open arms of someone who was waiting there. His mouth was full of sand and stones, and his teeth and jaws were broken to bits. I only glanced once at his face.

At the same moment, just as we were scrambling down from the battery to get to the body, we heard a shout and saw a man running down the bank of the martello tower. He was the caretaker stationed there, and his keen old eyes had managed to descry through the mist that something was wrong. He had seen Paxton fall and had seen us a moment after, running up—fortunate this, for otherwise, we could hardly have escaped the suspicion of being concerned in the dreadful business. Had he, we asked, caught sight of anybody attacking our friend? He could not be sure.

We sent him off for help and stayed by the dead man till they came with the stretcher. It was then that we traced out how he had come on the narrow fringe of sand under the battery wall. The rest was shingle, and it was hopelessly impossible to tell whither the other had gone.

What were we to say at the inquest? It was a duty, we felt, not to give up, there and then, the secret of the crown, to be published in every paper. I don't know how much you would have told, but what we did agree upon was this: to say that we had only made acquaintance with Paxton the day before and that he had told us he was under some apprehension of danger at the hands of a man called William Ager also that we had seen some other tracks besides Paxton's when we followed him along the beach. But, of course, by that time, everything was gone from the sands.

No one had any knowledge, fortunately, of any William Ager living in the district. The evidence of the man at the martello tower freed us from all suspicion. All that could be done was to return a verdict of wilful murder by some person or persons unknown.

Paxton was so totally without connections that all the enquiries that were subsequently made ended in a No Thoroughfare. And I have never been at Seaburgh, or even near it, since.

NUMBER 13

by M.R. James

Among the towns of Jutland, Viborg justly holds a high place. It is the seat of a bishopric; it has a handsome but almost entirely new cathedral, a charming garden, a lake of great beauty, and many storks. Near it is Hald, accounted one of the prettiest things in Denmark, and hard by is Finderup, where Marsk Stig murdered King Erik Glipping on St Cecilia's Day in the year 1286. Fifty-six blows of square-headed iron maces were traced on Erik's skull when his tomb was opened in the seventeenth century. But I am not writing a guidebook.

There are good hotels in Viborg—Preisler's and the Phœnix are all that can be desired. But my cousin, whose experiences I have to tell you now, went to the Golden Lion the first time that he visited Viborg. He has not been there since, and the following pages will, perhaps, explain the reason for his abstention.

The Golden Lion is one of the very few houses in the town that were not destroyed in the great fire of 1726, which practically demolished the cathedral, the Sognekirke, the Raadhuus, and so much else that was old and interesting. It is a great red-brick house—that is, the front is of brick, with corbie steps on the gables and a text over the door, but the courtyard into which the omnibus drives is of black and white wood and plaster.

The sun was declining in the heavens when my cousin walked up to the door, and the light smote full upon the imposing façade of the house. He was delighted with the old-fashioned aspect of the place and promised himself a thoroughly satisfactory and amusing stay in an inn so typical of old Jutland.

It was not business in the ordinary sense of the word that had brought Mr Anderson to Viborg. He was engaged in some research into the Church history of Denmark, and it had come to his knowledge that in the Rigsarkiv of Viborg there were papers, saved from the fire, relating to the last days of Roman Catholicism in the country. He proposed, therefore, to spend a considerable time—perhaps as much as a fortnight or three weeks—in examining and copying these, and he hoped that the Golden Lion would be able to give him a room of sufficient size to serve alike as a bedroom and a study. His wishes were explained to the landlord, and after a certain amount of thought, the latter suggested that perhaps it might be the best way for the gentleman to look at one or two of the larger rooms and pick one for himself. It seemed a good idea.

The top floor was soon rejected as entailing too much getting upstairs after the day's work; the second floor contained no room of exactly the dimensions required; but on the first floor, there was a choice of two or three rooms which would, so far as size went, suit admirably.

The landlord was strongly in favour of Number 17, but Mr Anderson pointed out that its windows commanded only the blank wall of the next house and that it would be very dark in the afternoon. Either Number 12 or Number 14 would be better, for both of them looked on the street, and the bright evening light and the pretty view would more than compensate him for the additional amount of noise.

Eventually, Number 12 was selected. Like its neighbours, it had three windows, all on one side of the room; it was fairly high and unusually long. There was, of course, no fireplace, but the stove was handsome and rather old—a cast-iron erection, on the side of which was a representation of Abraham sacrificing Isaac and the inscription, "1 Bog Mose, Cap. 22," above. Nothing else in the room was remarkable; the only interesting picture was an old colored print of the town, dated about 1820.

Supper time was approaching, but when Anderson, refreshed by the ordinary ablutions, descended the staircase, there were still a few minutes before the bell rang. He devoted them to examining the list of his fellow lodgers. As is usual in Denmark, their names were displayed on a large blackboard, divided into columns and lines, the numbers of the rooms being painted at the beginning of each line. The list was not exciting. There was an advocate, or Sagförer, a German, and some bagmen from Copenhagen. The one and only point which suggested any food for thought was the absence of any Number 13 from the tale of the rooms, and even this was a thing which Anderson had already noticed half a dozen times in his experience of Danish hotels. He could not help wondering whether the objection to that particular number, common as it is, was so widespread and so strong as to make it difficult to let a room so ticketed, and he resolved to ask the landlord if he and his colleagues in the profession had actually met with many clients who refused to be accommodated in the thirteenth room.

He had nothing to tell me (I am giving the story as I heard it from him) about what passed at supper, and the evening, which was spent unpacking and arranging his clothes, books, and papers, was not more eventful. Towards eleven o'clock, he resolved to go to bed, but with him, as with a good many other people nowadays, an almost necessary preliminary to bed, if he meant to sleep, was the reading of a few pages of print, and he now remembered that the particular book which he had been reading in the train, and which alone would satisfy him at that present moment, was in the pocket of his great-coat, then hanging on a peg outside the dining-room.

To run down and secure it was the work of a moment, and, as the passages were by no means dark, it was not difficult for him to find his way back to his own door. So, at least, he thought; but when he arrived there and turned the handle, the door entirely refused to open, and he caught the sound of a hasty movement towards it from within. He had tried the wrong door, of course. Was his own room to the right or to the left? He glanced at the number: it was 13. His room would be on the left, and so it was. And not before he had been in bed for some minutes, had read his wonted three or four pages of his book, blown out his light, and turned over to go to sleep, did it occur to him that, whereas on the blackboard of the hotel there had been no Number 13, there was undoubtedly a room numbered 13 in the hotel. He felt rather sorry he had not chosen it for his own. Perhaps he might have done the landlord a little service by occupying it and given him a chance to say that a well-born English gentleman had lived in it for three weeks and liked it very much. But probably, it was used as a servant's room or something of the kind. After all, it was most likely not so large or good a room as his own. And he looked drowsily about the room, which was fairly perceptible in the half-light from the street lamp. It was a curious effect, he thought. Rooms usually look larger in dim light than a full one, but this seemed to have contracted in length and grown proportionately higher. Well, well! sleep was more important than these vague ruminations —and to sleep, he went.

On the day after his arrival, Anderson attacked the Rigsarkiv of Viborg. He was, as one might expect in Denmark, kindly received, and access to all that he wished to see was made as easy for him as possible. The documents laid before him were far more numerous and interesting than he had at all anticipated. Besides official papers, there was a large bundle of correspondence relating to Bishop Jörgen Friis, the last Roman Catholic who held the see, and in these, there cropped up many amusing and what are called "intimate" details of private life and individual character. There was much talk of a house owned by the Bishop but not inhabited by him in the town. Its tenant was apparently somewhat of a scandal and a stumbling block to the reforming party. He was a disgrace, they wrote, to the city; he practised secret and wicked arts and had sold his soul to the enemy. It was of a piece with the gross corruption and superstition of the Babylonish Church that such a viper and blood-sucking Troldmand should be patronized and harboured by the Bishop. The Bishop met these reproaches boldly; he protested his own abhorrence of all such things as secret arts, and required his antagonists to bring the matter before the proper court—of course, the spiritual court— and sift it to the bottom. No one could be more ready and willing than himself to condemn Mag Nicolas Francken if the evidence showed him to have been guilty of any of the crimes informally alleged against him.

Anderson had not time to do more than glance at the next letter of the Protestant leader, Rasmus Nielsen before the record office was closed for the day, but he gathered its general tenor, which was to the effect that Christian men were now no longer bound by the decisions of Bishops of Rome and that the Bishop's Court was not, and could not be, a fit or competent tribunal to judge so grave and weighty a cause.

On leaving the office, Mr Anderson was accompanied by the old gentleman who presided over it, and, as they walked, the conversation very naturally turned to the papers of which I have just been speaking.

Herr Scavenius, the Archivist of Viborg, though very well informed as to the general run of the documents under his charge, was not a specialist in those of the Reformation period. He was much interested in what Anderson had to tell him about them. He looked forward with great pleasure, he said, to seeing the publication in which Mr Anderson spoke of embodying their contents. "This house of the Bishop Friis," he added, "it is a great puzzle to me where it can have stood. I have studied carefully the topography of old Viborg, but it is most unlucky—of the old terrier of the Bishop's property which was made in 1560, and of which we have the greater part in the Arkiv, just the piece which had the list of the town property is missing. Never mind. Perhaps I shall some day succeed to find him."

After taking some exercise—I forget exactly how or where—Anderson went back to the Golden Lion, his supper, his game of patience, and his bed. On the way to his room, it occurred to him that he had forgotten to talk to the landlord about the omission of Number 13 from the hotel board and also that he might as well make sure that Number 13 did actually exist before he made any reference to the matter.

The decision was not difficult to arrive at. There was the door with its number as plain as could be, and work of some kind was evidently going on inside it, for as he neared the door, he could hear footsteps and voices, or a voice, within. During the few seconds in which he halted to make sure of the number, the footsteps ceased, seemingly very near the door, and he was a little startled at hearing quick hissing breathing as of a person in strong excitement. He went on to his own room, and again he was surprised to find how much smaller it seemed now than it had when he selected it. It was a slight disappointment, but only slight. If he found it really not large enough, he could very easily shift to another. In the meantime he wanted something—as far as I remember it was a pocket handkerchief—out of his portmanteau, which had been placed by the porter on a very inadequate trestle or stool against the wall at the farthest end of the room from his bed. Here was a very curious thing: the portmanteau was not to be seen. It had been moved by officious servants; doubtless, the contents had been put in the wardrobe. No, none of them was there. This was vexatious. The idea of a theft he dismissed at once. Such things rarely happen in Denmark, but some piece of stupidity had certainly been performed (which is not so uncommon), and the *stuepige* must be severely spoken to. Whatever it was that he wanted, it was not so necessary to his comfort that he could not wait till the morning for it, and he, therefore, settled not to ring the bell and disturb the servants. He went to the window—the right-hand window it was—and looked out on the quiet street. There was a tall building opposite, with large spaces of the dead wall; no passers-by; a dark night, and very little to be seen of any kind.

The light was behind him, and he could see his own shadow clearly cast on the wall opposite. Also, the shadow of the bearded man in Number 11 on the left, who passed to and fro in shirtsleeves once or twice and was seen first brushing his hair and later on in a nightgown. Also, the shadow of the occupant of Number 13 is on the right. This might be more interesting. Number 13 was, like himself, leaning on his elbows on the window-sill looking out into the street. He seemed to be a tall thin man— or was it by any chance a woman?—at least, it was someone who covered his or her head with some kind of drapery before going to bed, and, he thought, must be possessed of a red lamp-shade— and the lamp must be flickering very much. There was a distinct playing up and down of a dull red light on the opposite wall. He craned out a little to see if he could make any more of the figure, but beyond a fold of some light, perhaps white, the material on the window-sill, he could see nothing.

Now came a distant step in the street, and its approach seemed to recall Number 13 to a sense of his exposed position, for very swiftly and suddenly, he swept aside from the window, and his red light went out. Anderson, who had been smoking a cigarette, laid the end of it on the window-sill and went to bed.

The next morning he was woken by the stuepige with hot water, etc. He roused himself and after thinking out the correct Danish words, said as distinctly as he could:

"You must not move my portmanteau. Where is it?"

As is not uncommon, the maid laughed and went away without making any distinct answer.

Anderson, rather irritated, sat up in bed, intending to call her back, but he remained sitting up, staring straight in front of him. There was his portmanteau on its trestle, exactly where he had seen the porter put it when he first arrived. This was a rude shock for a man who prided himself on his accuracy of observation. How it could possibly have escaped him the night before, he did not pretend to understand; at any rate, there it was now.

The daylight showed more than the portmanteau; it let the true proportions of the room with its three windows appear and satisfied its tenant that his choice, after all, had not been a bad one. When he was almost dressed, he walked to the middle of one of the three windows to look out at the weather. Another shock awaited him. Strangely unobservant he must have been last night. He could have sworn ten times over that he had been smoking at the right-hand window the last thing before he went to bed, and here was his cigarette end on the sill of the middle window.

He started to go down to breakfast. Rather late, but Number 13 was later: here were his boots still outside his door—a gentleman's boots. So then Number 13 was a man, not a woman. Just then, he caught sight of the number on the door. It was 14. He thought he must have passed Number 13 without noticing it. Three stupid mistakes in twelve hours were too much for a methodical, accurate-minded man, so he turned back to make sure. The next number to 14 was number 12, his own room. There was no Number 13 at all.

After some minutes devoted to a careful consideration of everything he had had to eat and drink during the last twenty-four hours, Anderson decided to give the question up. If his eyes or his brain were giving way, he would have plenty of opportunities for ascertaining that fact; if not, then he was evidently being treated to a very interesting experience. In either case, the development of events would certainly be worth watching.

During the day, he continued his examination of the episcopal correspondence, which I have already summarized. To his disappointment, it was incomplete. Only one other letter could be found that referred to the affair of Mag Nicolas Francken. It was from the Bishop Jörgen Friis to Rasmus Nielsen. He said:

"Although we are not in the least degree inclined to assent to your judgement concerning our court, and shall be prepared if need be to withstand you to the uttermost in that behalf, yet forasmuch as our trusty and well-beloved Mag Nicolas Francken, against whom you have dared to allege certain false and malicious charges, hath been suddenly removed from among us, it is apparent that the question for this time falls. But forasmuch as you further allege that the Apostle and Evangelist St John in his heavenly Apocalypse describes the Holy Roman Church under the guise and symbol of the Scarlet Woman, be it known to you," etc.

Search as he might, Anderson could find no sequel to this letter nor any clue to the cause or manner of the "removal" of the casus belli. He could only suppose that Francken had died suddenly, and as there were only two days between the date of Nielsen's last letter—when Francken was evidently still in being—and that of the Bishop's letter, the death must have been completely unexpected.

In the afternoon, he paid a short visit to Hald and took his tea at Baekkelund; nor could he notice, though he was in a somewhat nervous frame of mind, that there was any indication of such a failure of eye or brain as his experiences of the morning had led him to fear.

At supper, he found himself next to the landlord.

"What," he asked him, after some indifferent conversation, "is the reason why in most of the hotels one visits in this country the number thirteen is left out of the list of rooms? I see you have none here."

The landlord seemed amused.

"To think that you should have noticed a thing like that! I've thought about it once or twice myself, to tell the truth. An educated man, I've said, has no business with these superstitious notions. I was brought up myself here in the high school of Viborg, and our old master was always a man to set his face against anything of that kind. He's been dead now this many years—a fine upstanding man he was, and ready with his hands as well as his head. I recollect us boys, one snowy day—"

Here he plunged into reminiscence.

"Then you don't think there is any particular objection to having a Number 13?" said Anderson.

"Ah! to be sure. Well, you understand, I was brought up to the business by my poor old father. He kept an hotel in Aarhuus first, and then, when we were born, he moved to Viborg here, which was his native place, and had the Phœnix here until he died. That was in 1876. Then I started business in Silkeborg, and only the year before last I moved into this house."

Then followed more details as to the state of the house and business when first taken over.

"And when you came here, was there a Number 13?"

"No, no. I was going to tell you about that. You see, in a place like this, the commercial class—the travellers—are what we have to provide for in general. And put them in Number 13? Why, they'd as soon sleep in the street, or sooner. As far as I'm concerned myself, it wouldn't make a penny difference to me what the number of my room was, and so I've often said to them; but they stick to it that it brings them bad luck. Quantities of stories they have among them of men that have slept in a Number 13 and never been the same again, or lost their best customers, or—one thing and another," said the landlord after searching for a more graphic phrase.

"Then, what do you use your Number 13 for?" said Anderson, conscious as he said the words of a curious anxiety quite disproportionate to the importance of the question.

"My Number 13? Why, don't I tell you that there isn't such a thing in the house? I thought you might have noticed that. If there was it would be next door to your own room."

"Well, yes; only I happened to think—that is, I fancied last night that I had seen a door numbered thirteen in that passage; and, really, I am almost certain I must have been right, for I saw it the night before as well."

Of course, Herr Kristensen laughed this notion to scorn, as Anderson had expected and emphasized with many iterations the fact that no Number 13 existed or had existed before him in that hotel.

Anderson was in some ways relieved by his certainty but still puzzled, and he began to think that the best way to make sure whether he had indeed been subject to an illusion or not was to invite the landlord to his room to smoke a cigar later on in the evening. Some photographs of English towns which he had with him formed a sufficiently good excuse.

Herr Kristensen was flattered by the invitation and most willingly accepted it. At about ten o'clock, he was to make his appearance, but before that, Anderson had some letters to write and retired for the purpose of writing them. He almost blushed to himself at confessing it, but he could not deny that it was the fact that he was becoming quite nervous about the question of the existence of Number 13, so much so that he approached his room by way of Number 11, in order that he might not be obliged to pass the door, or the place where the door ought to be. He looked quickly and suspiciously about the room when he entered it, but there was nothing, beyond that indefinable air of being smaller than usual, to warrant any misgivings. There was no question of the presence or absence of his portmanteau tonight. He had himself emptied it of its contents and lodged it under his bed. With a certain effort, he dismissed the thought of Number 13 from his mind and sat down to his writing.

His neighbours were quiet enough. Occasionally a door opened in the passage, and a pair of boots was thrown out, or a bagman walked past humming to himself, and outside, from time to time, a cart thundered over the atrocious cobblestones, or a quick step hurried along the flags.

Anderson finished his letters, ordered whisky and soda, and then went to the window and studied the dead wall opposite and the shadows upon it.

As far as he could remember, Number 14 had been occupied by the lawyer, a staid man who said little at meals, being generally engaged in studying a small bundle of papers beside his plate. Apparently, however, he was in the habit of giving vent to his animal spirits when alone. Why else should he be dancing? The shadow from the next room evidently showed that he was. Again and again, his thin form crossed the window, his arms waved, and a gaunt leg was kicked up with surprising agility. He seemed to be barefooted, and the floor must be well laid, for no sound betrayed his movements. Sagförer Herr Anders Jensen, dancing at ten o'clock at night in a hotel bedroom, seemed a fitting subject for a historical painting in the grand style; and Anderson's thoughts, like those of Emily in the "Mysteries of Udolpho", began to "arrange themselves in the following lines":

"When I return to my hotel,

At ten o'clock p.m.,

The waiters think I am unwell;

I do not care for them.

But when I've locked my chamber door,

And put my boots outside,

I dance all night upon the floor.

And even if my neighbours swore,

I'd go on dancing all the more,

For I'm acquainted with the law,

And in despite of all their jaw,

Their protests I deride."

Had not the landlord at this moment knocked at the door, it is probable that quite a long poem might have been laid before the reader. To judge from his look of surprise when he found himself in the room, Herr Kristensen was struck, as Anderson had been, by something unusual in its aspect. But he made no remark. Anderson's photographs interested him mightily and formed the text of many autobiographical discourses. Nor is it quite clear how the conversation could have been diverted into the desired channel of Number 13, had not the lawyer at this moment begun to sing, and to sing in a manner which could leave no doubt in anyone's mind that he was either exceedingly drunk or raving mad. It was a high, thin voice that they heard, and it seemed dry, as if from long disuse. Of words or tune, there was no question. It went sailing up to a surprising height and was carried down with a despairing moan as of a winter wind in a hollow chimney or an organ whose wind fails suddenly. It was a really horrible sound, and Anderson felt that if he had been alone, he must have fled for refuge and society to some neighbour bagman's room.

The landlord sat open-mouthed.

"I don't understand it," he said, at last, wiping his forehead. "It is dreadful. I have heard it once before, but I made sure it was a cat."

"Is he mad?" said Anderson.

"He must be; and what a sad thing! Such a good customer, too, and so successful in his business, by what I hear, and a young family to bring up."

Just then came an impatient knock at the door, and the knocker entered without waiting to be asked. It was the lawyer, in déshabille and very rough-haired, and very angry he looked.

"I beg pardon, sir," he said, "but I should be much obliged if you would kindly desist—"

Here he stopped, for it was evident that neither of the persons before him was responsible for the disturbance, and after a moment's lull it swelled forth again more wildly than before.

"But what in the name of Heaven does it mean?" broke out the lawyer. "Where is it? Who is it? Am I going out of my mind?"

"Surely, Herr Jensen, it comes from your room next door? Isn't there a cat or something stuck in the chimney?"

This was the best that occurred to Anderson to say, and he realized its futility as he spoke; but anything was better than to stand and listen to that horrible voice and look at the broad, white face of the landlord, all perspiring and quivering as he clutched the arms of his chair.

"Impossible," said the lawyer, "impossible. There is no chimney. I came here because I was convinced the noise was going on here. It was certainly in the next room to mine."

"Was there no door between yours and mine?" said Anderson eagerly.

"No, sir," said Herr Jensen rather sharply. "At least, not this morning."

"Ah!" said Anderson. "Nor tonight?"

"I am not sure," said the lawyer with some hesitation.

Suddenly the crying or singing voice in the next room died away, and the singer was heard seemingly laughing to himself in a crooning manner. The three men actually shivered at the sound. Then there was a silence.

"Come," said the lawyer, "what have you to say, Herr Kristensen? What does this mean?"

"Good Heaven!" said Kristensen. "How should I tell! I know no more than you, gentlemen. I pray I may never hear such a noise again."

"So do I," said Herr Jensen, and he added something under his breath. Anderson thought it sounded like the last words of the Psalter, "omnis spiritus laudet Dominum," but he could not be sure.

"But we must do something," said Anderson —"the three of us. Shall we go and investigate in the next room?"

"But that is Herr Jensen's room," wailed the landlord. "It is no use; he has come from there himself."

"I am not so sure," said Jensen. "I think this gentleman is right: we must go and see."

The only weapons of defence that could be mustered on the spot were a stick and an umbrella. The expedition went out into the passage, not without quakings. There was a deadly quiet outside, but a light shone from under the next door. Anderson and Jensen approached it. The latter turned the handle and gave a sudden vigorous push. No use. The door stood fast.

"Herr Kristensen," said Jensen, "will you go and fetch the strongest servant you have in the place? We must see this through."

The landlord nodded and hurried off, glad to be away from the scene of action. Jensen and Anderson remained outside looking at the door.

"It is Number 13, you see," said the latter.

"Yes; there is your door, and there is mine," said Jensen.

"My room has three windows in the daytime," said Anderson, with difficulty suppressing a nervous laugh.

"By George, so has mine!" said the lawyer, turning and looking at Anderson. His back was now to the door. At that moment, the door opened, and an arm came out and clawed at his shoulder. It was clad in ragged, yellowish linen, and the bare skin, where it could be seen, had long grey hair upon it.

Anderson was just in time to pull Jensen out of its reach with a cry of disgust and fright when the door shut again, and a low laugh was heard.

Jensen had seen nothing, but when Anderson hurriedly told him what a risk he had run, he fell into a great state of agitation and suggested that they should retire from the enterprise and lock themselves up in one or other of their rooms.

However, while he was developing this plan, the landlord and two able-bodied men arrived on the scene, all looking rather serious and alarmed. Jensen met them with a torrent of description and explanation, which did not at all tend to encourage them for the fray.

The men dropped the crowbars they had brought and said flatly that they were not going to risk their throats in that devil's den. The landlord was miserably nervous and undecided, conscious that if the danger were not faced, his hotel was ruined, and very loth to face it himself. Luckily Anderson hit upon a way of rallying the demoralized force.

"Is this," he said, "the Danish courage I have heard so much of? It isn't a German in there, and if it was, we are five to one."

The two servants and Jensen were stung into action by this and made a dash at the door.

"Stop!" said Anderson. "Don't lose your heads. You stay out here with the light, landlord, and one of you two men break in the door, and don't go in when it gives way."

The men nodded, and the younger stepped forward, raised his crowbar, and dealt a tremendous blow to the upper panel. The result was not in the least what any of them anticipated. There was no cracking or rending of wood—only a dull sound as if the solid wall had been struck. The man dropped his tool with a shout and began rubbing his elbow. His cry drew their eyes upon him for a moment; then Anderson looked at the door again. It was gone; the plaster wall of the passage stared him in the face, with a considerable gash in it where the crowbar had struck it. Number 13 had passed out of existence.

For a brief space, they stood perfectly still, gazing at the blank wall. An early cock in the yard beneath was heard to crow, and as Anderson glanced in the direction of the sound, he saw through the window at the end of the long passage that the eastern sky was paling to the dawn.

"Perhaps," said the landlord, with hesitation, "you gentlemen would like another room for tonight—a double-bedded one?"

Neither Jensen nor Anderson was averse to the suggestion. They felt inclined to hunt in couples after their late experience. It was found convenient when each of them went to his room to collect the articles he wanted for the night that the other should go with him and hold the candle. They noticed that both Number 12 and Number 14 had three windows.

The next morning the same party reassembled in Number 12. The landlord was naturally anxious to avoid engaging outside help, and yet it was imperative that the mystery attaching to that part of the house should be cleared up. Accordingly, the two servants had been induced to take upon them the function of carpenters. The furniture was cleared away, and, at the cost of a good many irretrievably damaged planks, that portion of the floor was taken up which lay nearest to Number 14.

You will naturally suppose that a skeleton— say that of Mag Nicolas Francken—was discovered. That was not so. What they did find lying between the beams which supported the flooring was a small copper box. In it was a neatly-folded vellum document with about twenty lines of writing. Both Anderson and Jensen (who proved to be something of a palæographer) were much excited by this discovery, which promised to afford the key to these extraordinary phenomena.

I possess a copy of an astrological work which I have never read. It has, by way of the frontispiece, a woodcut by Hans Sebald Beham, representing a number of sages seated around a table. This detail may enable connoisseurs to identify the book. I cannot myself recollect its title, and it is not at this moment within reach; but the fly-leaves of it are covered with writing, and, during the ten years in which I have owned the volume, I have not been able to determine which way up this writing ought to be read, much less in what language it is. Not dissimilar was the position of Anderson and Jensen after the protracted examination to which they submitted the document in the copper box.

After two days' contemplation of it, Jensen, who was the bolder spirit of the two, hazarded the conjecture that the language was either Latin or Old Danish.

Anderson ventured upon no surmises and was very willing to surrender the box and the parchment to the Historical Society of Viborg to be placed in their museum.

I had the whole story from him a few months later, as we sat in a wood near Upsala, after a visit to the library there, where we—or, rather, I—had laughed over the contract by which Daniel Salthenius (in later life Professor of Hebrew at Königsberg) sold himself to Satan. Anderson was not really amused.

"Young idiot!" he said, meaning Salthenius, who was only an undergraduate when he committed that indiscretion, "how did he know what company he was courting?"

And when I suggested the usual considerations, he only grunted. That same afternoon he told me what you had read, but he refused to draw any inferences from it and to assent to any that I drew for him.

THE MAN OF SCIENCE

by Jerome K. Jerome

I met a man in the Strand one day that I knew very well, as I thought, though I had not seen him for years. We walked together to Charing Cross, and there we shook hands and parted. The next morning, I spoke of this meeting to a mutual friend, and then I learnt, for the first time, that the man had died six months before.

The natural inference was that I had mistaken one man for another, an error that, not having a good memory for faces, I frequently fall into.

What was remarkable about the matter, however, was that throughout our walk, I had conversed with the man under the impression that he was that other dead man, and, whether by coincidence or not, his replies had

never once suggested to me my mistake.

As soon as I finished, Jephson, who had been listening very thoughtfully, asked me if I believed in spiritualism "to its fullest extent."

"That is rather a large question," I answered. "What do you mean by 'spiritualism to its fullest extent'?"

"Well, do you believe that the spirits of the dead have not only the power of revisiting this earth at their will, but that, when here, they have the power of action, or rather, of exciting to action? Let me put a definite case. A spiritualist friend of mine, a sensible and by no means imaginative man, once told me that a table, through the medium of which the spirit of a friend had been in the habit of communicating with him, came slowly across the room towards him, of its own accord, one night as he sat alone, and pinioned him against the wall. Now can any of you believe that, or can't you?"

"I could," Brown took it upon himself to reply, "but before doing so, I should wish for an introduction to the friend who told you the story.

Speaking generally," he continued, "it seems to me that the difference between what we call the natural and the supernatural is merely the difference between frequency and rarity of occurrence. Having regard to the phenomena we are compelled to admit, I think it illogical to disbelieve anything we are unable to disprove."

"For my part," remarked MacShaughnassy, "I can believe in the ability of our spirit friends to give the quaint entertainments credited to them much easier than I can in their desire to do so."

"You mean," added Jephson, "that you cannot understand why a spirit, not compelled as we are by the exigencies of society, should care to spend its evenings carrying on a laboured and childish conversation with a room full of abnormally uninteresting people."

"That is precisely what I cannot understand," MacShaughnassy agreed.

"Nor I, either," said Jephson. "But I was thinking of something very different altogether. Suppose a man died with the dearest wish of his heart unfulfilled. Do you believe that his spirit might have the power to return to earth and complete the interrupted work?"

"Well," answered MacShaughnassy, "if one admits the possibility of spirits retaining any interest in the affairs of this world at all, it is certainly more reasonable to imagine them engaged upon a task such as you suggest than to believe that they occupy themselves with the performance of mere drawing-room tricks. But what are you leading up to?"

"Why, to this," replied Jephson, seating himself straddle-legged across his chair and leaning his arms upon the back. "I was told a story this morning at the hospital by an old French doctor. The actual facts are few and simple; all that is known can be read in the Paris police records of sixty-two years ago.

"The most important part of the case, however, is the part that is not known and that never will be known.

"The story begins with a great wrong done by one man unto another man.

What the wrong was, I do not know. I am inclined to think. However, it was connected with a woman. I think that because he who had been wronged hated him who had wronged him with hate, such does not often burn in a man's brain unless it is fanned by the memory of a woman's breath.

"Still that is only conjecture, and the point is immaterial. The man who had done the wrong fled, and the other man followed him. It became a point-to-point race, the first man having the advantage of a day's start. The course was the whole world, and the stakes were the first man's life.

"Travellers were few and far between in those days, and this made the trail easy to follow. The first man, never knowing how far or how near the other was behind him, and hoping now and again that he might have baffled him, would rest for a while. The second man, always knowing just how far the first one was before him, never paused, and thus each day, the man who was spurred by Hate drew nearer to the man who was spurred by Fear.

"At this town the answer to the never-varied question would be:—

"'At seven o'clock last evening, M'sieur.'

"'Seven—ah; eighteen hours. Give me something to eat, quick, while the horses are being put to.'

"At the next, the calculation would be sixteen hours.

"Passing a lonely chalet, Monsieur puts his head out of the window:—

"'How long since a carriage passed this way, with a tall, fair man inside?'

"'Such a one passed early this morning, M'sieur.'

"'Thanks, drive on, a hundred francs apiece if you are through the pass before daybreak.'

"'And what for dead horses, M'sieur?'

"'Twice their value when living.'

"One day, the man who was ridden by Fear looked up and saw before him the open door of a cathedral and, passing in, knelt down and prayed. He prayed long and fervently for men when they were in sore straits, clutching eagerly at the straws of faith. He prayed that he might be forgiven his sin and, more important, still that he might be pardoned the consequences of his sin and be delivered from his adversary; and a few chairs from him, facing him, knelt his enemy, praying also.

"But the second man's prayer, being a thanksgiving merely, was short so that when the first man raised his eyes, he saw the face of his enemy gazing at him across the chair tops, with a mocking smile upon it.

"He made no attempt to rise but remained kneeling, fascinated by the look of joy that shone out of the other man's eyes. And the other man moved the high-backed chairs one by one and came towards him softly.

"Then, just as the man who had been wronged stood beside the man who had wronged him, full of gladness that his opportunity had come, there burst from the cathedral tower a sudden clash of bells, and the man, whose opportunity had come, broke his heart and fell back dead, with that mocking smile still playing round his mouth.

"And so he lay there.

"Then the man who had done the wrong rose up and passed out, praising God.

"What became of the body of the other man is not known. It was the body of a stranger who had died suddenly in the cathedral. There was none to identify it, none to claim it.

"Years passed away, and the survivor of the tragedy became a worthy and useful citizen and a noted man of science.

"In his laboratory were many objects necessary to him in his researches, and, prominent among them, stood in a certain corner a human skeleton.

It was a very old and much-mended skeleton, and one day the long-expected end arrived, and it tumbled to pieces.

"Thus, it became necessary to purchase another.

"The man of science visited a dealer he well knew—a little parchment-faced old man who kept a dingy shop, where nothing was ever sold, within the shadow of the towers of Notre Dame.

"The little parchment-faced old man had just the very thing that Monsieur wanted—a singularly fine and well-proportioned 'study.' It should be sent around and set up in Monsieur's laboratory that very afternoon.

"The dealer was as good as his word. When Monsieur entered his laboratory that evening, the thing was in its place.

"Monsieur seated himself in his high-backed chair and tried to collect his thoughts. But Monsieur's thoughts were unruly and inclined to wander and to wander always in one direction.

"Monsieur opened a large volume and commenced to read. He read of a man who had wronged another and fled from him, the other man following.

Finding himself reading this, he closed the book angrily and went and stood by the window and looked out. He saw before him the sun-pierced nave of a great cathedral, and on the stones lay a dead man with a mocking smile upon his face.

"Cursing himself for a fool, he turned away with a laugh. But his laugh was short-lived, for it seemed to him that something else in the room was laughing also. Struck suddenly still, with his feet glued to the ground, he stood listening for a while: then sought with starting eyes the corner from where the sound had seemed to come. But the white thing standing there was only grinning.

"Monsieur wiped the damp sweat from his head and hands and stole out.

"For a couple of days, he did not enter the room again. On the third, telling himself that his fears were those of a hysterical girl, he opened the door and went in. To shame himself, he took his lamp in his hand, and crossing over to the far corner where the skeleton stood, examined it. A set of bones was bought for three hundred francs. Was he a child, to be scared by such a bogey!

"He held his lamp up in front of the thing's grinning head. The flame of the lamp flickered as though a faint breath had passed over it.

"The man explained this to himself by saying that the walls of the house were old and cracked and that the wind might creep in anywhere. He repeated this explanation to himself as he recrossed the room, walking backwards, with his eyes fixed on the thing. When he reached his desk, he sat down and gripped the arms of his chair till his fingers turned white.

"He tried to work, but the empty sockets in that grinning head seemed to be drawing him towards them. He rose and battled with his inclination to fly, screaming from the room. Glancing fearfully about him, his eye fell upon a high screen standing before the door. He dragged it forward and placed it between himself and the thing so that he could not see it—nor it sees him. Then he sat down again to his work. For a while, he forced himself to look at the book in front of him, but at last, unable to control himself any longer, he suffered his eyes to follow their own bent.

"It may have been a hallucination. He may have accidentally placed the screen so as to favour such an illusion. But what he saw was a bony hand coming round the corner of the screen, and, with a cry, he fell to the floor in a swoon.

"The people of the house came running in, and lifting him up, carried him out, and laid him upon his bed. As soon as he recovered, his first question was, where had they found the thing—where was it when they entered the room? And when they told him they had seen it standing where it always stood and had gone down into the room to look again because of his frenzied entreaties and returned trying to hide their smiles, he listened to their talk about overwork and the necessity for change and rest and said they might do with him as they would.

"So, for many months, the laboratory door remained locked. Then there came a chill autumn evening when the man of science opened it again and closed it behind him.

"He lighted his lamp, gathered his instruments and books around him, and sat down before them in his high-backed chair. And the old terror returned to him.

"But this time, he meant to conquer himself. His nerves were stronger now, and his brain clearer; he would fight his unreasoning fear. He crossed to the door and locked himself in, and flung the key to the other end of the room, where it fell among jars and bottles with an echoing clatter.

"Later on, his old housekeeper, going her final round, tapped at his door and wished him good night, as was her custom. She received no response at first and, growing nervous, tapped louder and called again, and at length, an answering 'goodnight' came back to her.

"She thought little about it at the time but afterwards, she remembered that the voice that had replied to her had been strangely grating and mechanical. Trying to describe it, she likened it to such a voice as she would imagine coming from a statue.

"Next morning, his door remained still locked. It was no unusual thing for him to work all night and far into the next day, so no one thought to be surprised. When, however, evening came, and yet he did not appear, his servants gathered outside the room and whispered, remembering what had happened once before.

"They listened, but could hear no sound. They shook the door and called to him, then beat with their fists upon the wooden panels. But still no sound came from the room.

"Becoming alarmed, they decided to burst open the door, and, after many blows, it gave way, and they crowded in.

"He sat bolt upright in his high-backed chair. They thought at first he had died in his sleep. But when they drew nearer and the light fell upon him, they saw the livid marks of bony fingers round his throat; and in his eyes there was a terror such as is not often seen in human eyes."

Brown was the first to break the silence that followed. He asked me if I had any brandy on board. He said he felt he should like just a nip of brandy before going to bed. That is one of the chief charms of Jephson's stories: they always make you feel you want a little brandy.

THE MARK OF THE BEAST

by Joseph Rudyard Kipling

Your Gods and my Gods-do you or I know which are the stronger?

Native Proverb.

East of Suez, some hold, the direct control of Providence ceases; Man being there handed over to the power of the Gods and Devils of Asia, and the Church of England Providence only exercising an occasional and modified supervision in the case of Englishmen.

This theory accounts for some of the more unnecessary horrors of life in India: it may be stretched to explain my story.

My friend Strickland of the Police, who knows as much of natives of India as is good for any man, can bear witness to the facts of the case. Dumoise, our doctor, also saw what Strickland and I saw. The inference which he drew from the evidence was entirely incorrect. He is dead now; he died in a rather curious manner, which has been described elsewhere.

When Fleete came to India, he owned a little money and some land in the Himalayas near a place called Dharmsala. Both properties had been left to him by an uncle, and he came out to finance them. He was a big, heavy, genial, and inoffensive man. His knowledge of natives was, of course, limited, and he complained of the difficulties of the language.

He rode in from his place in the hills to spend New Year in the station, and he stayed with Strickland. On New Year's Eve, there was a big dinner at the club, and the night was excusably wet. When men foregather from the uttermost ends of the Empire, they have a right to be riotous. The Frontier had sent down a contingent o' Catch-'em-Alive-O's who had not seen twenty white faces for a year and were used to riding fifteen miles to dinner at the next Fort at the risk of a Khyberee bullet where their drinks should lie. They profited from their new security, for they tried to play pool with a curled-up hedgehog found in the garden, and one of them carried the marker around the room in his teeth. Half a dozen planters had come in from the south and were talking 'horse' to the Biggest Liar in Asia, who was trying to cap all their stories at once. Everybody was there, and there was a general closing up of ranks and taking stock of our losses in dead or disabled that had fallen during the past year. It was a very wet night, and I remember that we sang 'Auld Lang Syne' with our feet in the Polo Championship Cup and our heads among the stars and swore that we were all dear friends. Then some of us went away and annexed Burma, and some tried to open up the Soudan and were opened up by Fuzzies in that cruel scrub outside Suakim, and some found stars and medals, and some were married, which was bad, and some did other things which were worse, and the others of us stayed in our chains and strove to make money on insufficient experiences.

Fleete began the night with sherry and bitters, drank champagne steadily up to dessert, then raw, rasping Capri with all the strength of whisky, took Benedictine with his coffee, four or five whiskies and sodas to improve his pool strokes, beer and bones at half-past two, winding up with old brandy. Consequently, when he came out, at half-past three in the morning, into fourteen degrees of frost, he was very angry with his horse for coughing and tried to leapfrog into the saddle. The horse broke away and went to his stables, so Strickland and I formed a Guard of Dishonour to take Fleete home.

Our road lay through the bazaar, close to a little temple of Hanuman, the Monkey-god, who is a leading divinity worthy of respect. All gods have good points, just as have all priests. Personally, I attach much importance to Hanuman and am kind to his people—the great gray apes of the hills. One never knows when one may want a friend.

There was a light in the temple, and as we passed, we could hear the voices of men chanting hymns. In a native temple, the priests rise at all hours of the night to honour their god. Before we could stop him, Fleete dashed up the steps, patted two priests on the back, and was gravely grinding the ashes of his cigar butt into the forehead of the red stone image of Hanuman. Strickland tried to drag him out, but he sat down and said solemnly:

'Shee that? 'Mark of the B-beasht! I made it. Ishn't it fine?'

In half a minute the temple was alive and noisy, and Strickland, who knew what came of polluting gods, said that things might occur. He, by virtue of his official position, long residence in the country, and weakness for going among the natives, was known to the priests and he felt unhappy. Fleete sat on the ground and refused to move. He said that 'good old Hanuman' made a very soft pillow.

Then, without any warning, a Silver Man came out of a recess behind the image of the god. He was perfectly naked in that bitter, bitter cold, and his body shone like frosted silver, for he was what the Bible calls 'a leper as white as snow.' Also, he had no face because he was a leper of some years' standing and his disease was heavy upon him. We two stooped to haul Fleete up, and the temple was filling and filling with folk who seemed to spring from the earth when the Silver Man ran in under our arms, making a noise exactly like the mewing of an otter, caught Fleete round the body and dropped his head on Fleete's breast before we could wrench him away. Then he retired to a corner and sat mewing while the crowd blocked all the doors.

The priests were very angry until the Silver Man touched Fleete. That nuzzling seemed to sober them.

At the end of a few minutes' silence, one of the priests came to Strickland and said, in perfect English, 'Take your friend away. He has done with Hanuman, but Hanurnan has not done with him.' The crowd gave room, and we carried Fleete into the road.

Strickland was very angry. He said that we might all three have been knifed and that Fleete should thank his stars that he had escaped without injury.

Fleete thanked no one. He said that he wanted to go to bed. He was gorgeously drunk.

We moved on, Strickland silent and wrathful, until Fleete was taken with violent shivering fits and sweating. He said that the smells of the bazaar were overpowering, and he wondered why slaughterhouses were permitted so near English residences. 'Can't you smell the blood?' said Fleete.

We put him to bed at last, just as the dawn was breaking, and Strickland invited me to have another whisky and soda. While we were drinking, he talked of the trouble in the temple and admitted that it baffled him completely. Strickland hates being mystified by natives because his business in life is to overmatch them with their own weapons. He has not yet succeeded in doing this, but in fifteen or twenty years, he will have made some little progress.

'They should have mauled us,' he said, 'instead of mewing at us. I wonder what they meant. I don't like it one little bit.'

I said that the Managing Committee of the temple would, in all probability, bring criminal action against us for insulting their religion. There was a section of the Indian Penal Code which exactly met Fleete's offence. Strickland said he only hoped and prayed that they would do this. Before I left, I looked into Fleete's room and saw him lying on his right side, scratching his left breast. Then. I went to bed cold, depressed, and unhappy at seven o'clock in the morning.

At one o'clock, I rode over to Strickland's house to inquire after Fleete's head. I imagined that it would be a sore one. Fleete was breakfasting and seemed unwell. His temper was gone, for he was abusing the cook for not supplying him with an underdone chop. A man who can eat raw meat after a wet night is a curiosity. I told Fleete this, and he laughed.

'You breed queer mosquitoes in these parts,' he said. 'I've been bitten to pieces, but only in one place.'

'Let's have a look at the bite,' said Strickland. 'It may have gone down since this morning.'

While the chops were being cooked, Fleete opened his shirt and showed us, just over his left breast, a mark, the perfect double of the black rosettes—the five or six irregular blotches arranged in a circle—on a leopard's hide. Strickland looked and said, 'It was only pink this morning. It's grown black now.'

Fleete ran to a glass.

'By Jove!' he said,' this is nasty. What is it?'

We could not answer. Here the chops came in, all red and juicy, and Fleete bolted three in a most offensive manner. He ate on his right grinders only and threw his head over his right shoulder as he snapped the meat. When he had finished, it struck him that he had been behaving strangely, for he said apologetically, 'I don't think I ever felt so hungry in my life. I've bolted like an ostrich.'

After breakfast, Strickland said to me, 'Don't go. Stay here, and stay for the night.'

Seeing that my house was not three miles from Strickland's, this request was absurd. But Strickland insisted and was going to say something when Fleete interrupted by declaring in a shamefaced way that he felt hungry again. Strickland sent a man to my house to fetch over my bedding and a horse, and we three went down to Strickland's stables to pass the hours until it was time to go out for a ride. The man who has a weakness for horses never wearies of inspecting them, and when two men are killing time in this way, they gather knowledge and lie the one from the other.

There were five horses in the stables, and I shall never forget the scene as we tried to look them over. They seemed to have gone mad. They reared and screamed and nearly tore up their pickets; they sweated and shivered and lathered and were distraught with fear. Strickland's horses used to know him as well as his dogs, which made the matter more curious. We left the stable for fear of the brutes throwing themselves in their panic. Then Strickland turned back and called me. The horses were still frightened, but they let us 'gentle' and make much of them and put their heads in our bosoms.

'They aren't afraid of US,' said Strickland. 'D'you know, I'd give three months' pay if OUTRAGE here could talk.'

But Outrage was dumb and could only cuddle up to his master and blow out his nostrils, as is the custom of horses when they wish to explain things but can't. Fleete came up when we were in the stalls, and as soon as the horses saw him, their fright broke out afresh. It was all that we could do to escape from the place unkicked. Strickland said, 'They don't seem to love you, Fleete.'

'Nonsense,' said Fleete, 'my mare will follow me like a dog.' He went to her; she was in a loose box, but as he slipped the bars, she plunged, knocked him down, and broke away into the garden. I laughed, but Strickland was not amused. He took his moustache in both fists and pulled at it till it nearly came out. Fleete, instead of going off to chase his property, yawned, saying that he felt sleepy. He went to the house to lie down, which was a foolish way of spending New Year's Day.

Strickland sat with me in the stables and asked if I had noticed anything peculiar in Fleete's manner. I said that he ate his food like a beast; but that this might have been the result of living alone in the hills out of the reach of society as refined and elevating as ours, for instance. Strickland was not amused. I do not think that he listened to me, for his next sentence referred to the mark on Fleete's breast, and I said that it might have been caused by blister flies or that it was possibly a birth-mark newly born and now visible for the first time. We both agreed that it was unpleasant to look at, and Strickland found occasion to say that I was a fool.

'I can't tell you what I think now,' said he, 'because you would call me a madman, but you must stay with me for the next few days if you can. I want you to watch Fleete, but don't tell me what you think till I have made up my mind.'

'But I am dining out tonight,' I said. 'So am I,' said Strickland, 'and so is Fleete. At least if he doesn't change his mind.'

We walked about the garden smoking but saying nothing—because we were friends and talking spoils good tobacco—till our pipes were out.

Then we went to wake up Fleete. He was wide awake and fidgeting about his room.

'I say, I want some more chops,' he said. 'Can I get them?'

We laughed and said, 'Go and change. The ponies will be round in a minute.'

'All right,' said Fleete. I'll go when I get the chops—underdone ones, mind.'

He seemed to be quite in earnest. It was four o'clock, and we had had breakfast at one; still, for a long time, he demanded those underdone chops. Then he changed into riding clothes and went out into the verandah. His pony—the mare had not been caught—would not let him come near. All three horses were unmanageable—-mad with fear —-and finally, Fleete said that he would stay at home and get something to eat. Strickland and I rode out wondering. As we passed the temple of Hanuman, the Silver Man came out and mewed at us.

'He is not one of the regular priests of the temple,' said Strickland. 'I think I should peculiarly like to lay my hands on him.'

There was no spring in our gallop on the racecourse that evening. The horses were stale and moved as though they had been ridden out.

'The fright after breakfast has been too much for them,' said Strickland.

That was the only remark he made through the remainder of the ride. Once or twice I think he swore to himself, but that did not count.

We came back in the dark at seven o'clock and saw that there were no lights in the bungalow. 'Careless ruffians my servants are!' said Strickland.

My horse reared at something on the carriage drive, and Fleete stood up under its nose.

'What are you doing, grovelling about the garden?' said Strickland.

But both horses bolted and nearly threw us. We dismounted by the stables and returned to Fleete, who was on his hands and knees under the orange bushes.

'What the devil's wrong with you?' said Strickland.

'Nothing, nothing in the world,' said Fleete, speaking very quickly and thickly. 'I've been gardening-botanising, you know. The smell of the earth is delightful. I think I'm going for a walk-a long walk-all night.'

Then I saw that there was something excessively out of order somewhere, and I said to Strickland, 'I am not dining out.'

'Bless you!' said Strickland. 'Here, Fleete, get up. You'll catch a fever there. Come into dinner, and let's have the lamps lit. We'll all dine at home.'

Fleete stood up unwillingly and said, 'No lamps-no lamps. It's much nicer here. Let's dine outside and have some more chops-lots of 'em and underdone—bloody ones with gristle.'

Now a December evening in Northern India is bitterly cold, and Fleete's suggestion was that of a maniac.

'Come in,' said Strickland sternly. 'Come in at once.'

Fleete came, and when the lamps were brought, we saw that he was literally plastered with dirt from head to foot. He must have been rolling in the garden. He shrank from the light and went to his room. His eyes were horrible to look at. There was a green light behind them, not in them, if you understand, and the man's lower lip hung down.

Strickland said, 'There is going to be trouble-big trouble-to-night. Don't you change your riding things.'

We waited and waited for Fleete's reappearance and ordered dinner in the meantime. We could hear him moving about his own room, but there was no light there. Presently from the room came the long-drawn howl of a wolf.

People write and talk lightly of blood running cold and hair standing up and things of that kind. Both sensations are too horrible to be trifled with. My heart stopped as though a knife had been driven through it, and Strickland turned as white as the tablecloth.

The howl was repeated and was answered by another howl far across the fields.

That set the gilded roof on the horror. Strickland dashed into Fleete's room. I followed, and we saw Fleete getting out of the window. He made beast noises in the back of his throat. He could not answer us when we shouted at him. He spat.

I don't quite remember what followed, but I think that Strickland must have stunned him with the long boot-jack or else I should never have been able to sit on his chest. Fleete could not speak, he could only snarl, and his snarls were those of a wolf, not of a man. The human spirit must have been giving way all day and have died out with the twilight. We were dealing with a beast that had once been Fleete.

The affair was beyond any human and rational experience. I tried to say 'Hydrophobia,' but the word wouldn't come because I knew that I was lying.

We bound this beast with leather thongs of the punkah-rope, tied its thumbs and big toes together, and gagged it with a shoe-horn, which makes a very efficient gag if you know how to arrange it. Then we carried it into the dining room and sent a man to Dumoise, the doctor, telling him to come over at once. After we had despatched the messenger and were drawing breath, Strickland said, 'It's no good. This isn't any doctor's work.' I also knew that he spoke the truth.

The beast's head was free, and it threw it about from side to side. Anyone entering the room would have believed that we were curing a wolf's pelt. That was the most loathsome accessory of all.

Strickland sat with his chin in the heel of his fist, watching the beast as it wriggled on the ground but saying nothing. The shirt had been torn open in the scuffle and showed the black rosette mark on the left breast. It stood out like a blister.

In the silence of the watching, we heard something without mewing like a she-otter. We both rose to our feet, and, I answer for myself, not Strickland, felt sick—actually and physically sick. We told each other, as did the men in Pinafore that it was the cat.

Dumoise arrived, and I never saw a little man so unprofessionally shocked. He said that it was a heart-rending case of hydrophobia and that nothing could be done. At least any palliative measures would only prolong the agony. The beast was foaming at the mouth. Fleete, as we told Dumoise, had been bitten by dogs once or twice. Any man who keeps half a dozen terriers must expect a nip now and again. Dumoise could offer no help. He could only certify that Fleete was dying of hydrophobia. The beast was then howling, for it had managed to spit out the shoehorn. Dumoise said that he would be ready to certify the cause of death and that the end was certain. He was a good little man, and he offered to remain with us, but Strickland refused the kindness. He did not wish to poison Dumoise's New Year. He would only ask him not to give the real cause of Fleete's death to the public.

So Dumoise left, deeply agitated, and as soon as the noise of the cartwheels had died away, Strickland told me, in a whisper, his suspicions. They were so wildly improbable that he dared not say them out aloud and I, who entertained all Strickland's beliefs, was so ashamed of owning to them that I pretended to disbelieve.

'Even if the Silver Man had bewtiched Fleete for polluting the image of Hanuman, the punishment could not have fallen so quickly.'

As I was whispering this, the cry outside the house rose again, and the beast fell into a fresh paroxysm of struggling till we were afraid that the thongs that held it would give way.

'Watch!' said Strickland. 'If this happens six times I shall take the law into my own hands. I order you to help me.'

He went into his room and came out in a few minutes with the barrels of an old shotgun, a piece of fishing line, some thick cord, and his heavy wooden bedstead. I reported that the convulsions had followed the cry by two seconds in each case, and the beast seemed perceptibly weaker.

Strickland muttered, 'But he can't take away the life! He can't take away the life!'

I said, though I knew that I was arguing against myself, 'It may be a cat. It must be a cat. If the Silver Man is responsible, why does he dare to come here?'

Strickland arranged the wood on the hearth, put the gun barrels into the glow of the fire, spread the twine on the table and broke a walking stick in two. There was one yard of fishing line, gut, lapped with wire, such as is used for mahseer-fishing, and he tied the two ends together in a loop.

Then he said, 'How can we catch him? He must be taken alive and unhurt.'

I said that we must trust in Providence and go out softly with polo sticks into the shrubbery at the front of the house. The man or animal that made the cry was evidently moving around the house as regularly as a night watchman. We could wait in the bushes till he came by and knocked him over.

Strickland accepted this suggestion, and we slipped out from a bathroom window into the front verandah and then across the carriage drive into the bushes.

In the moonlight, we could see the leper coming around the corner of the house. He was perfectly naked, and from time to time, he mewed and stopped to dance with his shadow. It was an unattractive sight, and thinking of poor Fleete, brought to such degradation by so foul a creature, I put away all my doubts and resolved to help Strickland from the heated gun barrels to the loop of twine from the loins to the head and back again—— with all tortures that might be needful.

The leper halted on the front porch for a moment, and we jumped out on him with the sticks. He was wonderfully strong, and we were afraid that he might escape or be fatally injured before we caught him. We had an idea that lepers were frail creatures, but this proved to be incorrect. Strickland knocked his legs from under him, and I put my foot on his neck. He mewed hideously, and even though my riding boots, I could feel that his flesh was not the flesh of a clean man.

He struck at us with his hand and feet-stumps. We looped the lash of a dog whip round him, under the armpits, and dragged him backwards into the hall and so into the dining room where the beast lay. There we tied him with trunk straps. He made no attempt to escape but mewed.

When we confronted him with the beast, the scene was beyond description. The beast doubled backwards into a bow as though he had been poisoned with strychnine and moaned in the most pitiable fashion. Several other things happened also, but they cannot be put down here.

'I think I was right,' said Strickland. 'Now we will ask him to cure this case.'

But the leper only mewed. Strickland wrapped a towel around his hand and took the gun barrels out of the fire. I put half of the broken walking stick through the loop of the fishing line and buckled the leper comfortably to Strickland's bedstead. I understood then how men and women and little children could endure seeing a witch burnt alive; for the beast was moaning on the floor, and though the

Silver Man had no face, you could see horrible feelings passing through the slab that took its place, exactly as waves of heat play across red-hot iron—gun-barrels for instance.

Strickland shaded his eyes with his hands for a moment, and we got to work. This part is not to be printed.

The dawn was beginning to break when the leper spoke. His mewings had not been satisfactory up to that point. The beast had fainted from exhaustion, and the house was very still. We unstrapped the leper and told him to take away the evil spirit. He crawled to the beast and laid his hand upon the left breast. That was all. Then he fell face down and whined, drawing in his breath as he did so.

We watched the face of the beast and saw the soul of Fleete coming back into the eyes. Then a sweat broke out on the forehead, and the eyes-they were human eyes—-closed. We waited for an hour, but Fleete still slept. We carried him to his room and bade the leper go, giving him the bedstead and the sheet on the bedstead to cover his nakedness, the gloves and the towels with which we had touched him, and the whip that had been hooked around his body. He put the sheet about him and went out into the early morning without speaking or mewing.

Strickland wiped his face and sat down. A night gong, far away in the city, made seven o'clock.

'Exactly four-and-twenty hours!' said Strickland. 'And I've done enough to ensure my dismissal from the service, besides permanent quarters in a lunatic asylum. Do you believe that we are awake?'

The red-hot gun barrel had fallen on the floor and was singeing the carpet. The smell was entirely real.

That morning at eleven, we two together went to wake up Fleete. We looked and saw that the black leopard rosette on his chest had disappeared. He was very drowsy and tired, but as soon as he saw us, he said, 'Oh! Confound you fellows. Happy New Year to you. Never mix your liquors. I'm nearly dead.'

'Thanks for your kindness, but you're over time,' said Strickland. 'To-day is the morning of the second. You've slept the clock round with a vengeance.'

The door opened, and little Dumoise put his head in. He had come on foot and fancied that we were laying out Fleete.

'I've brought a nurse,' said Dumoise. 'I suppose that she can come in for... what is necessary.'

'By all means,' said Fleete cheerily, sitting up in bed. 'Bring on your nurses.'

Dumoise was dumb. Strickland led him out and explained that there must have been a mistake in the diagnosis. Dumoise remained dumb and left the house hastily. He considered that his professional reputation had been injured and was inclined to make a personal matter of the recovery. Strickland went out too. When he came back, he said that he had been to call on the Temple of Hanuman to offer redress for the pollution of the god, and had been solemnly assured that no white man had ever touched the idol and that he was an incarnation of all the virtues labouring under a delusion.

'What do you think?' said Strickland.

I said, '"There are more things . . ."'

But Strickland hates that quotation. He says that I have worn it threadbare.

One other curious thing happened, which frightened me as much as anything in all the night's work. When Fleete was dressed, he came into the dining room and sniffed. He had a quaint trick of moving his nose when he sniffed. 'Horrid doggy smell, here,' said he. 'You should really keep those terriers of yours in better order. Try sulphur, Strick.'

But Strickland did not answer. He caught hold of the back of a chair and, without warning, went into an amazing fit of hysterics. It is terrible to see a strong man overtaken with hysteria. Then it struck me that we had fought for Fleete's soul with the Silver Man in that room and had disgraced ourselves as Englishmen forever, and I laughed and gasped and gurgled just as shamefully as Strickland, while Fleete thought that we had both gone mad. We never told him what we had done.

Some years later, when Strickland had married and was a church-going member of society for his wife's sake, we reviewed the incident dispassionately, and Strickland suggested that I should put it before the public.

I cannot see that this step is likely to clear up the mystery; because, in the first place, no one will believe a rather unpleasant story, and, in the second, it is well known to every right-minded man that the gods of the heathen are stone and brass, and any attempt to deal with them otherwise is justly condemned.

The End... Or Is It?

You have reached the end of your journey through the shadowy realms of *Spooky Stories to Tell in the Dark*. We hope these tales have chilled you to the bone, entertained you, and perhaps even haunted your dreams.

But remember, the world of the uncanny is vast and filled with endless possibilities. These stories are merely a glimpse into the darkness that lurks beyond the veil.

If your appetite for the macabre has been whetted, fear not! There's more terror in store. Keep an eye out for *Spooky Stories to Tell in the Dark II*. It promises to delve even deeper into the shadowy corners of the human psyche, with fresh horrors and chilling suspense.

Until then, sleep tight... if you dare.

www.ingramcontent.com/pod-product-compliance
Lightning Source LLC
Chambersburg PA
CBHW051002180726
48291CB00006B/1939